MICROWA   ᴸA.
by
E. S. Lange.

(Title suggested by Su Andi D.Litt, D.Arts, O.B.E., Dir. National Black Arts Alliance.)

Dedicated to "All My Relations."

Contents.

Soul Food.
St. Timothy's.
Choir Boy.
Museum.
Masjid.
Drivin' With Pop.
Mexicana.
Car Trouble.
Grand-Folks.
Pop's Youth.
Scrap Book.
Gaby and Mo's.
Chillin' Like A Villain.
Fambo.
Americana.
Barton Springs.
Texas TV.
A Quiet Night In.
Pop's Two Guns.
Hill Country.
Sun Ra.
Bombay Bicycle.
Austin Radio.
Confession.
Way Down South.
Heartical Vibes.
Islamophobia.
Confession.
Uncertainty.
Casa De Luz.
Ruta Maya Revisited.
Theme Park Ethnics.
The Calabash.
Slavepool.
Valkyrie.
Lorna.

Cheltenham Cathedral.
Pop's Flack Jacket.
Pop & Eve.
Diamond.
Gladys Street.
Shine.
Good Byes.
Back To Blighty.
Brown Babies UK.
Sacred Hoop.
Sarah.
Devon.
Heaven.
Nu Tribes.
Deeper Roots.
Back Up North.
The Mixed Museum.
Mixed Relations.
Grammar School.
Irene.

Newark Nexus.

I'm at Newark Airport, New Jersey, stuck in a time-warp again, with a four hour wait for my connection. I'm standing in an airport bookstore, browsing through a book of African-American daily wisdoms. The Black girl behind the counter, is talking to her friend about a third girl, who she says "Wants to eat her". She seems to be talking extra loud for my benefit. She says; "I think I might just let the bitch eat me". Ok so she's trying to shock me. She must think I'm a Square. It's the fine looking suit I'm wearing, and the white shirt, and blue and black striped tie. It's not my old school tie, but it is the same colours, Liverpool Collegiate Grammar School for Boys. The girls remind me this is not England, but I know that already. This is my third time in the States now. But this time I felt like a Soul in limbo, or in the Barzakh the intermediary zone, Orpheus about to embark on his journey through the Netherworld, or Luke Skywalker, as described by Joseph Campbell in 'Myths to Live By', the bar scene they filmed at the Neolithic-site/Hotel in Matmata, Tunisia. I had lunch there once with an ex of mine, named Esoteric, a raven haired damsel stunningly beautiful, face of a Persian princess. It's the place that Joseph Campbell describes as; "That point from where Luke jumps off into deep space". I'd been there before, but not like this, not in this way. I could see Manhattan, and I considered trying to pop over for an hour or so, and walk around. But I decided against it. I had to face my growing fear, and insecurity. I had no choice but to trust and wait, and try and prepare myself for what was to come. A friend of mine back in Liverpool called Jabba, had told me that, "If you ever go to New York try and catch a sunset from on top of the Empire State building, it's magnificent, Manhattan turns pink." I was around by there once, around about that time, so I tried it. It's true. Thanks Jabba. I stood at the top of the Empire State building looking down towards the Statue of Liberty. It took me back to the little bronze figurines from our old mantle piece in 5 Eastbourne Street, gifts from Arturo. Arturo Villado was my step-dad, my sister Tracie's dad. Our Tracie had never really knew him. She was the same age as I was when my own biological Father vanished. I've never thought of that. I can be so selfish. They were still selling them down stairs. I was gonna buy one, but I let it go. I had noone to give it too that would recognise it's significance. Who was there left to remember ? Me Mother had died by then. I ponder some times, how many of us in the Black Diasporan Community, grow up not ever knowing, who our Father's are, or even if we do, never ever seeing them, or meeting them, or having the benefit of just having them around. I thought of my little Sister, now a woman in her late thirties. She was only twenty when my Mother died from a tumour, after being treated with a migraine for twelve months. I can see how my sense of injustice can go one way or the other. Tears or anger, like the Puerto Rican poet on the Last Poets Live at The Cubiculo Theatre, Harlem, 1966 bootleg tape that my homey Kif, and I found in an old flea market down Camden Lock in London one time. The Brother did a poem called, "A Rifle and a Prayer", that he performed in English, then in Spanish, and one line always sticks in my mind; "I shoot, and I cry, I shoot, and I cry." I think of this, and I think of poor Tracie, and how I've scolded her in the past, and she's so sunny, so forgiving. I love her a lot, we're a close family, even though she's so scatty at times. I would have loved for her to have gone over with me, when I visited Pancho, Maria, and Alejandro, after all they were her blood relatives. Maybe one day, if God's good. I wish I could be more aware of how other people feel sometimes. Especially the people that I love. I brought Tracie a photo of her Cuban grand-Dad back with me, he was the image of Arturo, lighter, more Spanish. Apparently the custom in his family was brown men marrying Black African looking women. I brought her Arturo's cab drivers ID, and various bits of memorabilia. That was my first time in New York, I would visit America three times before I would eventually get to write about it. Each time will be more tumultuous than the next. I had always been a point of Human existence were borders over lapped. I could always see that Human truth transcends most people's conditioned notions of race, biology, religion, class or creed. One image that sticks in my mind from that trip, is an old Black guy sitting on the corner by the bank where I used to exchange pounds for dollars, shining shoes, and wearing a "Million Man March" t-shirt. Irony never escapes my poets gaze.

If your ever in Newark Airport I must warn you don't pay ten dollars for the Universal fonecards, cos they work on everything except ATS phonelines. And at Newark all the phones are ATS, but they don't sell ATS phonecards, and the phones don't take coins. So I realise I'm cut off can't phone out. I start to think about where I'm going. I'm looking over at the Manhattan skyline thinking I got four hours to wait. I consider again that, maybe I should shoot across and see some people.

Then I remember how I missed my Frankfurt connection once on my way to Hamburg to do a gig, made the recording session the next day, but missed the gig the night before stranded in Hamburg Air Port. Don't want a repeat of that little non-performance. Apprehension starts to set in. What if we don't get on. What if we hate each other. What if ? What if ? My life ran by me in cinema-scope, like it's been doing ever since I got the call. I weighed it all up, Urban -Jazz Creature with an arty-background. Cultural nomad, unsettled, ageing, becoming increasingly reclusive. Getting on top of my drinking, clubbing, serial-mono-polygamy, and various states of advanced Quadrefenia. Weed still a problem that shifts in significance, depending on externals like work for example.

Irremovable chip on shoulder, associated with the Human Rights-Eco-struggle, and counter-culture in general.

Growing up through those 1970's teen years, religion had become simply the power in the Soul. Soul music was my first love.

The G.I.'s brought it to Liverpool first, then the Merchant Seaman known as the Cunard Yanks. My long lost biological father was one of those G.I.'s. Gospel music was always lurking in the background somewhere. Soul power.

And all the time, last thing at night before going to sleep, some freestyle praying and testifying, smoothed off with The Lord's Prayer, later to be replaced with Al Fatiha. It was all churning over in my mind, like a field that's been laying fallow, just waiting for the tractor to come along, and turn that soil.

I was carrying a lorra baggage, that's generally what being a peasant-poet is all about. Ask John Clare. You just do what you know you have to do to keep from going totally crazy, and hope that enough people get onto it for it to be validated, as some form of liberating creative expression worthy of the word culture. I told myself, "It's the being on the journey that matters." I mean you've gotta tell yourself something haven't you.

Much has transpired since then, like how I eventually ended up here back in the USA, right now looking over at

Manhattan from an airport lounge window in Newark, New Jersey, on my way to Texas to parlé with my biological Father, after more than forty years of contemplation, finding out that he was now a Bible teacher, and was also a chaplain, during his thirty years service in the USAF. Never imagined that I would be discovering his songs, and his poetry, finding out he was Mohawk not Cherokee, and from Austin not Houston, finding out so much about my Mom and my Pop, so much new stuff about life, about myself. About my diverse roots, and 'All my Relations'. Time passes. It's 18:50 pm, time to embark on my Boeing 737 for Austin, Texas. I was about as focussed as I was gonna get. The rest is in God's hands. I told myself.

Austin Aria.

Unpredictably, the flight gets in to Austin early, so there's noone there to meet me. But I don't know the plane's early, I mustn't have been listening to the Captain on the plane, so at this point I don't realise. I'm just standing at the massive terminal window, looking out into the darkness of Austin's periphery. It's about 10.30 at night, the city twinkles in the beckoning distance. I think to myself, "Maybe they had a problem. Car trouble or something ?" Texas is a big place 276,000 square miles, the Lone Star State, 23.4 million acres of fresh forests, and woodlands, 624 miles of coast, 6.3000 square miles of lakes, what a place. I scan the baggage terminal for Black faces, or even one that might just slightly resemble mine. I don't see anyone. The place has emptied pretty quickly since we touched down. An empty air-port terminal, is a spooky place. I'm going through plan B. "I'll phone 'em." So I phones 'em. No answer. I wait for a while phone again. Plan C, "If no one shows I'll call TJ's brother." You see a few weeks before I got my ticket I had been talking to a guy from Doncaster, T J, whose married to a girl that I know, DJ, whose in Community Arts in Liverpool. TJ's brother Nigel is married to a Mexican woman called Patricia, in Austin. Just one small coincidence in a string of synchronicities that thread themselves throughout this story like pearls on a necklace. It's a long story, but I'm having a coffee with this guy TJ, in the Coffee Union, on Bold Street, in Liverpool, and he says, "If your going to Austin call me before you go, and I'll give you my brother Nigel's number. He's cool, he'll hook you up over there". So I calls him the day before I'm set to fly, and his brother Nigel's actually there in Liverpool, at TJ's place. TJ puts their Nigel on the line, and I get to talk to him in person. I tell him about Pop, and explain the glorious reason why I'm making the journey. He really is a cool guy, easy to talk with. He says he's flying back tomorrow. The same day as me, coincidentally, but a different flight. But he gives me a couple of contact numbers for him back in Austin, his work number, and his home number, and tells me to hook up with him when I reach the State's Side.

So I'm State's Side and panicking cos I'm early, and I think that Pop's late. I'm thinking about calling Nigel up, and I remember that they're only travelling the same day as myself, so the chances are that they'll be, either jet lagged, or still in transit. I guess my sublimated apprehensions we're starting to surface slowly in the face of an imminent confrontation with part of my past, and a part of myself, that up until this point had remained a mystery to me. Even the silhouetted city scape that sparkled enticingly on the not so far horizon, was some how a hidden part of me. It was still hard to absorb the fact that this place was connected to my origins, a big part of who I am, but largely unknown. Unknown but about to be revealed, and God is the Knower.

I sigh in desperation at my reflection in the polished glass, as I turn around to scan the arrival's lounge one more time before putting plan C into operation. I turn around from the window, and I see myself again, but stouter, older, more grey, silver even. It's my Pop, next to him is my second oldest Sister Grace, she's the one like me and Pop, we got our Grand-Mother's Mohawk features, it's in the nose, and the eyes. Graces's hair is pulled back, to reveal her classic features. She's serious looking. We stare in each other's direction, recognise, and smiles and waves come next, and I walk towards them. We hug instinctively, Pop and I, then Grace and I, and as I recognise my Spirit in Pop, there's some tears, from me. Grace is silent, studious. Pop is ebullient, standing there in his blue and white, sports shirt, anorak, and jeans. Grace is traditionally the beauty of the family, I later discover, and she's known as the serene one. She studies me, kinda suspiciously. She's wearing a dark brown cardigan, over a beige dress, gold loops hang from her ears, and a gold locket hangs around her neck. It must be as strange for her as it is for me. She don't know me, but here I am crying over meeting her Pop. Outside Wanda-Jean, the oldest Sister is waiting in her brand-new car. Wanda has hair like Oprah. She's wearing a navy blue dress, with a large white floral design, and a black cardigan, with similar jewelry to Grace, but smaller earings. By now I kinda feel like I know Wanda a little bit, cos we've already written to each other, and talked over the phone several times. And she's sent me photo's of her, and her family, and so I kinda recognise her. She's short, very cute looking, more like her Mother Doris than Pop. Dinky. We're driving from the airport towards Pop's place. I'm with my family State's Side, and they're cool, we're cool. The air is cool. It feels strange, but not awkward, kinda casual, the atmosphere is very relaxed as we drive to Pop's house on Singleton Avenue. I'm taking it all in out the passenger window as we chat. On first impressions, Texas reminds me of the Caribbean, sort of, the heat, the dryness of the night air, one-level plank built houses, and some tin shacks like the chattel houses in the Island's. One level, bungalow type houses, cactus, tumble weed, and wide dusty roads. It's all reminiscent of the drive from the airport to Holetown, on my first visit to Barbados. It was like the story of the prodigal son from the Bible, only I hadn't run away, it was more like a part of me, had never actually been home in the first place. Back at Pop's they make me a cup of tea in the micro-wave. They think it's quaint that I drink tea. Pop shows me how to do it for future reference. I get out the camera that I found in a yellow cab in New York, and start taking photo's of Pop and my Sisters, then Wanda takes one of Grace Pop and I, then Grace takes one of Pop, Wanda and me, and we work through various configurations. My Sisters all the time commenting on my features, and who else I look like in the Family besides Pop. It's agreed that I look a lot like most of the Mohawk side of the Family, like Pop, Grace, Pamela, and Sheila the youngest, while Wanda- Jean the eldest Sister looks more like their Mother's side of the Family.

After a while, and much welcomes, and greetings, and hugs, and arrangements to meet on the morrow, and good nights, and God's Blessings, Wanda and Grace leave, and Pop and I chew the cud. I make more tea in the microwave. "You English as your Momma, aint Yah", Pop says in relation to my tea drinking. "I guess so", I reply proudly, for whatever reason. It suddenly dawns on me why I feel so familiar around Pop, despite the fact that by now we have struck up a pretty good relationship over the phone, he sounds so much like Arturo. That's what it is, that's where I get the ability to do a good Pan-American accent. "Of course !" I think to myself, "It's starting to make sense already."

We talk mostly about the flight at first, and then Pop starts to talk about Mom. I get out the birthday cards he sent me, and his photo, and some photos of Mom. I can see him going back in his mind. "Yep that's your Momma alright ", he says somewhat winsomely. "I did love her son, and I was prepared to give up everything over here for her, but she didn't want that... She sent me a photo of you and I destroyed it in case Doris ever found it, now I wished I'd have kept it so you could see t."I would have like to have seen it. It would have been one of the earliest photos of me in existence. Apart from a big ink-tinted one when I'm about three months old, there are very few photos of any of us, from way back then", and then I realise maybe that was the same picture, Mom would have got more than one copy. We chat for a bit but it's been a long day, and we are both exhausted. I yawn, a big tired yawn. "If you don't get sleep Son, Sleep'll get you", Pop says smiling. "I know", I say smiling back. He shows me to my room. "This is the room that Evelyn's two evil grand-sons used to sleep in, till I caught them upto no good, and they got shipped down to Evelyn's Sister's down in Georgia, cos I wasn't having those evil-minded sons o' bitches living in my house." Pop was like Mom in a lorra ways, a Bible Teacher/Preacher that cussed like a trooper. I was already beginning to see how I turned out like I did, and I'd been here less than an hour. We had the same Soul. We just kinda vibrated at the same frequency it was hard to explain.

The room I'm in has a double bed, it used to be the room belonging to Evelyn's two Grand Sons, their photos are hung on the walls, along with photo's of Evelyn and Diamond, and someone who I can only assume is Evelyn's absent daughter. Facing the bed is a clothes rack full of Pop's old stuff, I route through it out of curiosity, there's so much I don't know about this man, that everything about him is of interest to me. I see some of his ex-military clothes in there, a yellow baseball jacket and cap, with blue piping, and the name "Sweet Gene", embroidered in blue, Air Force style across the left breast. I discover later that this was Pop's informal-military wear while on a mission as trouble shooter, and diplomat over in Isfahan, in Iran. "Sweet Gene the Peacemaker", they called him back then. Apparently he was about to close some lucrative deals over there, that would have made him a rich man, but the Ayatollah kicked off a revolution, and it ruined his play over there. He was pissed off about that. He explained it to me one day as we were going through the photo albums and I came across some excellent Polaroid's of Iranian mosques, and various other examples of famous Islamic architecture that I recognised from Islamic Society calendars. I also came across a green flack jacket, it had Pop's full name inside the collar, Above the left breast pocket was a standard "United States Air Force", embroidered patch, in blue and white. I tried it on. It fitted me well. It felt good on me. It looked good on me. I liked it, it gave me a sort of ex-Vietnam veteran look, especially if I wore my bandanna with it.

After playing around with my image in the mirror, I decided this is me. "I'm having this jacket", I told myself, "It's got my name written over all it". That night I slept like a frog in a hollow log. Texas was feeling like home from home already. My first night in Austin, felt like scoring a home-run, and a touch- down, all in the same game.

Morning Has Broken.

It's early morning. I am awakened by the sound of a train passing through the railway-crossing, at first I think it's a boat, or a ship cos I know the Colorado River runs through Austin, I saw it on the map. It sounds like somebody blowing an "A" natural minor chord, on a giant blues harmonica. A sweet lonesome Cowboy, Hill Country Blues... Hummm. There's a gecko on the window of my room, I study it's silhouette, and I think of the cactus by the airport the night before, and I think. The environment speaks to you when you travel. Yep, Texas has a definite Caribbean feel to it. I get up. Pop's in his office, but there is noise around the house, and I can smell something appetising cooking. I meet Evelyn, Pop's fancy woman, Pop's seventy five, Evelyn's forty eight, they met in the Air Force. Evelyn's got a pleasant, warm and friendly face, she's plumpish and wears glasses, and comes from Oklahoma City originally. Her nine year old grand daughter Diamond, who Pop dotes on, and adores, also lives with them. Little Diamond's cute as pie, a skinny little thing, but intelligent, and she has a sunny disposition. For some reason I didn't see them last night. "We got in early hours. You were asleep", Evelyn explains, as she's cooking breakfast. It smells good. My first Texas breakfast. I can't wait to sample some down home country cooking.

I get a shower and get dressed, and go back to my room. I try the green flack jacket on again, and I start to reminisce about the Green Jackets, a sort of Liverpool version of the Black Panthers. A memory from my turbulent youth. I think to myself,

"I'll offer him money for it and he'll refuse and say just keep it Son." And then I think again, "But I'll leave it for a while, cos it's only the first day give it some time, I don't want him to get the impression that I'm here on the make." I put my headset on to listen to the recital of the, "Ninety Nine Most Beautiful Names of Allah", on my Walkman, while I'm posing like a Vietnam Vet in the mirror. I'm trying to memorise them. I put on my Liverpool Football Club, baseball cap, and I'm standing there posing, jeans, t- shirt, trainers, LFC base-ball cap, and flack jacket. I look the part, I feel the part. I used to be called "Bongo Veteran" on some of my later, more Dub orientated, "African Head Charge", type recordings. I still am in some circles. I point at myself in the mirror and say, "Bongo Veteran ! Soy el Bongocero! Que barbaro!"

It's a sunny Texas morning in East Austin. Little Diamond, Evelyn's Grand Daughter comes into the room. Diamond is keen to hear what I've got playing in my head-set.
"What are you listening to Uncle Gene ?"
I hand her the Walkman. "Here you are babe, have a listen."
She's all smiles. She listens intently. "That's like what my Momma listens to." Her voice lights up. "It sounds like Muslim."
"That's very good Diamond", I say surprised. "It is Muslim. It's a recital of the 'Ninety Nine Most Beautiful Names Of Allah', in Arabic." Her eyes are bright with an intellectual glimmer.
"My Momma is Muslim", Diamond bleats, eyes shining. "Of course", I think to myself. Diamond's Mother is Muslim. She seems really focussed. "She's a bright kid", I think to myself. She bleats on like a little lamb: "This reminds me of when my Mom was home. She used to play tapes of the Quran, kinda sounds like this". "That's right it's the same type of sound, babe. In fact it's like a poem based on the Koran. So your absolutely correct." She starts to mimic the recital on the cassette, "Ar-Rahman-ir-Raheem." L'il Diamond's shiny, freshly-scrubbed-for-school-face, is so gleeful as she expectantly asks, "Can I borrow it for a while? " "Sure Baby, I won't need it. I've almost memorised it all by now". As grave, and sedate as the recital sounds, to my surprise, she likes the sound of it. She starts to mimic

13

the recital on the tape, mouthing the words in Arabic, and her pronunciation is quite good. I imagine her Mother, Evelyn's eldest, used to recite Koran with her, before she got put in lock-down in the Georgia State pen. Kids aquire language, much easier than adults. Evelyn pops her head in the room,
"Would you like some breakfast Eugene ?"
I'd been waiting for this. "Oh yes please! That'd be cool actually, I'm starving." I take off Pop's flack jacket, and put on my Royal Blue Karrimor fleece, with the three bears on it, that I bought in Betws-Y-Coed during an outdoor pursuits trip, back in my Youth worker days. Evelyn's cooked a fine Texas breakfast, Longhorn chuck steak patties, Texas eggs, long oblong Mexican tomatoes and Texas home made biscuits. A biscuit in Austin is something like a scone without the currants and raisins in it, and savoury for dipping in red-eye gravy like Jethro from the Beverley Hill Billies, not something sweet and crunchy to be eaten with strawberry jam and cream, with tea by the way, and unlike English biscuits they go hard when they're stale, and not soft. Pop's out of his private office, and sitting in his chair of office in the kitchen. He sits at a big old wooden table facing the TV, next to him and behind him is a pile of competitions, some filled in some waiting.

Diamond, Pop, and I, and all seated at the table as Evelyn serves up a breakfast fit for a King, a Prince, and a Princess. Pop's explaining that Evelyn's home early from visiting her folks in Oklahoma City for thanks giving, "Yep ! She came back especially to see you Son", Pop says. "I'm honoured", I say to Evelyn who is dishing out hot biscuits onto my plate. I pour Tabasco sauce all over my food. "Are you gonna eat it like that !", gasps Diamond. "Yeah ! I always eat it like that. It's nice." Pop, Evelyn, and Diamond all seem surprised. "Don't it burn your mouth?", Diamond asks amazed.
"Nah. I'm used to it. This is weak compared to what I'm used to back home."
Diamond winces, "Mostly it's the Mexicans are the ones that eat a lot of chilli sauce, over here."

"Yeah well this aint even like hot sauce to me".
She stares in disbelief as I swallow a piece of biscuit, drenched in hot-sauce. I start to show off a little. "Now the hot sauce in Barbados, is made with Scotch Bonnet peppers. Now that's what you call hot sauce." Pop's looking at me curiously. I'm English but I can literally drink Tabasco, straight from the bottle without even flinching. He's bemused. I continue with my boasting, "I heard that if you go into any of the Tijano bars, or Mexican juke-joints, they have chillies on the bar along with the peanuts and stuff. The game is that if your a stranger, and you wander in there by mistake, then they make you eat some chillis. It's kind of a macho game they play, especially on unsuspecting tourists." Pop's amazed at me, I can tell, so I play up to it.
"I was thinking of bringing some Scotch Bonnet's with me, and playing them at their own game."
Pop laughed a wicked laugh. We had the same dark sense of humour.

I'm just taking it all in as I have my breakfast, checking out Pop's place. The place looks lived in, and some, there are these plastic, kitsch, illuminated crosses, and statues of Jesus, and the Virgin Mary, sort of like small icons, that kinda plug straight into the electric sockets on the walls, but none of them are working. I notice that the switches go up for on, and down for off. The doors and gates swing outward, and some even have their locks on the left hand side. Evelyn's telling me about the work she does, and the course she's on. "Women coping with motherhood, widowhood, and living in the Hood." She's at the Anderson, Austin's Black College, and she's a big fan of someone called Shirley Fowler-Dunn, whom I assume she was quoting. She adds, "Life is Our Choice. Choose Life-Peace-Love-Joy." I'm impressed with Pop's lady. She sounds like a conscious Black woman. I'm flattered because I can see that she's just trying to give a good impression, for Pop's sake more than her own, but it seems like Pop keeps trying to undermine her. I get the feeling that something ain't right between them. He tells me jokingly, "Monkey'd leave her. Monkey'd say "Me man ! You foolish !" Cos monkey got more common sense." He grinned his warm tooth-less in parts, grin. I can see that Pop's got a real cruel streak in him, and he's a bit of a control freak. I guess being in the military for thirty years'll do that to you. But what happened to chivalry.

Pop was a chaplain for the Air Forces Black Masonic Order also. He shows me how to tie the bread. "A place for everything and everything in it's place. And if it don't have a place, make one for it, and then keep it there so you always know where to find it. And then if someone else needs to know, you can always tell 'em where to find it." He goes on about organisation, and personal property, and finance accounts, but all in such a way that it allows him to cuss out certain people for their slackness. He spices up maxims like, "If he don't need me, then I don't need him", with spiteful stuff like, "I'm gonna get me a pair of Stacy Adams (which I assume are shoes), with ice-picks in the toes, that'll wake Yah up. Kick some butt then." He seems to be partly talking to Evelyn, as a subtext. He stops reflects, and continues, "Success is a journey not a destination", he says underlining a point, that seems to have just popped into his head, momentarily. Pop's turning out to be one ornery old horn-backed toad. He senses my feelings, and he draws me in with a story about Cogewea, Mourning Dove the half-blood, celebrated as the first Native American novelist. He's quite the poet and philosopher. I'm impressed with my old Pop, and it's not even 8 am in the morning yet.

It's actually 7.43 am to be precise, Saturday 28th November, 1999, and Pop and I are standing outside of Pop's house looking at the rear-right wheel of Pop's car. It's an old coffee coloured Lincoln Town car, with a cream vinyl covered roof. I can see clearly now in the brightness of the morning hours, the over grown garden, with the towering pecan trees, that virtually shield the house from the road. It's a bungalow, that looks like it's made from wooden planks, until you get closer and investigate them, and then you discover that they're actually aluminium planks, made to look like wood for that cabin effect.

There's a porch with cushioned seating for sitting out front, and whittling. Just in front of the porch is a fragrant Japanese plum tree. The "Iwan", or porch under which the Sufi sits, symbolises the transitional space between the temporal world "Dunya," and the spiritual worlds "Ruhani".

Up and down the street, all the house's are differently designed, but all variations on the same down-home Hill-Billy theme, or so it seems like to me. Some are quite affluent looking, and made of bricks and mortar, others are literally nothing more than genuine, authentic wooden shacks, and they nearly all have a basket-ball hoop outside of them, either front, back, or at the side. Each place has at least one really flash looking jalopy, either parked outside in the street, or up side the house. Pop reckons the neighbours across the way are drugs dealers. The guy spends all day out front of his house, maxing, and relaxing in his four-wheel drive jeep, talking into his mobile phone.

Cousin Jesse.

We examine Pop's car. "Wheel trouble, Son. Some jive-ass peckerwood ran into me side on. I had right of way, but the sucker moved out too soon and now my rear wheels all messed up. I want to take you on a drive around Austin, but I gotta try and sort it out first", Pop says apologetically. "That's cool Pop. I'm happy just being here, don't worry about me". A guy about fifty-something in a blue denim jacket, plaid shirt, dungarees, and a Mini-Mall base-ball cap shows up, and says "You must be Li-l Gene. I heard you was coming." "This is my Son, Eugene" Pop says to Cousin Jesse. Jesse is Pop's second Cousin. He calls me "Li'l Gene", even though I'm about four, or five inches taller than him. "What's the problem ?". "This is Cousin Jesse", Pop says to me. Jesse takes off his jacket, and rolls up his sleeves to help out. We jack up the right-rear end of the Lincoln. Jesse checks it out; "Yep the nuts keeping the wheel on are coming loose, cos the axle's bent up slightly. See that there." Pop and I study the underside of the car. "Yep" says Pop. "That's why the wheel keeps working it self lose. When that sucker has hit you side on, he's buckled your whole axle." That aint gonna be easy to fix". "Hmmm" Pop says. Jesse messes with it for a bit, and says, "That aught to do you for while, but it won't last out for ever". "Well that'll do for now", Pop says briefly relieved. Pop goes into the house to wash his hands. "So how long you here for Li'l Gene?"... "Just a couple of weeks". "Wouldn't you think of coming over to stay here with your Pop". "This is my first day Cousin Jesse. I got a lot of things I'd need to think about before I made a decision like that. I mean I got a life back in England". "What you mean Li'l Gene, it aint shit here ?." "That's not what I'm saying cuz, and that's not what I meant. It's just that I got things in England that I need to be there for". In reality that wasn't true. As a matter of fact I didn't have anything to go back to, not really, nothing except maybe a long distance Aedipal affair, with a married German woman from Surrey, whose husband was 20 years her senior and allowed her to have flings by the way. So it's sort of kosha. I guess I was just a bit stunned by the idea of moving to Austin, or even the invitation to move over here being thrust upon me, on my first day in town. Jesse changes the subject. "I was just on my way over to pay my rent to my ex. She used to be my woman, now she's my land-lady. I don't know how I ended up in this situation, but here I am at the mercy of that gold-digging Mona Lisa. Cousin Jesse's talks about his sitch like it's a stand up routine. I like him he's warm, and down to Earth. He's only known me no more than fifteen or twenty minutes and he's treating me like he's known me all his life. He explains it like this, "I knew we was related as soon as I seen you. You look too much like Big Gene. I said to myself, if that aint one of Big Gene's chickens come home to roost, I'll be damned".

After we'all finish messing with Pop's car Jesse goes about his affairs, and Pop and I go back into the house. Pop sits at his table for a while filling in his competition forms, and watching cable tv. I sit a spell with him and get off on the TV evangelist Dr Jack Van Impe, and his glamorous assistant-wife,

Rexella Impe taking about the World Peace Bell, from Newport, Kentucky, the largest free swinging bell in the World. There's a news flash about Governor Bush, and how he can be contacted by a link with the George Bush Presidential Library and Museum. There's a lot of web sites, and e- mail addresses accompanying everything on TV, which for me is a new phenomenon. The whole internet thing hasn't really kicked off like this yet in England, but then Austin is Silicone City, and new technology is it's claim to fame.

Austin is situated in the prairies on the edge of the Hill Country, and yes those hills have eyes. Being the capital of Texas, and as host to the largest Live Music Festival in the World, Austin claims to be the Live Music Capital of The World, as it also holds the South by South West Music, Media, and Film, and Multi-Media Conference every Spring. One of the things that Texans in general seem mighty proud of, is the fact that they are notorious for also being, the best boasters in the World. I can dig that.

The news is less welcoming. Over a hundred bodies found on the Mexican border near El Paso. Mass graves, and hundreds of bodies according to CBS, near, and around El Paso, Laredo, Amarillo, San Antone, Albuquerque. It's Bill Clinton now on K Eye Witnesses News, talking about, "drug related killings", and "the Jauraez Cartel" . Another student goes missing, car found in the Nevada Desert. Yoghurt shop shooting, four girls shot dead. Brother accused of killing sister. Abilene body found. Student goes missing again, there's a lot of it in Austin, due to there being a big University of Texas campus not far from the Ghetto. It's just like back home in that respect. Texas Uni, generally caters for the kids of rich ranchers, and oil tycoons, such as they are today. The dark news ends, then a less threatening news article is popped into the menu, just to lighten the daily load, telling us to "Eat bugs", cos crickets are the new food source, they're cheap, nutritious, and plentiful.

I micro-wave a cup of Texas tea, and retire to the front room still within speaking distance, and full view of Pop, so as I can surf the local radio stations, a favourite pass-time of mine, when ever I hit an unknown environment. Tex-Mex, Rhythm and Blues, Gospel, Salsa, Tijano, old time Reggae, Hip-Hop, Rap, Merengé, Jazz, Blues, Rock, Country, Soul. Skywatch Traffic cuts in on Lone Star 93.3 FM, Lucy in the Sky. Then I hear "Stay tuned for a genuine retromercial". I buzz on the concept, before encountering what was to become one of my favourite stations, KASE 101 the sound of Country, I tune into Scarlet's Country Kitchen. I've never been a big fan of Country music, in fact I've always hated it. It's something that I associate with Red Knecks, and good ole' boys and lynchings. I kinda grew up thinking that Black folks shouldn't listen to Country. A stereo-type that was exploded for me, when I was in Barbados, and I hit a karaoke bar where only the local Bajans went. All they played was Country, and those good ole' Bajun boys knew the lyrics to all of them, and did some pretty good renditions. I could see that they were into it big-time, even down to the wearing of cowboy hats, and rodeo shirts. When I was there the only track on the play list that I knew, was a Funk track by Kool & The Gang. So I freestyled over "Celebrate", and got the crowd coming in on the chorus, like a call and response. It went down well. A fellow approached me to see if I had a manager, and had started fixing me up with some gigs, around the island. I told him I was on holiday. I switch channels, not being Bajun, or even slightly interested in Country music at this point, I move on swiftly, and get hooked by some Radio evangelising, some sports, some cool adds, loads of really cool commercials, a lot of which is based around a very subtle form of self depreciation. They sort of parody the blind optimism of suburbia, and the self-deceit of White middle-class America. For example they will advertise the Arboretum, an Austin version of Cheshire Oaks, with a lampoon of some well spoken Americans, with compulsive shopping disorders, in a group therapy session, discussing with their counsellor, how hard it is to drive past this, all-encompassing mega-mall. The Austin version of the, "Say No to Drugs", campaign add, runs more like a Cheech and Chong sketch. "Your friend wants you to smoke that wacky weed. Here's what to say, "No way man !", says some obviously Chonged-out Slacker. This commercial comes complete with disclaimer, "No teenagers were harmed in the making of this commercial". Must remember to call Nigel.

Domestic Diva.

There are no post-boxes in Austin. The postman picks up the outgoing when he drops off the incoming. There's a grey post-box on the porch, and an ancient wind gauge. Pop collects the mail, it's mostly junk-mail, and conman competitions. He sifts through it all for news of a big win. Pop's big hope, like most poor folks, is winning the lottery, or some other big score, that's how he passes his time these days, that and watching Fox sports, game shows, the news, and the Black Comedy Channel. Pop's arguing with Evelyn over nothing in particular. Evelyn and Pop dialogue, and it's not good, the way he talks to her, slags her daughter and her grand sons. "I'll put my foot in her ass". Pop says forgetting himself again. "It's only breakfast time Pop", I'm thinking, but I don't say anything. "Ornery ! She want get ornery. I wouldn't touch her with a borrowed piece of somebody else's wood". I didn't like that, there was no need to go so low, especially not in front of me. He says he loves Diamond, but he forgets that Evelyn is her Grandmother, and Evelyn's daughter, who is in the State Pen for drugs, is Diamond's Mother. Cuss one and your cussing them all, hurt one, you hurt all three. But how can I preach to my Pop, he's a preacher himself.

Being intrigued by TV evangelism, I've added an extra portion of TV evangelists to the programming. A Black woman preacher of about fifty, in a straight nylon wig, dressed in ecumenical robes is running up and down, wailing, screaming, and generally throwing herself about hysterically, on an altar that doubles as a stage. I'm thinking of St Marks in the Field, a Church in Manhattan that doubles as a theatre, where the altar converts into a stage. The difference with what I'm watching is that there is no distinction, it's all one thing. The altar is the stage. Art and religion, creativity and spirituality fused in one performance. This is African syncretism, it's like Juju, a marriage of the sacred and the profane. I remember one scholar of African-American history saying that, Africans were not converted to Christianity, they converted Christianity to Africa. You can see this more easily in things like Santaria, Candomble, Haitian Voo Doo, and New Orleans Hoodoo. As it was in the beginning, so shall it be in the end. Amen. I channel hop. Fox Sports Net. I see Liverpool get beat one-nil by West ham, Michael Owen missed a sitter, through greed, then got booked for diving in the box. I'm sitting at the breakfast table browsing through brochures, and looking up every now and again to sip tea, talk, or catch something that flashes across the tv screen, like "Sweat shops in New York". I stop ponder how when I was in Harlem, I thought Harlem, seemed like a Third World situation in a First World country. Pop sees me lookup and comments; "When it comes to government or politics, people don't look at the root causes of the problem, cos if they solve it they're out of a job"."That's so true", I thought. Pop continued, "On the street that's how I came up. You always gotta have a ram in the bush", he said it like he was in church. "That's from Abraham and Isaac, isn't it", I chip in trying to trace the origins of his Texan proverb. He's surprised that I know so much about the Bible. He's on a roll now so I just listen with great interest. I love everything he says, I write it all down. "People easy forget the good you do, even if you do good for them, cos they always want some more of that. That's why you should rely on nobody except the Creator", and he finishes his line with a Gospel flourish. "La howla wallah quwwata ila billah", I think to myself, "There is no ability nor power save from God". I was beginning to see Pop as a Southern-Baptist-Sufi, in my Wilberian Integral sort of way. His Faith was a lot like Sheikh Badruddin of Simawna's. He was on the Path of the Blameworthy. A sort of Spiritual existentialism, based on his own lived experience. Knowledge of "Self" in the real sense. Knowledge as a rose, a precious stone. Where your worst enemy, and your best friend dwell within you.

Hood.

As I once wrote in a poem called "Hood"..."It was dark times. The Hood lay across my shoulders at first. A fashion statement. Then I noticed it in the mirror. I pulled it over my head. And I noticed him observing me. Self-scrutiny. Scratching the surface of the face With the eyes of a traveller. A gypsey. A Nomad. Watching, monitoring. The World, people, me. Looking for hidden meaning. The truest stories, the best stories. The Ancient story. The One story. The Only story.

Hating me at times. The look in his slow brooding eyes. Pain glowing darkest bright. Features shaded by the black hood of his sweat-suit top rising up from inside the upturned pointed collar of a black leather jacket. Cold eyes over my shoulder scolding with their heated gaze. Sneering at my naivité, my stupidity, my openness. Ignorance the true shackles of my serfdom. Running with the wind. Drinking in the freshness of the rain. The teachings tell us that our best friend and our worst enemy both dwell within us. Mine dwells at my right hand shoulder. A chip off the old block. Carved into a new environment. A panther at home amidst the dark shadows of the greenwood. Integrated. An organic creature. Complex and distinctive in it's: Language spoken; Rituals performed; Manifestation of the survival instinct; Raw expressions of Life's essence. And this time. This is a ritual time. We are stories made from stories. The act of speech. Us telling stories to ourselves. About ourselves. About who we are. Naming ourselves as people. Brothers and Sisters !"

The Jazz poem, 'Hood', was based on Umberto Eco's character, Richard of Baskerville, played by Sean Connery in The Name of The Rose, but transposed into my own personal archetype. A Jungian synthesis of Sherock Holmes, and Robin Hood. The Hip-Hop 'hoody', a symbol of streetwise counter-culture, conflated with the monks hood in my interpretation.

Meaning is defined as relative to context, and as the postmodernist Derrida pointed out, context is infinite. Pop continues, "Since the American Black has been freed he's only ever got on by siding with the Whiteman, or climbing up on his Brother's shoulders. The World's for the needy and not the greedy." He finishes with a cadence like an MC, or a Reggae DJ.

I see an add for a rare Sun Ra video as I'm scanning through, some of the music bumf that I collected, on my walkabout up and down the Drag, and around 6th Street. "The Sound of Joy". I wrote, or should I say vocalised some lyrics to this tune once. I make a mental note.

Pop's ailments are many, back in 1992, he had an operation for cancer of the colon. I'll need to get some colonic irrigation when I get back. An Indian friend of mine Sabitri, specialises in it. Pop's also had a heart attack, back in 1991, and now he's got diabetes. He experiments with his diabetes. I watch as he pricks his finger for blood, and tests it on his little meter thing. "I might not be what I wanna be, but I sure nuff ain't what I used to be", Pop says in his darkly philosophical manner. Pop's seventy five, and Evelyn's forty eight. It's been the spiritual journey that I didn't expect. Evelyn's cooked me grits, and biscuits and eggs for breakfast. She's playing a Gospel tape. I'm hearing Gospel on TV, Gospel on the Radio, the Lord is in my head, and in daily conversation. "Kindness'll sort anything", Pop says. I'm at home in Singleton Avenue, it's eleven thirty-three in the morning, and I'm waiting to go to town with Pop. Pop's cooking his own eggs, the way he likes them. He shows me how to cook eggs, and tie the bread again. He scolds everyone continually. I'm being forced to hold my tongue, being taught tolerance, restraint, and perseverance. The perseverance of Saints, like Pastor Reeves will have talked about on Sunday.

Three teen-age rappers walk past the kitchen window, their flow is distinctly Southern in tone, they sound good. The down-home Rootical-street stuff is always the best. "No noise is good noise", Pop chides with a mischievous grin. Amused by his variation on an old proverb he adds, "I come up with some off the wall stuff sometimes... ", and we both laugh out loud. Pop starts to tell me about his rhyming competitions as a youth, "We just hoot on, and when you just hoot on you just say anything to make it rhyme. Anything just to say the last word."

Pop is crooning one of his deeply plaintive, torch songs. He's so poetic, sensitive, and sentimental at times. "A quiet face is a quiet place. Seeing memories that it can't erase. Quiet eyes with a quiet stare. Seeing memories no longer there". It sounds like me being here, is dredging up as much silt, from the bottom of Pop's heart, as it is for me. He's the same star sign as me. He mentioned it first I wasn't going to. It's no coincidence that I'm a poet, and a singer song writer, Pop has an award from the American Song Festival for, "Excellence in creative writing, originality, technical skills, and talent in composition." He croons on, "Quiet eyes forget a lot concealing all the mind can not." He stops crooning to espouse some of his, tumble-weed philosophy to me, "The same wind blows on you that blows on me which shows you that the Supreme being does not respect personalities." I wasn't sure what he meant exactly, or who he was aiming at but, I understood the point. We are all part of something far bigger than our individual selves.

Diamond comes in from her room when she hears Pop singing. Pop responds by telling me about the Mexican's "Iddy-biddy life" song. Diamond loves it. "Sing it ! Sing it Gran-Pop !", she pleads all smiles, and she grins. So Pop sings it. Diamond joins in and they laugh at the funny parts. Then she asks him to sing the "Caribbean Trinidad song". He sings it, and they do a little dance, Pop with his arms and shoulders. "It's a calypso", I say amazed. I think of my Nephews, Ashur and Malik, singing Half-Cast-Shine Calypso's, composed, and taught to them in Liverpool by their Grand-Dad, Uriah. This is what it's all about for me as an artist, passing on the simple things that help to make us fully formed Human Beings. Stuff that keeps us in touch with our own Human Souls. Pop kisses Diamond on the forehead, and tells her to get ready to go to school, and we'll drop her off on the way to Capitol Plaza. Pop drops Diamond at school everyday, and picks her up like clockwork. At this point in his life, it's part of what's keeping him alive I reckon. The TV grabs my attention. Bill Clinton on internet shopping. An advert for Zanzibar World Treasures comes on. A couple use their personal travel tales to plug their World trade craft shop on TV, and radio. It's an us-we-toi-thang, located in the shadow of Shady Oak.

Diamond's ready, Pop and Evelyn exchange some hostile banter. He slags off her daughter, Diamond's Mom, and her grand sons, Diamond's brothers. It's getting to sound like a scratched record, with the needle stuck. Evelyn's trying to keep pleasant, to save face in front of me. I'm uneasy, but helpless to intervene. "Let's get the hell outa here", Pop says sounding like the Duke. So we do, but I'm perturbed by his philistine attitude.

Walkabout.

When ever I hit a new village, town, or city, I like to do as much of the exploring as I can on foot, and besides I never learnt to drive. Austin Texas, the World's coolest of capitals of culture, better known for it's "Slacker" mentality. Lionised by the local film-making sensation Richard Linklater, who holds a biannual film festival here in cahoots with Quentin Tarrantino. It's also famous for being the birth place of Head-knecks, who are the original 'Beatniks', known in Austin as 'Slackers', (but this could be just Texan hype), and Janis Joplin, Mike Nesbit of the Monkees, Willie Nelson, Waylon Jennings, and the whole "Outlaw Country" movement, with it's weed smoking Cool Cowboys, and it's long haired Cosmic Cowpokes for Peace, or did I make that bit up. No I didn't they're real. Rebel Country artists who thought Nashville had become too 'Square', too restrictive, and too darn formulaic, and last but not least the legendary Bill Hicks.

After gleaning what local awareness I could for one morning, from the tv and radio, I decide to go on a walk-about. Pop has some stuff he needs to do, and although it's only my first day, I really feel so at home in Austin that's it's no problem to just say to him, "Listen Pop. I'm gonna go on a walkabout, to check out the lay of the land, if that's cool with you." Of course it was cool, a few words of caution, "OK son, but remember this ain't England". "Yeah Pop... I know..." We both smile.

Pop lives on the East side, according to the guide books anywhere East of inter State Highway 35 is considered dangerous territory. They usually add because it's predominantly populated by Black and Hispanic peoples. Now it's time to take a walk on the West Side, and that's something that can get a lot more dangerous than the guidebooks would have you imagine, particularly if your like me a poet, just luxuriating in being here at this idyllic point in time. Of course it only gets dangerous on the West side, if like me you just happen to be Black or Hispanic.

"Don't Mess with Texas" the car sticker tells me. I don't intend to so I'm not worried. This place is my long lost roots. I'm on a mission ya'll as a Bluesologist, that is a self-styled bongo playing poet-philosopher, cultural- historian, with a Lee Oscar A Natural Minor harmonica, as prescribed by Mel Bay. I had always been aware that all culture, all racial identities were hybrid. The Engish language is primarily a fusion of Latin, from the Roman presence, French from the Norman invasion, and of course Anglo- Saxon itself being a hybrid identity, and a patoise that evolved as a lingua franca to help the dozen, or so Gemanic tribes that invaded England back in the day, to negotiate trade. Royal has French origins, as in Le Roi, Rex is Latin for king, which itself is related to Konig, which is German. Having at least three etymlogical threads to the fabric of my identity, as an English speaking person, just for starters, I find it hard to reduce myself to anything less than hybrid in origin. I celebrate a syncretic-eclecticism in the main. Like Kenneth McKenna I seek boundary dissolving activities, and cultural forms, in the service of building bridges between people. As Bob Marley sang in his song Revolution, "In I'se is Black, in Is'e is White, in Is'e is Red, inna deh egg". That sums me up. I actually met Bob Marley once. It was when some other youth workers, and myself took a coach load of youths from The Rialto Community Centre, and The Methodist Youth Club to see the Wailers in Manchester. An experience that I will cherish for ever. I had dreadlocks at the time and had been seriously into Rasta, and Reggae, and all things Red, Gold, and Green. We looked at each other, and recognised. It was a Joycian epiphany for me. Somebody once described my stuff as Gothic. Maybe that's the German in me. As I often tell people, "Dhey used to call Bob Marley the German. So goh run aan tell dhat to deh people dhem..!" But whatever shapes us it's always down to the 'contingency' of life in the end, and ultimately God. As the Sufis say, "Man plans and Allah plans, and Allah is the best of planners". Who can say what will happen in time ? "The Sufi has arrived at a point where the paint is mixed that colours the World", as Shabistari once said. Shabistari got his Sufism from Ibn Araby, and Al Ghazali, who had already lived and passed away.

If not for the Soul validation I got from the above, and a whole host of mucho-many more artists, poets, philosophers, and teachers, then who knows how long I would have been throwing my highest aspirations into the garbage can as unworthy. Growing up in the scientific-materialist, and largely Racist atmosphere of the time, there was a serious dearth of like minded people. People capable of appreciating my search for an identity beyond 'Race'. An identity based on the 'Inner' person, an identity based on Spirituality. As a result of which I hid it, and disguised it as a sort of Ju-Ju politics, for fear of victimisation, as the 'once upon a time' Radical Atmosphere of the Seventies and Sixties, gave way to an ultra conservatism, characterised by an inwardly spiralling sense of nihilism during the Punk years, and a general Redkneck type of Xenophobia, due to the influence of Thatcherism. In Liverpool, and the North in general at that time it was partly due to, an inherent lack of self esteem since the demise of the City as a great sea port, the decline of the docks, the unemployment, and the end of the industrial North. The chasm of difference between the Cosmopolitan awareness, of the outgoing past, and the inward looking, Nationalistic-parochial present we experienced during Brexit. As such, it's about separation and exclusion versus connection and inclusion, to put it in a nutshell.

Home On The Range.

After over forty years of great expectations I'm in Austin, Texas. Visiting, my long lost Poppa, "Me arl fellah", and lots of other "Fambo" as they say in my own Scouse dialect. I'm comparing the Texas tradition, "Come early ! Be loud ! Stay late!", with the Scouse tradition, "Late start ! Early dart !", sounds like a 'Slacker' sentiment don't it. There's a similar layed-back rhythm to life in Austin. It's a slow paced, slackish, laid-back, Beatcity, smell the ganja tea, coffee sort of place. A weird mix of the rebellious, the bohemian, and the retarded right wing. A bit like home. I like it so far. I turn North out of Pop's gate up Singleton Avenue, and then I take a left at the Meat Packing factory on the corner where the sign reads: "Long Horn Meat: Hot Links". Which I suppose sounds a tad less suggestive than: "Long Horn Meat: Hot Sausages".

For some reason this sign reminds me of one of Mom's old girl friend's Yvonne. I snap a shot of the damaged sign, it's a local landmark by which I can find my way back home once I hit Martin Luther King Boulevarde. Growing up I used to go to various US air bases to shop at the PX, with Mom, and her American friends, and their kids. It was a great day out. Some of Mom's friends where African-American like Tomasina, and others were English, but married to Americans. She had a White friend called Yvonne, who was married to a White Yank called Gerry Duckworth. They lived at the top of our street, Eastbourne Street in Everton, in later years. Yvonne was a

Scouser, a Beatnik. She had a flat on Huskisson Street, in what we called the South End, later called Toxteth, in the media, after the Toxteth Uprisings/Riots of 1981. At the time I was about 5 years old. John Lennon lived in the flat below them. She didn't like him, because she would sometimes hear him arguing with his girl friend, but that's another story. As for me as I grew up Lennon became one of my heroes, due to the fact that he married Yoko Ono, and supported the Black Panthers. The Beatles also single handedly challenged segregation in the Southern States, their stadium gigs were the first time many Black people had even seen inside a stadium in the South, let alone be part of a mixed audience. Lennon was what Ken Wilber would describe as "Healthy Green".

Gerry Duckworth was a happy, smiling sort of a guy, soft spoken, with a slow Deep-Fried Southern accent. Yvonne was like Joanna Lumley's character, the glamorous lush in 'Absolutely Fabulous', from what I can recall of those times anyway. I see her with a tall, heavily lacquered and back combed, peroxide blonde bee-hive hair-do. Big hair, eyes all blue eyeshadow, and heavy on the mascara. Slouching on a chaisse-lounge, in tight slacks, angora wool sweater with leopard print mules on. Long painted finger-nails, slim American Cool menthol ciggie, hanging from a black and gold cigarette holder, squirting soda into a short drink, in a chunky Scotch glass, from one of those stylish at the time, metallic soda siphons, that nearly everyone who had a bar... Had. And most people had bars at that time if I remember rightly. Often with a Spanish flamenco doll on the counter, and a tea-towel imprinted with the poster from a bull fight hanging on the back wall, along with a sombrero or a small artificial bulls complete with colourful pink red and yellow cocktail skewers sticking out of its kneck. I can hear her talking in an over the top, affected, Yankee accent, even though she was from Liverpool, and only lived in the states for about two years. They had a son called Jim-Bob, who was born this side, and we used to hang together when we had to. But he was a real spiteful kid, and we were just in competition over nearly everything most of the time. Once Mom, Yvonne, Jim-Bob, and me, we all went to stay on the US Air Base, down in the Norfolk Broads, for a week.

The night drive was amazing to me at the time, it was a mini road trip in between sleeping, and waking up drowsy. The atmosphere was electric. Full of adventure. Mystery and expectation. I remember seeing rabbits, foxes, pheasants, and various wild-life for the first time in their own natural environments. Mom and her posse were..., looking back as a life-long student of cultural history, they were some raucous Blues ladies in their time. Scouse Beatniks on the loose. The Black G.I.'s were in fact the inspiration for Liverpool counter-culture of the 1960's, and the adoption of Blues and Soul by the local L8/Toxteth music scene, including The Beatles. Once we stopped for five minutes down a country lane, so that Yvonne could go for a wee. She came back from the woods, with a leather belt that she'd found. It had a big Texan cowboy buckle, the head of a long horn steer. "Look what some dirty GI's left behind!", Yvonne drawled. The women laughed. I imagined some GI defecating in the woods, and leaving his belt behind. On reflection I think the women had laughed at a joke, that at the time, only they understood, those dames were thinking of something else.

As we drove through Berkshire, and Oxfordshire, pheasants kept running out into the road. "Little fuckers", my Mother called the pheasants. "Let's catch on of them", Yvonne slurred. So they used the belt as a snare, to catch a pheasant for dinner. Jim-Bob got to keep the belt eventually. I was peeved, but I'd forgotten once we'd reached the base at Lakenheath. It was Christmas from then on in, the PX was me Mother's favourite place.

I remember the women only parties back then, music and stand-up comedy albums. Mom and Yvonne would play Red Skelton, and Red Fox records, when we used to visit Yvonne's pad on Huskisson Street. They be drinking, and crack up laughing, at all the stuff we could never work out. I had an image of a red skeleton, talking in a Black American accent that's all, or a red cartoon fox like a Huckleberry Hound type of thing. I'll have to listen to some of those albums one day, and find out what that joke about making catapults out of knicker elastic was all about. I still can't work it out. It must be a Sixties thing. They had some cool times and some cool Blues&Soul party-nites. All of us kids would be bunked in together in one big double bed, with the older one's as baby sitters while the old folks was out clubbing in the Beacon Club on Upper Parliament Street, which was just across the road from Tomasina's top-floor flat, where we'd be spying out the window sometimes watching, and waiting for them to come out when we couldn't sleep, which was most of the time. Some in the top and some in the bottom of the bed, like sardines in a quilted can. We'd leave our socks on, and tie the feet together so that we wouldn't fall asleep until the folks got back. That was Wardell's idea. At least that was the plan. It depended on how late they stayed out how awake we'd be.

They'd all come in from the club, and we'd hear the music start up on the Dansette record player. From Chubby Checker, "The Twist", to Percy Sledge, "When a man loves a Woman", all them golden oldies. We'd leap up out of bed and run into the room, and start twisting along with everyone else, cos we knew we got money off our folks, and their friends when they were drunk. Just for being cute, and entertaining. We were just being Hip kids in tune with the vibes of the times.

Some of those Hip kids have been living in the States for over fourty years now. One in particular has been living in a Spanish speaking community for over 40 years, Mandy Chor. I was in touch with her on Facebook, and I sent her a photo of her brother Dino, and little sister Girna with their G.I. Pop Eddie, and myself in our back garden in Haven Road, Fazakerley. I was twelve years old, Dino was about nine, and Girna about seven. She sent me a photo of myself at seventeen years old, standing in front of the cenotaph on St George's Plateau, in front of St. George's Hall, with a massive Afro, two-tone flares, and a Jimmy Hendrex type jacket, that her Pop Eddie had taken on another occasion.   This was about the same time my aunty Mary, and her daughter Halima went to live in the States, and are still there, well... are still here in America.

I even came across Mom's old mate Yvonne, from Huskisson Street on Facebook. We were both amazed, and ecstatic to find each other. She was quite frail, and had cancer, but her face was still like a model. The last time I'd seen her I could only have been five years old. I know that because our Tracie hadn't been born, and she was born when I was seven. She spoke a lot about Mom and Pop, and those Huskisson Street days, the laughing, the singing, the dancing. Singing and dancing was how you got approval in those days. In fact everything was a song and dance. Soulfulness is a hard habit to break. Then you realise as you get older, and go to University, that this is the experience of a minority culture, it's popular culture. And it will keep you ghettoised. You also realise that you must now, try and assimilate to mainstream sobriety, or society, what ever. That's the script as it pans out to my eyes. Even now. But how can you turn your back on your own people, the masses of the people, and your own life. "There in lies the rub", as Will the Quill would say.

The Food Of Love.

All Black music was a cultural space, that had been running through my veins since before I was born. I was hearing the music, and the accent, the rhythms, and voice patterns of these places through my mother's stomach lining when I was in the womb. I know it because I am stilling feeling it now, but I've never been here before, and that's what makes it so surreal. Hyper-Reale. Did I just intuitively make that term up to describe an existential state? Hyper-Reale. All Quadrant Full On Awareness, as Wilber might say, sort of. I take one more look at the Longhorn sign, that'll be my landmark. I can locate Singleton from there. I stroll Westward along Martin Luther King Jnr Boulevarde, for about two blocks, then I cross the road just before Church Street, and head North past Alamo Park. I mean you know your in Texas when you have places with names like Alamo Park, then left and West along Manor Road. Pop lives on Singleton Avenue which slopes gently down hill South of MLK Boulevarde, looking down from the top Singleton looks like a bunch of shacks. It's almost completely hidden, amidst the jungle of over grown trees, and bushes, that tower above most of the single level houses, bungalows basically.

The Ghetto side of MLK Boulevarde, speaks in untended gardens, where the over-hanging branches, and wilderness of bushes overflow into the road, with the basket-ball hoops, and classic Americana rust buckets. Turn and look across MLK, and it's still Black and Hispanic, but the houses are more modern, more up-market with carefully manicured lawns striped like, Wembley on an FA Cup Final day. Flower beds, yellow rose of Texas rose bushes, sculptured hedge rows, and well rounded trees. A lot of the gardens and houses on MLK, and North of Singleton are clearly visible, the cars are newer, no beat-up old jalopies. Most of the gardens have really kitsch plaster replicas of the Statue of Liberty, or the map of Texas State, or the outline of the USA, or some form or other of cheesey patriotic garden ornamentation, usually decorated with the Stars and Stripes, or some reworking of the red, white, and blue semiotics of "Old Glory."

I eventually get to Inter-State Highway, Mopac 35 up by Calvary Cemetery, and find a place to cross where the 258B crosses over the Mopac 35. I stop halfway across the bridge that spans the motor-way and gaze South, then North it's as if the whole the USA slopes Southwards towards Mexico. I ponder the destination of the Big Mach trucks that are steaming along in both directions beneath me. There's a massive police strong hold at the intersection of East Austin and the University Complex, and a poster for the "Gray Panthers". I continue across the bridge and down an embankment to end up at East Campus Drive. I pass the University soccer pitch where some students from University of Texas are training, which takes me by surprise.

"English football, or Soccer as they call it in the States, at UT", I think, "OK-OK that's cool". Soon I find myself with the Texas Memorial Stadium to my left, and North to my right is the UT Performance Arts Centre, "Endowment For Performing Excellence", it says outside, along with compulsory motto,"Give the Gift that Keeps Growing". In the distance just behind that, I can see the LBJ Library and Museum. As I proceed all eyes, and ears past a bronze statue of "The Long Horn Band", the UT trad-jazz band whose motto is,"Till Gabriel blows his horn". I'm seeking The Drag on Guadaloupe Street it's supposed to be a good spot for cafes, records stores, and bookshops. In particular I'm heading for the Dobie Mall which houses the Book Market, and a place called Fringe Ware, an independant place that specialises in underground, banned, and heretical texts. I mean why wouldn't I ? Right !

Texas is known as the "Buckle of the Bible Belt". As I mosy across Jacinto Boulevarde I realise I am now deep within the University of Texas Campus Complex, and I'm aware how all of a sudden, how White the place is. Pop don't really like White Yanks, "Honkies", he calls them, or "Redkneck Peckerwoods". Three fifths of Americans are ethnocentric. Identity politics, although necessary up to a point, if not transcended only leads to a sort of inward looking narrowness, and a fragmentation into polarised tribes, and becomes quite toxic. As can be seen in most kinds of exclusivity. A few more yards, and I'm standing face to face with the famous statue of MLK that stands facing the Ghetto, arms outstretched in a token gesture of acceptance, and welcome towards the Hoody-Hood. I find out later that the statue was originally inside the Hood, but that the University has slowly, but surely spread into the area until now it has engulfed the statue in gentrification.

In My Element.

The campus is a nice place to wander about, having done

over ten years of higher education, at least five of those years at the John Moores University in Liverpool. Campus life is sort of a normal environment for me, it's a big part of my life, I'm at home in libraries, book stores, and stationary shops. I find the Dobie Mall, its discreet, sparse for Austin. There's more people visible now, but it's so spacious, and laid back that it leaves a lot more distance between people on a one to one level, so you get a sense that the place is under populated. I notice the birds, black with yellow eyes, they are Mocking Birds, I discover later in a book on local wildlife, they look like the birds in Barbados. We must be on the same latitude I think to myself, so many similarities in the land and the climate, and the fact that Barbados picks up Country Radio from here explains a lot. I stroll up the Drag looking for Antone's bespoke record store. I make a note of where the bike hire place is.

Everything rhymes in Texas, Buy and Fly, Surf and Turf, Guns for Nuns, Pedal to the Metal as Pop would say. I stop at Quackenbushes, a hip student hang out that does a nice daily lunch for four dollars. There's some Boho types playing chess, a reading room, free news papers, a cigar stand, a wooden Indian, and they sell "Texas" cigarette papers. I buy a bunch of them for souvenirs. "You plannin' to do a lot of smokin' ?", the girl serving me asks. The Philipino-American guy behind the counter with her points to the packet and says, "Texas". It dawns on her that I'm a tourist of sorts, and I'm buying them for the logo, more than anything. I'm buying them mostly for my Rasta Brother, Ras Kif, back inna Blighty, who has some impressive collection of skins, and rolling papers from Around the World. Quackenbushes is a cool place. It's so cool it was used as the back drop for an instant of fame in the film "Slackers". People are polite here, they say, "Sir" and "Maam". I like that. A cowboy walks past, in a tan leather jacket, he's unshaven, and wearing a beat up old cowboy hat, with the sides curled forward like a three cornered hat, and a sweaty red and white bandanna tied around his scrawny throat. His cowboy boots are a bit worn at the heels. He looks like a modern day saddle- tramp, without his horse. Somebody from a short story I wrote at school called the "Red Bandanna". But this isn't a costume, this is who he is. He probably owns a motorbike. It's all culture to me, all just as amazing as being in a movie. I make a guess that he's going to the pool hall I just passed, "The Hole in the Wall". I took a look in there, it looked a bit of a rough-kneck-cowboy sort of a place. I was gonna go in there, but after taking a peak inside. I thought twice.

I wander out along The Drag, buy a Texas Long Horns base-ball cap. That's the UT football team. I buy a "Take Six" Gospel crooners CD in Tower Music Mart. I continue my walkabout, I discover where Antone's is for future reference, and an amazing US surplus store, (Its like the old style Army and navy stores we used to have back in the day in Liverpool, and which you still see in London), with everything you could ask for, by way of utility clothing. Slackers hang-out, and sit-off on the side-walk, all up and down the Drag on Guadaloupe Street, generally busking or just begging. One little combo of young White dudes, all Rasta tams, and blonde Dervish/Dread locks are playing some serious, acoustic Nya- Binghi beat. They compliment it, with some sweet Reggae mandolin, wafting in and out of the groove, as soft as the balmy Texas breeze. I toss them some coins. "Blessings me Lion", one of them says to me inna a Dread-Texan styly. "One Love me Idren", I reply. We all share some smiles and each of us nods. The Sister just tosses her head to one side, and rocks to the riddim. It's all good. Reggae is the Roots-Rock-Rebel music Outer-National, well at least to 'dhem dhat' knows is not a colour ting… Not any more. Jah know dhat feh tru. Other guys and gals are sat-off, up against shop fronts on the pavement. Some are begging with lines of coins on the floor in front of them, spread out like street-I- Ching. One seedy looking guy, with a big bushy beard, and woolen hat pulled down over his bushy red hair, has spelt out a letter "B" with cents and quarters. "Help me spell beer buddy!" he asks. I don't drink, but I add a few coins, cos he called me buddy. As I'm placing the coins to make an " E", I notice that each state has it's own "quarter", for example, Georgia's has a peach on it. I'm keeping an eye out for the set, but there seems to be only about three types in circulation. Just up from the ZZ Top stunt man spelling out beer in coins, a group of feral Slackers, are seriously dishing out their liquor, from a bottle inside a brown paper bag. I'm beginning to get a feel for the demographics of the Drag. I probably look like a janitor, or service worker, or even, in my dreams a lecturer, or mature student. I walk a bit further down the Drag, taking in the laid-back hustling vibe on the ground. It's all wooly hats, fleeces, plaid shirts, baggy jeans, tie-dye t-shirts and skirts, and combat fatigues. A placidly poised, Hippy girl with coloured braids in her hair, and friendship bracelettes plaited around her wrists, has almost spelt the word "Love", with her coin collection. I add some more coins to complete her project. A Black brother in a demin shirt, army fatigues, shades, and a turquoise and orange, Miami Dolphins base-ball cap, is sauntering towards me down the Drag. He eyeballs me, recognises my vibe, smiles and enquires, "Bud brother?" "Nah ! Bro...Me kool yuh know." I reply without breaking my stride. He smiles and nods. Checking out my accent. The Brotherman smiles, and nods knowingly, in the instant that our eyes meet. Soul to Soul, maybe at my accent, maybe just out of Black recognition. He can see today, I'm an undercover Brother. On a mission. People seem so warm over here, so far, but no weed for me today. At least not while I'm staying at Pop's, I tell myself. I heard the way he was cussing out Evelyn, cos he suspects that she smokes weed. When I scoped the Big Youth, "Drealock Dread" album in Pop's record collection, it never dawned on me that it could be Evelyn's. But if she smokes herb, then that would make a lorra sense. You can't really dig Reggae without Sensi.

Mojo's Daily Grind.

It's a warm afternoon for November, sunny too. It's like being on holiday in a way, none of the gravity that I thought I

MICROWAVE TEA.

might face. Just a cool, mellow, laidback acceptance. I'm sat outside Mojo's Daily Grind, a friendly place full of Students from the Texas Uni, and a variety of intellectual, and arty types. It's known as a poetry, and live folk music haven, and I'm enjoying a well needed cup of tea. I like the chunky-wood DIY feel of the place. Their motto says it all,"Starbucks fuck off. Get out of my neighbourhood." I'm people watching and perusing the Rough Guide to Texas, and I see that there is a place called the Ruda Maya, this top Peruvian Coffee bar where they have a great poetry, and acoustic scene going on. I scribble it into my itinerary for the day, and I get up to make a move. It's on West 4th Street. I walk down Lavaca in the direction of West 4th Street, looking for Red River, and East Cesar Chavez Street, where the Austin Convention and Vistors Centre is. Being a would-be-wordsmith, I'm getting into checking out the characteristic names of the places I'm passing on the way. It becomes a walk-about game. Boots and Saddles, Guns'R'Us, Ego's, Steamboat Sally's, Oil Can Harry's. The Black Cat Lounge, sounds like a cat-house, as does Maggie Maes, which now you come to mention it does sound like a Hill Billy name, as well as a Scouse name. The Buffolo Club, the Cactus Club, a folksy feel to it, the Caucus Club, a Jazz hot-spot, the Broken Spoke, a Country and Western watering hole, Club Latino a spicey Tijano bar, the Flamingo Cantina, good place for Reggae and World Beat, La Zora Rosa, Casino el Camino, two nice sounding Mexican dames, sorry I meant two nice sounding Mexican names. Travelling from Toxteth to Texas only the day before, I'm taking my walkabout directions from my "Rough Guide". What the "Rough" guide doesn't tell me, is that down town Austin's silently segregated. Well it does mention it actually, but I haven't got to that bit yet. It warns Black people from the U.K. that it's, Whites on the Westside, Mexicans and Blacks on the Eastside. In actuality it's Blacks, Mexicans, and the odd poor White Trash family, who might have just moved up from the trailer park, down by Threadgills. As I hit the corner of Lavaca and East 17th I see some graffiti, "World Peace Through Tex-Mex". As I turn the corner, next thing I see is the magnificent Capitol Building built from Texas, sun-set red, limestone. As the guide book says, taller than the Capitol in Washington DC at 311 foot high, if you count the Goddess of Liberty figurine that sits on top of it's dome. I'm in the metropolitan centre. I pass the Scottish Lodge House. It's a magnificent, austere, towering stone edifice, actually designed like a Scottish Church but larger. I ponder going in, and talking to someone about my Scottish relatives, the McCleans, as a sort of Ali G type experiment. Thinking back to a documentary I saw once about WASPisms, I imagine that it's most probably the local KKK HQ. I let the idea dissolve in the hazy pink Texas light. I make my way across Capitol Hill's rich-lush green parklands, that contrast so vividly with the red stone architecture.

A statue of Daniel Boone has me spellbound in historical revery for a good five to ten minutes, child-hood hero-worship, and cinematic imaginings, remembering the movie the Alamo. My Aunty Mary made me a Daniel Boone "Racoon skin" hat, from an old fox fur, when I was a kid. I loved it. On the way to the Capitol Visitors Centre, I take notes from the public artifacts that surround me; Austin; population 567, 000. Texas; State of the Arts, pecan pies, armadillos (Pop has some burrowing under his house out back), mocking birds, road runners, blue bonnets (a type of flower), red chilli peppers, barbed wire museums (Texas invented barbwire), oil wells, and long horn steer. I see a birch-bark, open canoe on top of a Winnebago, at the lights. It's designs are so familiar to me. They speak to me. The whole thing invokes an inner vision of mountains, and cool clear lakes surrounded by pine forests, and braves fishing with bows and arrows from canoes just like this one. Scenes from my very first Native American Indian book, that Arturo had brought me back from the States when I was five years old. The couple in the Winnebago are both silver haired. Both probably retired, and living out their dream of touring the still existent wildernesses of this vast, and varied land. I feel mixed emotions, a sense of awe at this symbol of a lost civilisation, and a feeling of envy, bordering ever so slightly on resentment. I wanted to float that canoe on a lake amidst the dancing pines, with the Ghosts of my Red ancestors, and show them my skill with a bow. I let it pass. There was too much to see of wonder, right here in the present moment, to be dwelling on lost treasures of yester-year, and unattainable dreamings. Texas has existed under six different flags since Estevan, the first recorded African-American, to explore the region North of the Rio Grande, was washed ashore near Galveston in 1528. Since then it's been under Spain, France, Mexico, Republic of Texas, The Confederacy, and the United States. I marvel at the detail in a larger than life painting of Davy Crocket in the Austin museum. Stand mesmerised by paintings of scenes from The Alamo, and various other scenes taken straight from the Texas history, and what is for me the mystery of Texas. I keep thinking it's a dream being so close to this history, so close to my roots that I can feel it in me. Everytime I see a wooden Indian, or a cowboy hat, or a gun, or a Mexican, or a lingering sign of the original Native American culture like the Oklahoma Indian license plate, or the Otoe Indian decals on a tractor, Redman chewing tobacco, with the Chief's head, and Eagle feathered head-dress emblazoned across it. I am spellbound. It all takes me back to my wig-wam days as a kid, playing Cowboys and Indians in my buckskins, eagle feathers, and beaded mocassins. In the big toy room upstairs in the big old family house, on Eastbourne Street, Everton, Liverpool. It takes me back to myself.

Burnt Soul.

One of my most important teachers in the Jazzgriot tradition, was Sheikh Suleiman Al Hadi of the Last Poets as stated, a student of Malcolm X, and a veteran of the prison Da'wa programme. Like Malcolm he taught us that, "Anger is oppression's burn on the Human Soul. Depression is when the self-hate takes control." Malcolm taught us that the antidote to that dark state is to learn to love ourselves. You may be unemployed, but your still somebody, you may feel null and void, but your still somebody. As Martin Luther King told us to say, "I am somebody". That whole era was the cultural hot-house, in which the seeds of my artistic aesthetics were nurtured. This book, like the art of most of my contemporaries, is also about trying to say, despite all of these things that have tried to negate my existance, and reduce it to something that can be easily dismissed, without wishing to seem egotistical, "I am somebody !" That's all folks.

The Ruta Maya Coffee House.

Down town Austin is hot, lazy, hazy, and dusty, but fairley deserted for a Saturday afternoon. Even the student area was relatively desolate once you moved away from The Drag. Maybe it's because it's a bank holiday of sorts. Liverpool goes dead once all the students go home for the holidays. I mosied on down the dusty streets, and I saw a young Slacker couple. The guy was wearing what looked to me like a white woolen topi, a Muslim prayer cap to the uninitiated. "Cool", I thought. "They got some Womadism going on over here." Then just as I reach a cross roads I look around to get my bearings. Lo and behold there in front of me is the Ruta Maya, looking like a cantina from an old movie set to me. So I mosies into this cool looking palace of poetry, philosophy, and people. It's a weird time of day, and it's virtually empty but for a couple of silent, mean looking White dudes sitting facing the door. And one or two other silent shady-looking Bad Cowboy types, looking directly at me as I walk in. A young woman who looks a bit like a Goth, with dyed Red hair, nose piercings, tats and a black t-shirt with the Coffe Shop logo and name in white text across the front, is serving behind the counter. There's a kind of a head shop-tobacconist place, that runs into the coffee house, at the side of the bar by the door. It's a sort of small arcade. I mosey on in there and browse around.

The people in there seem friendly enough, outside on the veranda there are people playing chess. The coffee smells good, as a rule I generally drink tea, but when I'm travelling I like to try the coffee if it's notoriously good. So I double back into the coffee house. I'm chilling at the counter waiting to get served, and I turn around for a second, and this fellah stands in front of me. I think nothing of it, until another guy gets up and stands in front of him. It's the same two guys. One is wearing a black shirt, and a black leather waist coat, and looks like the Ysabel Kid, an outlaw from a comic-strip back in the day called The Dakotas. He has long, greasy, lank hair falling into his eyes, and is hunched over like someone with low self-esteem. I can feel a weird sort of silent hostility coming from him, but it's been so nice up to now, that I am loathe to believe it. The other one is less memorable, he was just sort of fair, with a Zapata moustache, and in a corderoi shirt, but menacing as such. If somebody that wears corduroy, can possibly be menacing, then they can in Austin. So I'm musing to myself just trying to make some sort of pleasant sense of it all, and it looks like they're saying with their body language that, maybe they're before me in the queue. So being sociable I say, "I'm sorry I didn't realise you were waiting to get served." Before he can answer, the kid with the white woolen hat, that I saw a minute earlier, has doubled back on himself, and is coming through the main door, behind me. He's got the sun to his back, and I can just make out a sardonic sneer, as he starts advancing on me, chanting, "No Chics ! No Bucks ! No Cokynuts !" Which I didn't know at the time being my first day there, was supposed to tell me that they didn't serve Mexicans, that is Chicano's, Buck Negro's, or even Coconuts, that is someone of colour, white on the inside brown on the outside. I am genuinely oblivious at this point, because the accents pure Hill-Billy, and he's sung it with a, a sinister sing-songy-nursery-rhyme, mocking tone to it. So although the words never computed fully. The macabre vibe he was projecting did. So I says to the girl wiping coffee cups behind the counter, "So have you got any coffee then? I'll try a house coffee, one of those Peruvian coffees if you have one, please luv."

At which point a couple more of these, by now overt Rednecks, started appearing from nowhere, and crowding in on me. One was cross-eyed, and had a piece of straw, sticking out between his evil clenched, tobacco stained teeth. Next it was the Ysabel Kid who chipped in with the malicious mantra, "No Chics ! No Bucks ! No Cocynuts!" As the Corderouy Cowboy echoed his leather vested amigo, "No Chics! No Bucks! No Cocynuts!", the words started to sink in slowly. I'm standing there absorbing all of the possible implications of finding myself, in my worst case scenario of walking into a Redneck bar, full of KKK sympathisers. A small amount of fear may have registered, all of a sudden on my gob- smacked face, which in turn may have prompted the young woman behind the counter to say, "Listen to how he's talking. He's ain't one the Nigres from around here!" So of course one of them says, "Where you from boy?" So I says, "Liverpool like." And so you can guess what they ask me, "Do you know the Beatles?" Well not long before I'd arrived in Austin, a Black Brother had been dragged through Jasper County behind a pick-up truck by some Red Knecks, and his body parts had been found scattered over a twelve kilometer radius. So I'm thinking, "Do I know the Beatles. I've got Ringo Starr's drum kit in the house. My mate, the Beatles original manager was Lord Woodbine, an old Calypsonian from Liverpool, blah blah, who had a second hand shop on Granby Street through the Sixties and Seventies, blah, blah blah... And he sold this old Beverley Kit to me around 1975... Blah blah..." And I'm just trying to blagh me way out of there at this point ('blagh' is slang taken from the Arabic word Balagha, meaning eloquence, but used as English slang for 'bullshit'), but the guy in the white woolen hat seems to have it in for me. I think maybe because he's with his girl he feels the need to prove something, I don't know. He comes up real close to me, right in my face and says, " Kangol huh!" And he gave my Kangol Jacket a dirty look like it meant something bad to him. So I'm trying to compute, maybe it's Kangol equals Hip-Hop, equates with Black? Who knows what his problem was...? But all at once I realise I'm deep in potential Ku Klux Klan territory.

I start humouring them. So I ask them if they know ... "Willie Nelson, Janis Joplin, Stevie-Ray Vaughn, or Mike Nesmith from the Monkees", and they seem a bit perplexed. So I say, "They're all from Austin I thought you just might know them. Do you know the first record I ever bought was, "I'm a Believer" by the Monkees. Blah-blah-blah... My first album was "Rubber Soul" by the Beatles blah blah blah. They weren't amused, and I thought to meself, "Woh ! Buck... wind your kneck in kidder." I could hear this guy starting up the pick-up truck out back, and I had visions of getting a worms eye view of Travis County, which I couldn't imagine to have been much, better than Jasper County at that level. Have you ever had that feeling that your about, five minutes away from a serious truck- dragging. It was one of them moments. Then the hostility dissipated into a reluctant tolerance on realising it was my first day in Austin. And never the less I actually managed to get a cup of coffee after I'd chatted to the waitress. It was her, that had helped them, and me to realise, that I was from out of town, and I didn't know the rules. I took my coffee, and sat down near the open door. Remembering what Mom had told me, about the Scotsborough Boys. Just in case I'd talked to the waitress just a tad too long. I felt like I'd been stung by a WASP-ism, and me an ex-member of the Orange Lodge, Masons on both side of the family, and a big Stingray fan, World Aquanaut Security Patrol. Though on reflection Phones sounded like a Red Kneck puppet, now that I come to think of it. I was sitting there summoning up Big Chief Kalamkooya, from Four Feather Falls, to put a Mojo on their Cracker arses, or even a magic feather, or a fire cracker up their arse crack, or what ever, then in swans this Hippy woman in a swirl of white cotton skirts, cheesecloth blouse, coloured scarves, Indian beads, and bright coloured cotton hair braids, handing out flyers for tarot readings. I took one from her, she smiled, on the flyer was a picture of , "The Hanged Man." I thought to myself, Billy Holiday, "Strange Fruit. Then I said to myself, "I'll not stay where I'm not welcome", in a George Formby voice. So I got ready to leave, and on the way out I saw the shifty eyed, vengeful looking guy, with what looked to me like a little white Muslim prayer cap on his head, and I was gonna say, "Salaam alay koum" as I was leaving, but... I thought, "Woh ! Buck !" And I just got on my horse drank me milk, and moseyed on out of town, or at least back over to the East Side.

Austin's Shadow.

That was the first day in Austin. When I told my Pop, he said, "Son stay away from them Red-Kneck Peckerwoods. They'll shoot yuh. This isn't England yuh know !" I said, "When was the last time you was in England Pop?" I was getting that feeling. That shadow of slavery feeling. And if a "Slavery" moment hits you all I know is it's time to pray, or meditate, same difference. 'Embodied cognition', consciousness as a holistic social, and sensory phenomenon, with regards to Sarah Bakewell's summary of Maurice Merleau-Ponty's vibe, I go out, and sit on the porch. I start whittling on a piece of tree. Like Jethro Bodeen. I whittle away at my mind. Reflecting on the ambiguity, and complexity of the Human experience. Talking with my inner tutor, getting some inner-tuition. I started thinking about the scene in the coffee house, that ever so friendly, and fun sounding phrase, "No Chics! No Bucks ! No Cokynuts !", was bugging me, with it's smug tone of White Supremacy. I couldn't understand Racism, or cultural imperialism. I had grown up in the racially, and culturally diverse environment of my own Family, who lived in what was basically a mixed-race community. I'd studied many cultures, practised several religions.

As a Sufi of the Blameworthy Path, and a self-styled Mystic Knight of the Malamatiyya, following in the humble foot steps of the Unorganised, and unorthodox, in the words of Najm Din Al Kubra, "I am shapeless and colourless, like water", as all Soul's are. What was bugging me, was the fact that mixing on either side wasn't really allowed here, and this was going to seriously limit how much I was going to be able to partake of, and indulge in, the much-bespoke, cultural life of Austin. Maybe next time I'll try the Warehouse District, which is apparently a mellower, more diverse quarter, for the more mature punter seeking less of a carnivalesque atmosphere. Apparently not everyone in Austin, is thrilled by the prospects of being the World's live music capitol. In fact some locals call the "South by South West Fest", "the South by So What Fest".

I started reflecting on my own culturally diverse experiences growing up in the UK, and comparing them. I was feeling like a set of De-Luxe Jenga, the one with the Red, White, and Black bricks. I was pushing back into place, some of the bricks that had been slightly displaced. Consolidating my central point of balance, an internal place. A place where I am beyond the superficial, yet deadly perspectives that pollute the outer world, of postmodernist identity politics.

Pop's Church.

Texas is Southern Baptist country. It's Sunday and everyone's getting ready for church, Evelyn, and Diamond go to a different church than Pop. Pop's a Bible teacher at the St John's Heights Bible College, up in St John's Colony, so we're going there. I've always fancied myself as a Gospel Preacher, always wanted to go to a Gospel church, a Southern Baptist, hollering and testifying church. Now I was going there with my Pop. This was a dream of a lifetime. I was in my element. Only Allah knows. We drop off at Randals Food & Pharmacy for do-nuts on the way there. There's Mexican families everywhere, on their way to church. Remember the Alamo.

Pop tells me, "See, I always buys Ram-Rod Do Nuts, cos everybody swears by them. Every Sunday morning on the way to church, I buy some for the youngsters at break time". My first visit to the St John's College Heights Baptists Church was surreal. As I walked into the foyer of St John's chapel, I'm hit by an exquisite painting of John the Baptist and his followers in their white turbans and thaubs. Nabi Yah- Yah, as he is known to Muslims, is baptising the Faithful in the River Jordan. They look like Sudanese Muslims, or Ethiopian Orthodox Christians of the Tewahado, Church of the One God. Next I see a quote from Ephesians 4:2 "One Lord, One Faith, One Baptism". To me this is a clear sign. As I step into the main prayer hall, my eyes are scanning the frugal, minimalist interior. No images as such, and look up at the altar. They don't have any idols, or even an altar with a cross, they just have the words: "One God ! One Church ! One Religion !", just like you'd have in a Mosque. I'm thinking about some research I read, on how the Black Southern Baptist Tradition, had some ancestral trace-echoes of the Islamic practises, once performed by Muslim Slaves, during Plantation days. I remember a web site from the TV, WWW Onelord.org. Then my eyes fall upon a quote from John 8:31 "This do in remembrance of me". My Sufi spider-sense was tingling like pins and needles. The musical notes that ran up and, down each side of the altar, it all impressed me, right down to the way they perform free-style rap-prayers, like R&B-Gospel Sufi's. I could see the essence of an African Sufism, at the cultural root of this Black Baptist tradition.

One of the most talented musicians in Liverpool, is a homey called Junior sits with the other drinkers, on the benches outside St Luke's, the Bombed out Church, at the top of Bold Street, bottom of Hardman Street. He sold me this quote from Shakespeare for a fiver once, "For a man to hath music in his Soul: Surely hath heaven in his heart. For a man who has no music in his Soul is fit for only spoils, treason, and stratagem. Trust no such man". Junior is a preacher, a drunken master. I must have been called, cos from the word go I was a poet and a preacher. A ranter of dissident discourse, in the olde Englishe traditione, of course. Hence my choice of the name Urban Jazz Preaching, to describe my rhetorical releases of cerebral congestion. An indigestion caused by eating my food for thought to fast. A necessary habit when serving up the revolutionary remembrances of the streets of the mind, that fed me, and my kind, during my artistic apprenticeship during the Soulfully-Funky Seventies. A culinary knowledge that began as my, 'Make a Joyful Noise' DJ-ing days during The Granby Festival, back in 1972. I can still hear myself at seventeen chatting Yankee, on the crude home-made tapes that we used to make. "So I'm gonna urge you all to put on your big white Converse basketball boots, and street-dance with the Fatback Band". Way back then, I was already moulding myself onto, what was at the time, an Afro-American psychic infra-structure of faith, fun, and freedom fighting. It's uncanny how the fruit don't fall far from the tree.

We get to Church about 9am for the Elders meeting It's known as "Orientation". And I don't know what to expect. There's about fifteen to twenty of us, and we're all suited up like Mormons. Purple suits seem to be the rigour for the Elders. There are some opening prayers and addresses from the Pastor. I'm a stranger in their midst, so naturally everyone's casting curious glances in my direction, but nothing obtrusive. Just natural curiosity. A few more words from Pastor Reeves, and then, everybody starts taking turn to piece, testifying. In Islamic Sufism, "Testifying" is called "Wasayah". Which always sounds to me like someone saying, "What say you !" in English. As it happens this is just a teachers meeting for the Elders, before the Bible students, from the Sunday School arrive. "OK ", So we're sitting in a small room, in a prayer circle ". I say to myself. Cool, no worries. I'll just sit back, and relax, and blend in anonymously. One at a time people are standing up and introducing themselves, saying where they're from, and then saying what they believe. Testifying. One guy who seems fairly humble and meek, in a Southern sorta way, tells us that he's from Denver. He has an amazing country accent. I'm just watching, listening, and feeling the vibes. There's some serious Southern drawls, and a couple of good ole' Huckle Berry Hound Dogs in there. So I'm just buzzing. The "testifying" travels clockwise around the room, when it gets to me I imagine that it's just going to pass over me, and I'll just be an observer. A participant observer. It doesn't work like that. Pop says: "This is my son from England, he's a Mooslim. And he turns to me and says to me, "Just get up and testify son". So I just stand up, and I recite my basic testimony of Faith as a Muslim. First in Arabic: "Amanto billahi, wa Malakatihi, wa Kutubihi, wa Rusulihi, wal Akhari, wal Yaum al Qiyamma, wa kharihi wa sharihi minal lahi, ta'ala wal bathe ba'adal mowt". Then in English "I believe in the One God, His Books, His Prophets, His Angels, The Life After Death, The Day of Judgement, and that good and bad both come from Allah ". I end it with "Alhamdu-lillah". Which I explain is a Muslim thing, and it just means "Praise be to God !". And I explain to them that as far as I believe, Judaism, Christianity, and Islam are all just branches of the One religion of Abraham, passed on by Moses, and that there is no difference between those who Believe in the One God, whatever tradition they follow, and that in my tradition of Sufism anyone who pursues Truth, and works at softening their own heart towards their fellow Human Beings, is a Sufi. They go silent for a while, and then Pastor Reeves suddenly exclaims like a flash of lightening: "Praise the Lord!", and the roof rises about three inches, as they all respond with a thunderous, "Praise the lord !". I could feel Pop's pride oozing out of him. His body was sitting there sedately, but his Spirit was Moon walking up and down the room, in a top-hat, twirling a silver-topped cane, and crooning. Pop be crooning to himself like Bing Crosby, pulling a stunt on Bob Hope. It was like a test, or a challenge. Well, he was in the Military for thirty years.

After the round-Robin of Testifying, the Reverend Pastor W.M. Reeves, handed out two sheets of A5 with eighteen articles of Faith printed on them. He then asked for a Brother to volunteer to read article of Faith no 11, spelt as "Preserverance of Saints", which I kinda liked, even though I assumed it to be a spelling mistake. Brother Denver volunteered to read it out loud: "We believe that the scriptures teach that such only are real Believers as endure to the end; that their persevering attachment to Christ is the grand mark which distinguishes them from superficial professors; that a special Providence watches over their welfare; and they are kept by the Power of God through Faith unto salvation". I listen intently to the words, and make the intention to study the St John's College Heights Baptists Church's full eighteen articles of Faith, that The Reverend Pastor Reeves hands out to us all. We study article 11, and then we discussed the "Perseverance of Saints", by breaking it down and looking into the etymology of the words "perseverance" and "Saint". "That wasn't too bad", I confide to myself. It all boiled down to the fact that a Saint is someone who is orientated towards "Doing good works". The "Orientation" is sealed with a quote from Philippians 1:30. "You should honour men like him; in Christ's name he came near to death, risking his life to render me the service you could not give". In fact the "Orientation" was good, because it made it easier for me when Pastor Reeves, as he is known, requested that I, "Testify" Muslim style for the young people from the 9am to 10am Sunday School, Bible Class feed-back session, that would eventually follow. The words "Say What ?" sprang to mind.

The order of the days events at St John's starts with Orientation, which is for the Elders, who then split up to take the various Sunday School classes, up until 10am, this is called Baptist Training Union. That's followed by a short coffee break, and then the morning service. During the coffee break, while people start turning up for the main service, we all retire to the refectory. Pop starts giving out the Ram-Rod do-nuts, from behind the counter, and another Brother Elder starts pouring coffee, and the other Elders, and Grand Mother Elders, and young people start filtering into the refectory, talking, and laughing, and letting off a bit of steam. I'm snapping shots of Pastor Reeves, and Deacon Wayman Lamb, and the various folks that I've met so far, and it's all cool runnings, and level vibes.

Pop finishes do-nut duty, and comes over to introduce me to a light skinned, elderly, Mohawk woman, named Imogine Samster. "This lady is Mohawk, she was a good friend of your

51

Grand Ma Eva-May's. Her father was your Gran-Ma's preacher", Pop said in his officiating voice. "I'm pleased to meet you", I said. Imogine was a youthful seventy year old, with a high forehead, and large round, tinted glasses. She could have easily passed as one of my Sisters. She had a very gentle away about her. She told me a lot of stuff about Eva-May , like how Eva-May used to make a wonderful banana pudding, and how excellent a student she was. "Your Grand mother was from St John's Colony like me, my father was your Grand mother's Minister. She had a lot of Indian in her, looked like a White lady", she told me. "I've been to England. I lived in Stevenage for seven years, I got a son that was born in the UK", she added. It was good to be talking to somebody that was a spar of my Grand-Ma Eva- May, who wasn't around anymore, cos she had some good old stories, that I needed to hear. We were hitting it off so much that people were starting to get suspicious, old as we both were. Imogine's voice was almost a whisper, she spoke in a vary gentle manner, "I had cancer, and the doctors told me I had six months to live. So I just gave up trying with their methods. I gave up all my treatment, and medicines, and started praying seriously. I put my total trust in the hands of the Lord. That was eighteen years ago", she said this triumphantly, but with serenity. I couldn't doubt her Faith, or the power of her prayers. She was living proof of it, as far as I was concerned. We warmed to each other instantly. I have no doubt that it was due to the fact that, I looked as Mohawk as she did, and it just felt like I was talking to Family. In a way I was. After a while three other Mother-Elders joined in the chat, and I got Pop to take a photo of all four of us together, standing in front of a large mirror, ornately framed in a sort of gilt-edged Baroque, that they associate with "class", or "substance", in the States.

It wasn't long before the full service was in session, and we were all moving into the prayer hall. By now the whole place was ram-tam to the brim. There was the full congregation of local regulars, and then visitors from Macon Georgia, and Denver Colorado, and Houston, and other churches from around

Austin where somebody might know someone, and invite them over to their church for the day. The Morning Service starts with a Processional, which is similar to the Muslim practise of Tawaf, where people circumnambulate the Ka'aba at Mecca, reciting du'a, or supplications. Baptists circumnambulate the pews chanting, as they make their seven cycles, just like in Islam. Except everyone's marching, and chanting: "We're on the battle field ! We're on the battle field ! We're on the battle field for Jesus ! We're on the battle field !". Next comes a congregational song, then a "Responsive Reading", which is kinda of a call and response sort of thing. This particular Sunday, being so close to Thanksgiving, it was about Thanksgiving, and an beautiful call and response piece was created from the edited verses of especially selected Psalms. Then the Deacons take over for the Prayer Service.

Next comes another hymn or congregational song. Collection is known as "Benevolent Offering", then Sister TJ Collins read some announcements, and acknowledgement of visitors, after which the Male Chorus, Pop's crew, perform what is called "Service in Songs", then it's the "Altar prayer", where the Deacons kneel and engage in vocal prayer, freestyling Praises, one after the other in a line. There is then a "Hymn of Preparation", before Pastor Reeves delivers his sermon, in a James Brown meets Richard Prior styly. After the sermon there's the "Call to Discipleship". Then the Deacons and Ushers take care of the presentation of tithes and offerings, which is another sort of collection, and the whole thing ends with a "Benediction". I'm checking out the congregation. It's a very lively, friendly, family orientated atmosphere, a lorra Love flowing from person to person, and a lorra genuine warmth expressed on people's faces. There was a kind of Joy in the air. Pastor Reeve's is preaching charismatically, singing, rapping, chanting, moving and shaking, rockin'n'rollin'. I looked around at the congregation, most people were dressed in a modest fashion, muted colours, discrete styles, and then I saw a Brother in a white suite, wearing a bad-ass wide brimmed hat with a chunky gold hat band, wraparound mirrored shades, and some crocodile shoes that some brothers'd kill for in London. If I hadn't seen him in church, I'd have thought he was a Mack-Daddy pimp. Next to him was the only White woman for about a five mile radius. She was wearing a short, tight, low cut, sleeveless, off the shoulder, red little number, and matching lip-stick. Nobody seemed to be paying them much attention except me. I could hear John Lee Hooker singing: "Big legs... tight skirt... bound to drive me outa my mind".

The St John's Funky little rhythm combo, of guitar, bass, drums, congas, and organ is seriously cooking. The Angelic Lady's choir starts singing, and the Pastor's nephew, our exuberant keyboard, player is getting the spirit. Pastor Reeves introduced him, by telling us that he'd just got through to the finals, of some big-big Gospel music competition, and he's proud of him. Nephew is sitting there smiling righteously at the church organ, all teeth and spectacles, sat right in front of the 'Old Glory' flag, and rocking so hard his glasses come flying off, and shoot across the front of the altar. If I hadn't seen him in church, I'd have said he was high on something. The Women's choir are sounding sweet. I scan their faces, and I notice this reddish, Mohawk looking woman with hazel eyes. My gaze just rewinds for a double-pipe, and she's eyeballing me from the choir, and I'm thinking "OK. OK. Homey". So I'm looking back, then looking away to see if anyone's looking at me, and I'm just checking those light brown eyes, and I'm thinking so this is church. Church good. The choir real good. Choir good-good-good like you know it should.

It's time for the sermon. The main act, and Pastor Reeves is giving a talk about the perseverance of Saints.
"I was on the way to church one sunny Sunday, and I saw a certain man, a certain Brother, down by the river fishing. He didn't see me, but I sho' nuff saw him !"
Pastor Reeve's eyes scan the congregation by way of example.
"I got me to church on time, and his wife was there, and when I asked his wife where he was, she told me he was ill".

The Pastor shrieked in shrill voice that spelt incredulity, "Ill!"

"Next time I saw that man... the next time I saw that Brother, I asked him why he didn't make the prayer meeting last week, and the same Sunday-going-fishing man, told me that he'd been struck down with a severe cold. He's lucky the Lord didn't strike him down there and then."

The gentle murmur of uneasy laughter, washed over the walls of the prayer hall.

Feeling the congregation now, Pastor Reeves was starting to take it to the bridge.

"Now I would-na call him a fibber. I woulda just said he musta been a li'l confused".

He paused to give the congregation time to chuckle, then added deftly:

"But the Lord just might say he was fibbing".

He pause again. His comic timing was immaculate. Honed to precision by years of practise.

He continued, "I wouldn't call him a phoney. I'd say his memory must be bad or somethin', but the Lord just might just say this man is a phoney".

He repeats the procedure. There's a rhythm hidden in the story, and he's rolling with it.

"I wouldn't call him a fool. I'd maybe'd just say he's a l'il lost, somethin' like that, but Jesus just might say he's a God-damn fool!" And as he triple-made his point, which is a tradition of the Prophets, his voice rose in a classic Gospel cadence.

"Fibber, phoney, or fool he might be, but I wouldn't call him any of those things, but the Lord just might ! And the Lord knows !"

"Praise the Lord !", was the spontaneous response from the people. Pastor Reeves milked his alliterative hook-line for all it was worth, as he repeats more passionately this time: "Fibber, phoney, or fool !" You can almost see the exclamation mark hanging in the air above the altar. There is some more laughter, more ecstatic laughter this time, cos people can feel that the admonishing bits over, and it looks like noone else is gonna be reeled in on Pastor Reeves hook-line this week. The jollity and the glee die down. The sermon continues, as Pastor Reeves some how manages to relate this story to "perseverance". He even works in John the Baptist and his loin cloth of leather, and his camel hair shirt. I'm digging it, it's like stand-up comedy, and some cool cabaret singing, all rolled into one with some edifying discourse from scripture. Then he starts segueing into something else, and I realise that he's trying to tie me into his sermon, when he says, "We got a young man here today came six thousand miles to see his Daddy, all the way from England, and I'd like that young man to stand up and testify for us today!"

OK, so Orientation with the Elders wasn't hard, neither was Sunday School, but this was the full-on St John's Colony community, plus friends, and distant out of town relatives, all vibing on me now. I'm about three rows from the front, sandwiched in the middle of a row of people. So I can't just do a runner, but the thought crosses my mind. Pop's sitting on the front row, so he can move about to do his choir thing and stuff. He turns around and looks at me and just says, "Stand up son. Just say what you said before." It was good to see he had so much confidence in me, after only really knowing me for a day, and I didn't have much choice anyway. So I rose to the occasion, and I brought out the Urban Jazz Preacher. I get up and I'm talking to the people, "I'm Muslim. I believe in The God of Abraham and Moses, the One God who created Adam and Eve."

I start preaching how Jesus is in the Koran, and Mary, and how there is only One God, the same God of Abraham and Moses. I end with, "We have a saying in Islam, "Alhamdulillah!" It means, "All Praise is due to God!" And the congregation erupted. The old ladies in the A-men corner were crying, and praising. All manner of people where yelling "Praise the Lord". All eyes are on me now, as Pastor Reeves says again, "I want everybody to welcome this young man to the Community. I want everyone to give him a warm welcome in Jesus name. Praise the Lord !" In an instant people were queuing up all around me, to welcome me. People shaking my hands, hugging me, kissing me, giving me so much love, so much sincerity and warmth. Then came the people's testifying. A chair was set up in front of the altar, and people came down one after the other, and sat in it and told a part of their story, about them and God, or them and Jesus. First a lady from a Sister church came and testified, saying how she was just visiting, and bringing some Joy from her congregation to St John's. She had a long, straight haired nylon wig on, and she seemed like a lively sort of a person. If I hadn't seen her in church, I'd have thought she was one Hoochie Momma, in her time. That's the way it was, various converts of the moment stood up and testified, and got the Spirit. I think Pastor Reeves was hoping that in the fervour, and frenzy of such Soul inspiring free-styling that it would reach me, and that I would some how convert back to Jesus. It was a nice enough feeling just to be accepted for who I was. It was such a good feeling to be wanted, as part of the clan. Strange to be dissected by so many deeply Soul searching eyes.

After Church Chicken.

As the service drew to an end, everybody filed past me. Anyone who couldn't reach me during the service, made sure they did on the way out. Folks hugged me, or kissed me, or shook my hand, and everyone said something nice to me. As all this was going on, I was thinking to myself, "Where the choir at ?" An elderly woman in the choir was clocking me, clocking the choir, and Pop was clocking everything. It was like the Mosque, no statues or crosses just the words: "One God ! One Church ! One Religion !" over the alter, all that was missing was the Arabic writing. Unlike the Mosque, where most people wouldn't let their daughter marry a Black man, I could see that these folks'd have me fitted up for an arranged marriage no problem, if I wasn't careful. Never the less, some mischief is in me, and I'm waiting for the choir to come down off the stage, and embrace me, but by the time I deal with all the Love coming from congregation out front, I look up, and the choir stalls are empty.

Story of my life.

Outside I'm standing on the corner talking to Pop in his purple choir suit, with us are Pastor Reeves, Brother Clayton, Brother Leonard, several Deacons, and the bass player, who was a young dude about eighteen, or twenty. If we wasn't standing outside church, you'd thought we was Bootsey Collins. Brother Bassman had on some long Matrix coat, and some large striped trousers with broad braces, big shiny silver buckles on his shoes, a bootlace tie, and a Hombourg hat so crisp it was like crackers. Everyone's queuing up inside the door, as people are making their way out. "Nice metting yah!", says the old dear in her Sunday hat, all black mesh-veil, and hatpins. I ponder the corrupted English phrase, "Nice metting yah !", as oppposed to "Nice meeting you."

I'm clocking everyone in the queue, and everybody coming out of church. "I'm glad I got feeling in my Soul", Pop sings. My Poppa's has got me well clocked. He grins and sighs. I think it means that he's thoroughly enjoying the fact that, I'm so much like him. Pop's good buddy, Brother De Fay, is standing with us also. Brother De Fay is one real cool octogenarian. He looks a bit like John Lee Hooker, actually. He has on a sleek silver blue, scirocco suit, and the crispest white shirt in Christendom. In his tie he has a gold tie pin, with an exquisite diamond set into it. His hands are covered in precious stones, mostly diamonds, and gold. Gold chains drip from his wrists, and he's wearing, some sweetly subtle, gold links hanging around his kneck also. He must have been some sort of player back in the day. If I wasn't sure I'd just seen him in church, I'd have said he was a Mississippi gambler. Brother De Fay is telling me how close him and Pop are. He's so calm, like a still lake. His eyes deep, knowing, with that kinda bluish tint to the edges, that some old Black folks get. His skin is like oiled parchment, and his silver hair, hot combed immaculate, Duke Ellington style. Him and Pop pray together over the phone, last thing each evening. I get a lot of spiritual vibes off Brother De Fay, and fashion tips for the future.

By now everybodies outside whose coming out, and we're

all standing around in the car-park of St John's, for the after church conflab. I turn my head, to take a glance over my shoulder, just people watching, and I hear: "Hi!" I turn to face the voice, "Oh ! Hi !" So I'm talking to this visually stunning, hazel-eyed Mohawk woman, and trying not to appear overwhelmed by the sudden rush of such unexpected attention.

"What's your name?".

"Muhammad, but my Christian name's Eugene."

"Muhammad-Eugene. They sound good together. You can have two names joined as one. We do it all the time over here", she said unable to decide which name she preferred.

I said, "I know. My Sister's names Wanda-Jean, and I've heard people called Billy-Joe, and Jim-Bob, and Tammy-Lynn, like a Stevie-Ray Vaughn kinda thing."

"Yeah that's right!" she said in a sprightly manner.

"So what do people call you, Sister ?" I said.

"Colorado.".

"Isn't that the name of the river that runs through Austin."

"Yeah ! That's right", she drawled this time. Slow liked the Colorado itself. She seemed impressed, so I pressed on. I said, "Yeah I was down at Barton's Creek, in Zilker Park with Pop, the river runs right by there". She's studying me more intently now. Kind of amused.

"Colorado", that's a nice name. It reminds me of my Mother.

"Was your Mother called Colorado ?" she asked wide eyed, and expectant.

"No, actually my Mother's name was Florence. That's a place in Italy, but it's kinda geographical."

Now she looked bemused. It was a tentative link. The Scouse sense of humour doesn't always work outside of Liverpool, it can often come across as sarcasm, especially in a culture where everything can be taken so literally. But I'm English there is scope for some misunderstanding, and it all adds to the mystery that unfolds before us every step of this journey that we take.

"Do you like chicken?" she asks pulling out some tin foil, from a sort of Yogi Bear type picnic basket.

I said nonchalantly, "What? You mean like fried chicken. Yeah! I like fried chicken." She smiled. Teeth like pearls. She's curious about my accent. I notice.

"Say that again", she pleads. Thinking she couldn't understand me, I repeated what I'd originally said, but slower, and in clearer English. The corners of her mouth turned up, as she tried to copy the way I pronounced the word "chicken". She was imitating me saying, "fried chicken, chicken", exaggerating the "ck" sound making it sound more guttural, like Arabic, or Welsh even. She calls her friend over. "Come over here girl-friend. Listen to this." Her friend's only about six feet away from us, and she's been monitoring her every move any way, and earwigging as best she can from that distance. Girl friend's's like Queen Latifa, about six foot, and about sixteen stone, of pretty, but unassuming chaperone.

"Hi how yah doin", she sounds Texas to the bone.

"Pleased to meet you", I say conscious of how English I sound, and suppressing the urge to break into an Old-Skool Rap thing. We shake hands politely.

"Listen how he say this", Colorado gushed lazily, eye-lashes fluttering like a Black Monroe. "It's so cute", she jiggles as she says it. I'm slightly embarrassed, but flattered.

"Say it for her", she insists.

"How could I resist", I think almost going into a Rap.

So we're stood there after church, eating fried chicken, and chanting "Fried Chicken!", exaggerating the fricative in the word "chicken". It was fun. It was a nice ice breaker.

Soul Food.

The church musicians start loading up the gear, into a Chevvy pick-up truck. The drum kit sparks some nostalgia in me. Memories and fancies melt into each other, as I reflect back on how I ended up in Austin Texas, making a Joyful Noise unto the Creator at the age of forty three. I seemed to have come a long way from the DJ of Seventeen, who played a whole Summer of street parties during the Granby Festival of Seventy Two. Spinning solid gold soul, and the new-new super heavy funk in The Methodist Youth Club, and in all the street-parties off Granby and Lodge Lane. There's even some super eight footage of a street-party down Beaconsfield Street, with my sister Tracie, my cousins Helen, Tina and Miriam, and my Aunty Betty partying with, Sister Ebony a local Ju-Ju Priestess, and a Soul-mate of mine. I recall learning the "gum-boot" dance from South African Dance Troupe Themba, down at the Blackie the same Summer. Way back then in 1972, L8 was more like Soweto than the Liverpool that the tourists knew as they flocked in to see the legendary home of the Beatles.

Liverpool was the crucible that had fused music, into religion, into race, into memory, into the dissonant melody that was only faintly audible at that point in time. A murmur deep down from somewhere in the bluest depths of my Blue-beat heart. Faintly audible fears crying amidst the cacophony of disparate voices, all flailing about like wailing laments in need of solace, and reconciliation. I take off my mask, like a cracked actor, who realises that there is a world of stages out there, but once you've seen behind the scenery, the play's not all it's cracked up to be, and even the scripts a bit ripped. Especially for the bastard child of a long lost GI, born in Mill Road Hospital, Everton, Liverpool, during the mid- fifties. Yes I was born in the fifties, and it's now swiftly approaching the year 2000, Y2K. Tempus fugit.

After Church, and the after-church ritualising, we drove over to Singleton Avenue to pick up Evelyn and Diamond, and then headed on over to Doris's for Sunday Dinner. Doris was my Sister's Mother. Pop's ex-Wife. "Where going over to your Step-Mother's son", Pop said reassuringly. Evelyn had her Church, Pop had his, Wanda had hers, and Doris had hers. Church seemed to develop into a peer group thing, once you grew up. As a youth you might all go to the Family church together, but as you got older, and developed your own network of friends and acquaintances, it seemed like people just found their own more peer group-based, places of worship. I liked it. It was all good. Everybody had their own local, a chapel on every corner. It reminded me of the old Scotland Road in Liverpool, an ale-house on every corner. We arrive at Doris's, not far from Pop's place, but on the North side, of the Ghetto, the better part of East Austin. This is the house Pop and Doris had lived in together. "This is a double plot house. I left Doris and the kids with it when we split up. It's the only one on the block". It was a massive house, with lots of land out front, and out back. The sittin room was completed with a mounted TV screen, as big as a small art-house cinema. Doris's usual family household would include herself, Pamela who is my middle Sister, and is the only one who smokes. Pam was born in the same year as me 1955, me in July, her in September, so we're almost twins. Pam's son Nugent, named after his Grand-Dad also lives with them. Nugent is in Pop's bad books. He's got three children to three different Baby Mothers, and according to Pop, he's forged Pop's signature to pay their maintenance. But this all happens after I get back, and Wanda denies Li'l Nugent's role in the whole affair. Doris coins the phrase, "It's just a sneeze in the breeze", it reminds me that Austin is the allergy capitol of America. I make no judgement, but at this point he's kinda sheepish cos Pop's giving him some jib generally over just being a Slacker. "I'd rather clothe him than feed him. He can eat a wagon load of hay, and pick his teeth with the wagon tongue", Pop jests. Poor Nugent, my homeboy nephew.

Special guests this Sunday down from Fort Hood, are Sheila my youngest Sister, Pop's favourite, and the only one who really still talks to him. Her husband Will is with her, who I met at breakfast at Graces, and Baby Melissa. Cousin Kate is there, Sister Grace, Wanda, who is in training to be the next Big Momma. There are some of the little people, like Diamond and Quentin. Quentin is introduced as being, "creative like me", by Wanda- Jean. Quentin tells me: "I got another brother he's nine, I'm only six. He looks a little like you. But he's not grown up. He don't got a beard, but he's kinda light". I just love him for that. Kid's are just so direct. Colour's a major, but unspoken about, issue over here. As a rule people avoid using the words, Black and White in relation to people. It's a touchy subject. It's probably cos we're Deep South. People use the word "Clear", when they mean "White" in Austin. That's the polite thing to do over here. In Ku Klux Klan territory. I should keep this in mind, I could make a terrible faux pas, at some point. In fact I know I will. The language of Racism, it's my favourite obsession. The subtly salacious, Cousin Kaye is there. Kaye is wearing a pearl grey collar less jacket, over a demure black, church dress, with matching accessories. Pop's fancy woman, Evelyn's there, and I'm amazed at how well she is treated by Pop's Ex, Doris, and my Sisters. I mean she is waited on with so much grace, by Doris, and the girls, that I really am surprised, at how Christian, and tolerant an attitude they all show. Pop seems to be the Badd-Ass really, but Doris and the girls are being nice to him cos I'm over here. After dinner Little Jonni, Wanda's eldest turned up he's a musician, and an actor, and is introduced to me as being from the same seam as Quentin and myself. "Give me love", is how he greets me, and a big hug. He looks like he could be my son actually. Talking about his Mother, Wanda-Jean. Jonni says "She's a pistol". He's with his Mexican Homeboy, and Conjunto trumpet player, Fernando. Fernando looks like a friend of mine Tony Peers, a mixed race trumpet player, from Oxton on the Wirral, who is now living in France. That spooks me. The resemblance is enough, but the trumpet is spooky.

The food they laid on for the after church Sunday Dinner, was as good as a Thanks Giving banquet, which I'd missed by a week or so. But they made up for it, my long lost family did everything to welcome me, into their World. On the menu for Sunday Dinner were collard greens, ochra, sweet corn, yams, sweet potatoes, turkey, biscuits and gravy, brisket of beef, teriyaki chicken, rice, corn bread, iced tea, hot tea, cheese omelette. Us being in Texas the home of the Longhorn steer, and Texan cattle barons, and me being a big meat eater, there was so much delicious beef to eat. I thought Pop had just killed a fatted calf for me. It was like a vibing like a Homecoming already. Home cooking being an essential ingredient. Nobody at Doris's, or in Pop's household eats pork. In East Austin it's considered a Black thing, and a Baptist thing, and kind of a cool thing, although not all Families abstain from pork, mine did. That pleased me. I just thought: "God's in the man. God's in the plan!"

St. Timothy's.

In Everton during the late Fifties, early Sixties. The thing in them days was, outings. My Mutha and my Aunties, and their friends used to take all us kids on what they called, "Days Out". We never lived on a reservation, but we were a definite tribe. The whole of our family went to St Timothy's Church down Everton Brow. I sang in the choir Sunday morning, after which I went to Sunday School there. Then I'd return in the evening to sing in the choir for Evensong. After school I went to St Tim's youth club, and at weekends I'd sometimes go on hiking trips to Wales, and the Wirral Peninsula. Nature rambling we called it , or country rambles. We even used to go to Barnstondale on week long camps. That's how I got to love nature and the countryside so much, especially North Wales, Cheshire and the Wirral.

We'd do orienteering around Hoylake, Heswell, West Kirby, Irby, Greasby, Thurston Common, and Meols (where my good friend Dave Elwand lives now). We'd stay at Colomendy sometimes with my junior school, St. Augustine's, or later on with the Liverpool Collegiate, to study nature. Doing nature studies we'd walk all over North Wales, climb Moel Fammau via the catwalk, and luxuriate in the dark green forests of the Alyn Valley. Wales is still one of his favourite places. I love the rich foliage, red-laked mountains, sparkling waterfalls, shiny-silver rivers, and singing streams of Betws-Y- Coed, Dolgethlu, Beddegelert, Colwyn Bay, LLangollen, Llandudnow, and a million magical places, each complete with it's own inspiring castle.

On our Sunday school outings we had a cool youth leader, Paul Southern, his folks were middle-class, he was older than us, and he was in The Boys Brigade. He could run faster than us, throw a knife and make it stick in a tree, play split the kipper to breaking point, carve twigs, tie sheep-shanks, and various nautical knots we'd never seen. He was a good role model at the time. Disciplined, and upright. Like an Enid Blyton kids hero really, that's what we aspired to be on a good day, given the chance. Someone from Grey Towers, one of Bunter's chums, or an extra from just William. Yes ! St Timothy's Sunday School outings, that's were I got his taste for outdoor pursuits, camp-fire singing, and youth work, I suppose thinking back now.

Choir Boy.

I was Esu Elegba, the Trickster, Jack the Lad, and a bit of a Scallywag, but I was basically a good kid, me and all my Scallywag mates, they all were. We were into the mischief for the craic more than anything else. I sang in the Cathedral in the Liverpool Schools Choir, and in The Philharmonic Hall's Junior School's Choir, and as I said before I sang in the St Timothy's Church choir Sunday mornings, Sunday evenings, and at weddings and Christenings, and attended choir practise on a Wednesday night, and I went to Bible studies on a Thursday evening, as did all my Uncles, Ernie, Eddie, and Billy before me. This is something that I only found out at his Auntie Maggie's funeral, when my Uncles Ernie and Billy were winding up my Uncle Eddie, by telling the story of how Eddie had had swore at the priest and got thrown out of the choir. "I walked out of the choir of me own accord I'll have yiz know !", Eddie had argued. It had happened when he was about eighteen. It all boiled down to machismo, and coming of age in the end from what I could work out. But I realised then that I'd followed in their footsteps part of the way. How come I still didn't fit in, I asked myself. They were all good role models, Uncle Billy had even took him under his wing when he was home from sea, and treated him like the son he never had. He'd even stuck the choir out.

I loved it I must admit. In fact I used to love choir practise on Wednesday nights, six till nine. The church was empty, and every little voice, every little foot step echoed in the stony darkness. Candles flickered, the half-light played havoc with the imagination, shadows danced, and it took on a magical, spooky feeling. Especially on cold Winter's nights when the air in the chapel was so cold you could see the condensation on people's breaths. A sight that in that era was easily mistaken for ectoplasm. Mr Bramhall the choir master was a dead ringer for Boris Karlof, he had this old lived in face, his skin was like the yellow parchment of an ancient scroll, with a series big dark brown rings hanging under his eyes, like a cartoon hound dog. His voice was deep, and eerie. He wore a big old loose-fitting, grey pin-striped de-mob suit. He looked like a Chicago gangster from the prohibition era. At a mid-way point during choir practise, everybody would stop for cocoa. We'd all huddle around the church organ sipping our cocoa, and Mr Bramhall would tell ghost stories. His eye brows would be raised, as I remember, as if his face was mimicking a feeling of suspense.

With most of the lights out in the main area of the church, it was like a séance. It all aded to the spooky, Gothic ambience. It was the best setting you could imagine for such low key high jinx. You can't buy entertainment like that, we got ghost stories, local history, religion, and some times we often got a little theatre when some joker, usually Paul Southern's dad. A post war Basil Rathbone type of chap, would get dressed up in a Cardinal Red cassock, and snow white surplus as a head-less monk. Always at a crucial moment when old Bramhall was telling one of his well practised ghost stories, usually after a glass or two of Port. In fact there was a story of a headless monk that used to prowl around nd about Rathbone Street by the Anglican Cathedral. And then he'd retell the story around the camp fire at Summer Camp, and he'd laugh and slap his thigh.

But what I liked the most about being in the St Tim's choir was that every now, and again we got paid. Choir boys who wore the purple cassocks got five shillings, for singing in the choir. I wore a purple cassock, and sometimes a black one. I seem to remember though that purple cassock carried more status in terms of time served as such. Eventually everyone got equal pay though as I remember. Five shillings was a lot of money back in the late Fifties-early Sixties. I would spend ten big old copper pennies on a large bar of Galaxy, the first one ever in the shops in the cream and sky-blue wrapper, nothing ever tasted as creamy- and milky to me, and then I would give most of the rest of the money to me Mutha. And I would feel proud, like a little man taking on me responsibility, bringing home the shekels from Church, holding the fort till me Arfellah came back from the sea. I loved it, I'd skip along Shaw Street past The Anne Fowlers Home For Fallen Women, and the Croft that you can see on Everton Football Club's badge, with me money in me pocket, two big silver half-crowns, two shillings and six-pence in each one. After I'd bought me Galaxy, I'd go into the dusty old stationers shop next to Joe Macs Café where we'd often get a Holland's steak and kidney for lunch. The stationers again had the feel of an old curiosity shop. The shop keeper Mr Greyman was a bent over wizened old man in a navy blue pinafore, that a lot of shop keeper's wore. Thick glasses like a cartoon owl, and just wisps of steely grey hair like soft wire wool at the sides of his 'egg in the nest', as we would call it, scholarly bald dome. It's the place we'd all buy some foriegn stamps for our stamp albums, and search the packet for that elusive Penny Black. Our collective dream as kids. I'd be lost in the exotic images of birds and far away places as I sauntered home, singing Jerusalem, and sorting out me swaps, feeling sanctified, and serious about me Soulful hymn singing little self. It was a good feeling.

Even now. I will confide. I love going into old churches and cathedrals. The Lady Chapel of the Virgin Mary in Anglican Cathedral, I used to find especially soothing. I used to call it the Mariam Chapel. I used to magine leaping from the balconies,

swinging on the chandeliers, and filming a good old swash-buckler in there. Probably cos it was very Robin Hoodish in style to my young adventurous mind at the time. Even today the artist in me would like to film some sword play in there but, something worthy of the place, something like Sir Gawain and The Green Knight. A good old Romantic tale of Chivalry and sacred knowledge. A Sufi-Gnostic cross-over theme. Universal. It seems like the place for it, atmospheric, heroic even. I smile inwardly as I listen to myself. Feeling as nostalgic as I am infused with inspiration, enthused as I nostalgically muse, a laddish glee in my eyes. I can hear the young me still alive and kicking in there somewhere. Somewhere in the Sacred Space deep withing the Gothic cathedral of my heart. My Inner Sanctum. My sanctum santorum. My secret Green Chapel
deep within the forest of the Soul.

Yes! St Timothy's Church of England, and those happy clappy Sunday School outings, that's were I got me taste for outdoor pursuits, camp-fire singing, youth work, and Gothic architecture I suppose. I say suppose, cos I've only just noticed that fact just right now. As we grow up we forget, or deny things that don't fit what ever the current socially-coerced-self-image is trying to be at the time. Our socially coerced persona. I was beginning to see a pattern. All my life I have been trying to fit in with what ever the current socially acceptable, contrived by someone else I.D. was supposed to be. It's amazing what connections you make with the present, once you start trawling through the past. I have been slowly realising one important thing ever since I began to make this poetic journey into the shadows, of my inner self. The shadow of an unrecognised past rich with edifying experiences. The good of it and the bad of it. All of it no more than the cartoon Yin and Yang of the warm red sun, and the cool green moon, that signify the patchwork costume of a Holy Fool, or Majnun Allah. Allah's madman as the Sufi's say. In the end you realise that your identity is what is within you, not it's external limitations, as in names and labels.

Museum.

Back in Austin it's a hot, sunny afternoon, me and Pop
are out visiting the George Washington Carver, Branch Library
and Museum of African-American History, on Angelina Street.
It's named after that famous American educator, but unknown
to me at the time, George Washington Carver, the Peanut Doctor.
A local hero, whose work aided Black share croppers, and poor
farmers throughout the early Twentieth century. It's a compact,
but functional space, situated at the heart of Austin's Black
Community, and the first of it's kind in the country. I wouldn't
have expected anything else, culturally Austin cutting edge.
Like campus's, class- rooms, book shops, and stationary stores,
museums, and art galleries are water to a fish like me. The Carver
Museum has changing exhibitions, that explore the African-
American experience. Currently to my surprise, they have an
exhibition of Nigerian artifacts, and some modern Nigerian
paintings of musicians. Always looking for a chance to show
off a pathology of mine, I say with a connoisseurs tone, "That's
Nigerian influenced painting, in a Cubist style." Pop's checking
the label's to make sure, "Your right son it is Nigerian." "Yoruba,
I recognise the masks they've been taken from. It's all turning
full circle. Picasso's so called "Primitivism", and his "Cubism"
is inspired by African masks. Now Modern, Western Educated
African painters more influenced by the Jazz culture of the
West visually are reinterpreting the same ideas, as if reclaiming
them." Pop muses silently at my words. I'm not sure what he
makes of it.

A short, studious looking Black woman with glasses
hanging around neck on a golden safety chain, is listening in.
"Yes that's right!", she chips in. She turns out to be the curator, a
lady called Brunhilde Pfizer. She introduces herself with a hand-
shake, and a smile. She's an African-American. I say, "Pfizer,
isn't that a German name?" It's one of my attitude tests. "Yes it
is", she says pleasantly surprised at the recognition. I do recall

thinking that Friedriksberg, wasn't far from here, and that it had a community of German speaking people there, but I don't imagine she was from anywhere near there, although you never know. Even though she was Black, she liked that little bit of Teutonic exoticism, that she possessed. In much the same way that, many White Americans, like the idea of having some Native American genes in their DNA. In some places, being of mixed heritage, seemed to be the thing actually. It was in vogue, for a lot of Humanly healthy reasons. I met an African-American in Bray once who was there tracing his Irish roots, his mother was Irish, and he was proud of that. People seem to like being a bit different, a bit unusual. "His Mom was German", Pop chips in, putting "It" on me. She smiles at me, and says something relevant, to my comment to Pop, about contemporary Black Diasporan Art. I just remember talking about how, "A lot of Sixties Jazz artists, like Ted Joans travelled to Africa, from Tangier to Timbuktu, and how Modernism has a Black Jazz legacy attached to it, that is largely unspoken of." I asked her if she'd read the book, "Harlem: Vicious Modernism? " She'd heard of it. Pop's impressed with me. The three of us stroll around the gallery, as miss Pfizer, our Black-German curator, is showing us around this exhibition of Contemporary Yoruba art. "Are you an artist?", she asks at one point. Waiting for his chance Pop says proudly, "He's a Mooslim, he's been to Africa, he speaks Arabic." Miss Pfizer looked at me curiously. I told her that I painted a bit, and had sold some of my stuff at exhibitions in the past, and that I was involved in the Arts in general.

"Do you know Gallery 19, on Railton Road, in Brixton, London", she asked curiously.

"Wow ! It's a small world. I do actually."

" It is isn't it. Another Brown Baby turned up here once, whose Mother was German, and he stayed in Austin for two years, working in a voluntary capacity here at the museum", she told me. It felt like she was saying, "So if your planning on staying in town, we could use a hand over here, from someone who knows about this stuff." I kept it in mind. Even though I needed paid work, if I was going to stay on over here, it was an inspiring thought. We cruised around the exhibitions, chatting between the three of us. They had an exhibition of stuff about Austin's Airmen, pieces of flying gear behind glass cases, and a lot of WW2 posters. I put "It" on Pop this time, as I explained, "Pop's one of Austin's Veteran Airmen. He also sings, and writes poetry." Pop looked at me, with trepidation. She looked at Pop with admiration.

"Do you really write poetry?"

"Sure I do", Pop grinned, like a gummy bear.

Miss Pfizer started talking to Pop, and he started crooning one of his sweet Country tunes into her ear, and I'm thinking this guys a case. Next thing she's all friendly with Pop asking him, "Do you have any photos in uniform. If you do, maybe you should bring them in, and I could fit them in with the display on local Air Veterans." A Black Biggles and Algie peered down at me from a poster. It wasn't soon before Pop was engaged in story telling mode. It was kinda nice seeing him in action. He was a smooth, down home Southern-Gentleman, type of an operator. Huckleberry Hound meets Peppy Le Pew. Pop almost had her sorting me with a job at the local museum, as a local historian. I walked around the other exhibits taking notes, leaving them to talk. Dr Selma Burke started a school on one pound fifty, with only five students, that later became one of the first Black Colleges. Mary McCleod Bethne of Daytona started the Cookson-Bethne Black College, from scratch almost. Our host also informed me that there was a Mosque in Austin, newly built, all but three weeks old. All Praise be to Allah.

As we left I said to Pop, "She was sweet on you Pop. You got it going on with that crooning, and stuff." Pop laughed and pointed to the car, as if to say just get in, and lets move. We get into the car, and Pop says,"Do you want to visit this mosque son?"

"Yeah ! That'd be really good. I'll show you how we pray. Insha'Allah !" He decides to run one of his aptitude tests on me, and he asks, "Do you remember the directions son?". I say,

"Yeah, you go left here towards Malik's corner shop, then right after Singleton onto Martin Luther King Boulevard, then you go past those Rednecks that have moved into the hood, cos of the cheaper rents, where we turn off for the Mall, keep on across the tracks, till you reach the junction with Popeye's Fish Emporium, on your right and Taco Bel with the Chihuahua eating a burrito on your left, keep going due East, and you pass the old airstrip where you used to be based, and before we get to the new airport, it should be on the left just off the road. And when we got there, there it was, and Ole' Pop was so impressed at my sense of orienteering. "Well I was a Boy Scout", I explained. "25th Fairfield. Panther Division. We used to meet up at Holly Lodge, in West Derby." The last bit meant nothing to Pop, but that's how, when I eventually caught up with my own Poppa, my Father who was a Southern Baptist Preacher, I got to show him how we used water when we made our ritual ablutions (Wudhu), and took him in with me, while I prayed, in a three week old Mosque, in Austin Texas. When I'd first told him I was Muslim, after tracing him to Austin after forty years, Pop said to me, "I'm just glad you got religion son, cos if God got you by the hand, and the devil pulls at your feet the devil's never gonna get you !".

Masjid.

I was the son of a preacher man. As we got out the car and began to walk towards this brand new, work in progress, huge Texan mosque, that was probably destined to be, the biggest Mosque in the USA, people began to greet us. Some Chicano builders, were mixing some cement at the edge of the car park, they let on to us with waves, and healthy smiles. So many Latinos had been converting to Islam, following Malcolm X, and due to racist alienation, tracing their heritage, at least symbolically, back to their Moorish roots in Andalucian Spain. As we approached nearer to the mosque various other people, Asian people, and African-Americans, approached us cordially, and greeted us with, "Salaam alay koum". "As salaam alay koum, wa rahmatullah, wa baraketuh", I replied. I flashed a few extra, more elaborate, greeting etiquette's in Arabic, just to pose in front of Pop. Then I introduced my Pop: "This is my Father he's a Christian", I said with a grin. They welcomed him respectfully. Pop was impressed. He took his shoes off as we entered the Masjid, I explained that, "The word Mosque, Pop, is a European corruption of The Arabic word Masjid, which means literally a place of prostration. There is a hadith, a saying of The Prophet, salallahu alyhi wa selem/peace be upon him, that states that the whole World is a place of prostration". He likes hearing me talk like this. I like showing what I've learned. It's like I'm making up for all those lost years of wanting his approval. I explained to him that, "A third of Africa speak Arabic, two thirds of Africa is Muslim, and in many places it's like a lingua franca amongst Muslims. Even Swahili, Africa's own lingua franca, is made up of half-Bantu, and half Arabic." He was more impressed than I could have imagined. I could feel his sense of pride, at what I'd gravitated towards, left to my own devices. Especially amidst everything that his well travelled, well disciplined, well cynical, street-wise mind was aware of, as a potential alternative road that I could have taken.

I showed him how we use water to perform whudu, ritual purification before we pray, and I could see he was picturing the painting, in the foyer of St Johns Baptist College of John the Baptist in a White turban. Purifying his flock, by passing water over their heads, in the River Jordan. "I'm gonna pray Tahiyatul Masjid, Pop. That's two rakats for the House of Allah. It's traditional when ever you visit a town with a masjid, or when ever you pass a Masjid". He watched proud of his son's religiosity. After I prayed I put some money in the zakhat box, "That's the Charity box Pop", I explain. Pop just grinned, "Yeah... this is a lot like Church, son." I suppressed a smile.

Drivin' with Pop.

We drop Diamond off at the De Witty school on Rosewood Drive, and circle back towards the Mopac 35, in the direction of the Hancock's Shopping Centre, Capitol Plaza, and eventually the Highland Mall. Driving With Pop is a blast it's like being in a road movie. We head off in the beat up old Coffee coloured Lincoln, with the dimpled-vinyl, cream top. Pop has to visit the Veteran's Clinic, and there's a bunch of things he has to do, I need to change some money, buy some film, various stuff. As we pull away from the pinkish iron fire hydrant on the corner of Pop's block, the rear of the car reels over to the right, the wheel starts to go funny again. Pop curses the guy who crashed into him, the Police, White folks, anybody he can think of pinning it on. We talk a lot while we're driving. We discuss Sealand RAF base back in England, and I tell him that the old spitfire's still there, at the camp entrance, with it's red, white and blue target-like decal on the side. Pop tells me about the time he got put in the stockade in Wales, something about a decoy, and a fuel line. "Love'll end but friendship'll last for ever", Pop says.

We cruise in Pop's crippled cream and coffee Lincoln Town car, talking about Morocco, Mexico, News men, the forces. He has about one collision a year in his car, and it's always the other guy's fault, and poor Pop always has to shell out. Pop sings Country, Gospel, and old school R&B. As we're cruising along we're tuned into 'Lone Star 93.3 for New Country'. I come across some Soca Country, Country-Soul, Reggae-Country, Country-Funk. Pop don't like it, he's a purist. He says; "That's just a novelty son. Something like that'll fade from your memory quicker than a snowball in hell". He's used the word hell twice this morning, he's unhappy about the state of his car, and the accident, and him and Evelyn don't seem to be hitting it off too good. I know he's having hard times, and I seem to have turned up right at a crucial point. I start to surf the radio. I find "Local Live", Texas Uni Radio KBM, a big treat, Craig Ross "Nice and Indecent". KFMA 98.5 Classical. Queen Latifa from 9am on KLM radio. I discover Blue Indians. We drop into a place where Pop can change some Sterling into Dollars for me. Pop processes the money. I offer him some money for rent and stuff, but he refuses. "I should be doing for you son, after all these years". "It's not like that Pop. I didn't come here because I wanted something. You don't owe me anything. You give me life, that's all I need". I stuff 150 dollars in his pocket. He reluctantly accepts it. "If you need any help with anything while I'm here, just let me know. I'm just trying to help out Pop. I'm from the Ghetto just like you. I not the Englishman that you think I am. I understand more than you think about being a Blackman". He looks at me incredulous. I know I'm more of a mystery to him than he is to me. But there are stark parallels between being Black in the UK, and being Black in the USA, but he doesn't understand that. We cut East across town, towards Zaragosa Park. Pop listens to the Reverend Al Green mostly at home, sings mostly Gospel in the house. In fact he sings Gospel all the time. La Quinzas, Plantation House, Rawhide Texas BarBQ, the Steak Escape, all pass us by through the moving window on my left. Some of these places serve steaks, shaped like Christmas puddings. Texans like to eat meat, especially raw gobbets of flesh.

We come to a railway crossing. At the crossing we stop at the lights. The trains slow down to a Southern crawl as they roll across town. I hear the noise that woke me up this morning, and realise it's the trains that make that sweet-sweet Blues harp sound. It all falls into place as I see the open box cars go slowly rolling by in the hot Texas haze. "Now I see how those Hobo's back in the day used to ride these things from town to town. And I can see how it's got that link to the Blues, even that lonesome sound of the trains hooter. "Yeah" said Pop. "But the railway detectives put an end to all that. Killing bums on trains if they found 'em, and throwing them off freight trains alive, and out of empty box cars. Leaving them to die out in the desert" He looked at me; "You don't want to try it. You can meet up with some crazy, evil people out there". He knew the idea had flashed through my mind briefly, and he said it as if he'd seen it, done it, had the t-shirt, and burned it.

Pop's cussing Evelyn. The train's hooting them lonesome Blues, and it's blending in with what's cooking in Scarlet's Country Kitchen on KASE 101. "I really hate her. I'll think of a reason later", sings the honey voiced Hill Billy lady on the radio. Pop uses it as he lectures me on the art of the song writer. He rates Bing Crosby and Nat King Cole, I tell him I do a mean "Autumn Leaves" in a Nat King Cole styly, and accompany myself on tenor sax in the breaks. He's impressed. And I just love making an impression on him. Thundercloud Subs passes us on the right. Native American iconography is everywhere. As we pull into the car park of Capitol Plaza, some Mexicans are loading groceries into the back of a pick up truck. The Country music coming from Pop's car, makes them smile. Music is a universal currency, that's for sure. We don't spend a lot of time in Capitol Plaza. I'm just buying some post cards, and some candy for Diamond. I bought a wooden post card for The Married One. A woman I've seen on several week-ends away at festivals, and carnival week-ends. Someone I met while working with South Wales Intercultural Arts. She was a friend of some Community Arts people, who were mutual acquaintances of us both, down in Cardiff. Once we shacked up at her sisters in Brighton for a week end. She's German, a belly-dancer, and an amazing artist, an intellectual seeker on a Spiritual quest, and is two years my senior. She works on movie sets, she worked on the set of Star Wars, and was working on a film about Ancient Egypt in Morocco. What makes it seedy, is that she happens to be married to a man over twenty years her senior. A libertarian Frenchman, who just happens to be filthy rich. In the end I don't have much chance really, money'll win out every time of course.

I took some shots of Pop's license plate, and when I get the film developed I will make several copies of that particular photo, and use them as post- cards to send to certain people. Folks back in England, who I know will appreciate the special significance of it. In the car park of Capitol Plaza, I notice the variety of Inter-State logos, and designs on the various license plates on display. I photograph some. Everything here is potential art to me, the whole car park is like a specialist type of exhibition. A bird picks bugs off the wind screen wipers of Pop's car right in front of me. I get a birds eye view of it. I don't recognise the species. "High on the Hog", Pop says, as he turn off the engine. I turn towards him, and I realise he's hanging out the window talking to the woman in the car next to us. She appears charmed by his engaging manner. Even at seventy five the dames seem to spark for old Pop.

He's like the Bruce Forsythe of East Austin. "I'd like some of what's in those jeans", Pop jives. "That's two clicks today already", I muse to myself. "One at Malik's mini-mall, and now one at the Capitol Plaza". My Pop's a player to the bone. Stone to the bone. It may be an uncurable case of Narcissism, on Don Juanism, but I'm proud of him, in a laddish sort of way. As John Lee Hooker sang it, "My Moma done had, my Poppa done had it to. I gots to have it myself. We both be Blues born "Boogy Chillun'."

"Must Phone Nigel", I tell myself, it would be a shame to come all this way and not hook up with him. He seemed like such a cool guy. Pop and I are now on our way to the Veterans Clinic. Visiting the Veteran's Clinic with Pop was a lesson in itself. The place is like any hospital waiting room, but the clientele is composed of some of the most seasoned characters your gonna ever see this side of the Mason-Dixie line. Cowboy hatted trailer park trash, denim jackets, and bikers jackets, and the Texas equivalent to Oxfam designer-wear, and bandanna wearing brother's from the hood, in trainers, and jeans, track suits, I look around and I start to feel for the Tex-Mex's and the poor White trailer-park trash, and the Piney Wood Crackers as Pop called them, and the broke-ass Negroes, and ass-whooped-Indians. I can't help it. Texas moves me. "It's called buzzards luck, son. When you can't kill nuthin', and don't nuthin' die." Pop was bitter, "Thirty years in the Armed Services and then your thrown on the scrap heap. That's the military for you Son". It seemed like both Pop and I had transcended a certain amount of the racial and cultural baggage of our upbringings, and philosophically we'd both moved onto something more Spiritual, but between White Supremacy and the shackles of the Ghetto, it gave us that ghost of Slavery feeling, something kept dragging us down, and it wasn't just our own feet of clay. I related to Pop more than ever seeing him sitting there at the Veteran's Clinic with all the old Vet's. As a Community artist I was a Bongo-Veteran for over thirty years, now villified for holding onto Community values, and defending the "People", in the face of a cold, impersonal bureaucracy, corporate take-overs, gentrification, gobshiteism, coerced commodification, claim jumpers, and Blairite carpetbaggers by any other name.

We crawl through al Barrio like a sick armadillo, Austin's hot, dry and dusty Chicano Ghetto, trying not to abuse the already over-sensitive rear-right wheel. The Mexican area seems to lay in between Ceasre Chavez in the South, and Sixth Street in the North. The streets start to take on Mexican names, Gonzales Street, Hidalgo, Corta, Santa Rita, Santa Rosa, Santa Maria, and so on. We drift through the salmon-pink dusty haze like a ghost car, past a shop called "Labrador". "That's a type of dog back in England", I say thinking out loud. I ponder what that could mean to a Mexican. We pull into the Mexican Mega Mall, while Pop's doing his stuff I check out the base-ball, and basket-ball gear for my nephews. All the stuff in the Mexican shops is cheaper, but such a substandard quality that it's hardly worth buying. It reminds me of the first time I went into a tobacconists in Morocco. I bought a packet of Casa Sports cigarettes, the brand smoked by athletes, the packet proclaims as unashamedly as any Arab conmerchant, and I bought a bar of chocolate. The ciggies were like smoking cardboard rolled up, and the chocolate tasted like grease with a bit of sugar mixed in with it. It's that kind of thing that tells you your in a real poverty zone. Of course it's all relative. English luxury goods look impoverished compared to the Swedish , or Danish sense of opulence. Go to Germany or Holland from the UK, and the standard rises again in some areas of life. We stroll around the Barrio supermarket. I get my camera out and start to use up the last of my film. I see some interesting graffiti. It's not so much what it says, as what it implies. It simply says, "US. Indians-Mexicans and Cotton". The official Texas travel map I'm using has a photo of George W. Bush, then governor of Texas, and his wife Laura, inviting us to enjoy the 300,000 miles of road way that networks the Lone Star State. It meant nothing to me back in 1999, but as I write these notebooks up near the end of 2004, so much has changed in the World, and in the State of Texas.

Mexicana.

It's coming up to Christmas, there's a nice joint African-Mexican display in the supermarket, it's composed of two halves. One half has a Masai shield, and a Kenyan mask with some spears, and a drum, the other side has a sombrero, and a pancho, a guitar and a machete. Christmas is in the air, and it's only the first of December. Piñatas hanging from the ceiling, and everywhere the most ornately decorated cakes, in all manner of amazing colours schemes, and all incorporating the traditional Mexican bright pink icing. I'm taking photo's of the many, delightfully designed, confectioneries, when one of the Mexican girl's behind the counter takes umbrage. Next thing I'm being confronted by the Mexican store manager.
"Excuse me sir but could I ask you to put the camera away, please." He's extremely polite.
"Sure." I say, "I didn't realise it would be a problem."
"He's my son, and he's a tourist from England", Pop explains. The Mexican store manager looks me up and down.
"Your from England", he asks me.
"Yes", I confirm Pop's story.
"Do you work in catering in any way back home in England, or in connection with any know confectioners."
"No, not at all", I reply honestly.
"Can I ask you what you do back in England Sir ?"
"I teach English, usually to people to whom English is their

second language."

He looked at me, and I could gauge his thoughts. He was thinking I don't look English, so I'm probably teaching English to other Brown people like myself. Possibly even Mexican people. He smiled. "OK then, there shouldn't be any problem with the photo's that you've already taken, but I'll have to ask you to leave it at that, cos we get a lot of our competitors trying to steal our ideas, and we gorra be real careful, you know."

"No... I mean that's cool with me. I understand totally."

"OK Sir have a nice day, and enjoy your time in Austin."

"Thank you I will." And next minute he's gone.

"Security's tight over here son. People'll sue you, do you, or screw you for anything they can" Pop sneers.

"I think he was just amazed that anyone would want to photograph cakes."

"He seemed like a pretty cool guy", I said smiling.

We both laughed. A Mexican woman, and her teenage daughter stare at us. Their faces are so weathered, even the younger one. I smile at them, they smile back, surprised, but pleased by the rarity of such a cross- cultural exchange.

　　　"I need to buy some film Pop, let's pull in here"; I say as I notice a sign for 'One Hour Developing' . Pop pulls over, and we park up outside the City General Stores, along with an adverts that reads " Candles / Herbs / Incense / Herbs / & Intimate Items. "Weird advert", I thought to myself. "I wonder what kinda herbs they sell, and what on Earth are "Intimate items doing on a New Age looking shopping list. "What would intimate items be Pop ?" I ask. Pop looks at the notice in the window. "Who knows Son , Who knows ?" I buy a new film and put my old filmed in to be developed within the hour, and Pop buys some sundries, it takes about five minutes. As we're getting ready to drive off, I tell Pop that I've put the film in for a one hour process. He asked how much it was, and I tell him, and he takes off on me for spending silly money. I realised it was bugging Pop not having enough money to sort out the car, and police on his back for fines, and him wanting to represent good while I'm here but being thwarted everywhere he turned. I flare up instantly at his tone, I'm as proud as he is, and I can be as quick to ire as he is. He sees this in me, but I suppress it. I don't want to get into a confrontation with Pop outside the store, I bite my tongue, something I'm not used to at all, but I do it.

As we drive off the wheel's getting worse. We'll be lucky if we make it back before it comes off altogether. I'm thinking of what Pop was saying at the Veteran's Clinic, he was saying it with a sort of irony that bordered on sarcasm, "When they're trying to recruit you for the Forces, they'll promise you everything. Training, a career, pension, medical, but once you leave the service, it's like you never existed. No matter how much loyal service you give Massa, the Ghetto always waiting at the end to devour you back up." I dug where Pop was coming from. I also dug that the Ghetto was devouring my Poppa, through his thwarted sense of pride. I could feel it, and I knew that feeling, that Jim Crow feeling, cos the same thing was happening to me back home.

Car Trouble.

The car capriciously capers through the tumble weeds Texan streets, I'm thinking "Four Wheels on my Wagon and I'm still rolling along, So far so good". The Mexican Ghetto is like anywhere else in the Third World, full of Desperados, and deserted dreams, a lot of back street garages, cowboy mechanics, scrap yards, and tire- retreading operations. We drive away from the parking lot, and roll onto the wide, dusty street. We just about wobble over to the first place, that looks like they might have a wrench, or the right nuts to fix this wobbly wheel. This is humiliating for Austin, but maybe not in al Barrio, never the less it's bugging Pop no end, and the atmosphere is as tense as the past imperfect. I know the Museum Del Barrio, is just around the corner, turn left down Coricho Street, and onto Cesare Chavez, but now is not the time. Pop puts on the breaks next to a yard, where some Chicano brother is hosing down a shiny black hill of freshly retreaded tyres, and speaks to the guy. Blacks and Mexicans as a rule don't necessarily get on. Pop actually has a thing about them, just like his Momma Eva-May, so it's hurting him in a lot of ways to ask for a favour off this guy. So Pop's trying hard to suppress his rage, as he's trying to beg this mercenary, Chicano mechanic, for some Christian assistance, in tightening up the wheel nuts on the rear right wheel. The atmosphere is tense. The sun is cracking the flags, and the sweaty, oil smeared mechanic is making it quite clear, with his menacing eyes, "No money ! No deal ! Me no fix wheel Gringo!". It was a long shot anyway, I didn't expect any other response really, but Pop was desperate to save face. I'd said to Pop on the way to the Vet's Clinic, "Let me get the wheel fixed for you. It won't cost much I thought to myself", but Pop refused my offer . He was too proud to accept help from the son he felt he should be showing a good time to. I understood him, so I didn't push it. I just waited for Pop to pull out a giant shit pistol and shoot the guy with the hose pipe. The poet Hakim Sanai knew that, "Till you have endured dire straits on that road, your Soul is two-faced, though your form is one."

It's a hot, hazy, dusty December afternoon, in al Barrio as we head towards Rose Park, to Pop's old Buddy to get the wheel fixed. We wobble comically, wheel teetering on the brink of leaving us well and truly up Dawson's Creek without a spanner. It's all adding to Pop's anger, and his frustration at being broke when I eventually showed after all these years, and me being insensitively flash. In our mutual competition to impress each other, I'd been negligent of my duties as a Son. I had a duty not to try and out do my Pop, on a Paternalistic level. We leave al Barrio behind, but not the confrontation, as we keep miraculously rolling along.

"If we can make it to Rose Park, we could get help there" Pop says, still brooding.

"Cool" I say, sounding more like a Son than I can ever remember doing. Pop smiles briefly with optimism, "I gotta a buddy there with a garage. Rose Park is Austin's oldest Black community. I'll show you my old school house, son." We pass a Nation of Islam head quarters on Angelina Street, it looks like a Rastafarian shack somewhere in Jamaica, or a Bayfal Sufi zawiyya in Senegal the way it's painted, all DIY styly. "We pass my old school house on the way to this place I'll show it to yah." We drive a block or two and then Pop points, "There it is son!". I follow his gaze to an old wooden shack. We drive past it,"So that was Pop's old school house", I muse to myself.

This is Deep South Ghetto, it gets deeper in between al Barrio, and Singleton Avenue. We pass the House Park Stadium home of the Austin Lone Stars, and some more old wooden shacks. We scuttle humiliatingly up a broad, but dusty back alley, and Pop pulls up outside his pal's garage. "I'm gonna see my pal and see about getting this wheel fixed", Pop says in a voice that thinly conceals his anger, humiliation, and frustration. I nod, still fuming myself. I don't offer money again the air is too tense, there's too much pride at stake, and it's choking us both. I'm furious at the way Pop let off on me, for spending foolishly. And I'm vexed at myself because I should have read the subtext, but I'm in cloud cuckoo land.

We were getting on so well. Now we were both at odds, in Spirit, even if I was outwardly meek, and humble as a respectful son should be. I got out my side of the car and walked up the alley and stood on the corner just taking in the Austin street layout. It was so like the Caribbean in parts, especially, quelle surprise, the Ghettio. I stand on this Ghetto corner, and summon up my teachings. It's like an invocation. I need to mix some Black history in with my mysticism, or it doesn't make sense of the mayhem anymore. I use my Sufism to fuse my Black-Ass Blues, in the primal prism of my Eternal vision, to escape the internal prison of negative emotion. I invoke the Blues Dervish from deep within. The teachings of Al Haj Malik Ash Shabazz (Malcolm X), tell us that, "Anger is the wound of oppression, injustice the pain, deep sorrow the path to depression, as anger recedes deeper into self hatred". For many people living under a dark cloud of Soul destroying social conditions, he taught that, "Self hatred is internalised oppression". He taught us that the cure for this disease (Marad) of the Heart, was to first begin to learn to Love ourselves as people. He taught us to accept ourselves, and stop trying to be someone else to get acceptance. He taught us to Love, and learn to Live with, our own upfront shadows, our "Baad-Ass-Blues-based-Selves", and the implicit mainstream society's shadow projections. This was Brother Malcolm's advice to, what Amiri Baraka described as, us "Blues People". Poor people suffering from social exclusion, and the debilitating, damaging effects of racism, and class prejudice, using the Light seeping out from their broken Hearts, so that their Soul's could survive by it's guidance.

Malcolm describes how, social inequality is not just material, but transcendental, echoing Ken Wilber in my mind. Malcolm also stressed that due to the nature of cultural "repression, and social oppression", the "Pilgrim's life style could not be "limited by any form of organisation, or idealism." Improvisation being the key to all oral traditions. In changing times, the Way needs to be supple, flexible, flowing and fluid like water. What Dhul' Nun would describe as, "Truth without Formulation". Malcolm describes his mission as trying to help people "Reassert their Humanity, simply because they are oppressed Human beings", subjected to 400 years of ongoing dehumanising treatment, that is still ongoing in American, and elsewhere. He was getting the plight of African-Americans recognised as a HU-man Rights issue, by the United Nations.

My studies have always provided me with a rich source of coherent, lyrical sutures for patching up, the disparate parts of this "Yank'n'Stein's monster", that I sometimes fear I have become. In my alchemy of the heart, I attempt a Deutsch-Amerikan Freundshaft, that fuses the Anglo-Germanic, with the Celtic, with the African American-Native American in me, as I try to embrace my Totality, what I like to call, "The Versprung Durch-Technique". I simmer my Soul in the crucible of my inner sanctum-sanctorum, like Doctor Strange, from the Marvel comics I used to read as a kid.

When the wheel was sorted, I walked back to the car, and smiled at Pop. He was mellower, and things were a lot cooler, cos he'd been able to make a mark, and show me that he still had some moves, some influence, some power. As I got in the beat up old coffee coloured Lincoln town car, with the cream vinyl covered roof, and the wobbly rear-right wheel Pop said to me, " Your a lot like me Son, you got your own mind", and he looked me straight in the eye to read me before, I'd even responded with a sort of smug, "I know." There was warmth, and admiration in his face. There was a happy glow in my heart. I make a mental note, "Must phone Wanda over the Sun Ra video: The Sound of Joy".

Grand Folks.

I'm into what seems to be some sort of writing spree. All the inner-chatter and clutter has dropped in volume, I'm still conversing with me but it's not the whinging child in me. It's less emotive, more on the moment, just listening to what's happening at present. No past-No Future as such. Just in the moment. Feeling the influence of a brief revision of the basics of trans-actional analysis, as a language to interpret what's going. Anticipating new insights now, into each aspect of the overall self, or ego states as Berne describes them in TA. Also feeling the ideas of Rogers being assimilated into the overall Sufi head-space that I cultivate at my core of self. What I call The Blues Dervish, my backs-woods man of wisdom, who sits on the porch of a shack in a beautiful pine forest some where in my mind, looking out at the mountains and the trees and the blue skies, and contemplating serenity, tranquillity, and God manifest in the natural world around me. I go off on one like that. That shows me my muse, Sapho, is near. My Anima, the romantic poetry, meditating, one with nature side, not the banshee aspect of her, which is basically my Mother on a rant. I'm used to the

Jungian symbolism approach, as used in the deep-reading of creative texts, in the study of Literature, and culture in general. It's as if I'm saying "Look Mom no hands !" Yes the show off in me is definitely the kid in me, but as Erich Fromm states in his book on the language of dreams, myths, and folk-tales, "The child's spontaneity, it's ability to respond, it's delicate judgement of people, it's ability to recognise the attitudes of others regardless of what they say, it's unceasing effort to grasp the world; in short all these qualities... are the child like qualities"... these are what I can feel awakened at present, but within the spaces allowed by the rational directives, and disciplines of my previous spiritual, professional, academic training, and educational leisure pursuits, and personal interests. But what's happening is me clearing space, reorganising space to accommodate the quickening process that's been triggered again. I've done a lot of studying, what I'm getting from this journey, is the time to play with what I've crammed in, and sort out the wheat from the chaff.

What I often do as a poet is ramble, just get into the flow, Jazz poetry is based on spontaneity, improvisation, feeling the groove, getting in tune with the over-all vibe and just flowing. That's what I am as a poet, a Jazz writer of free-association prose, and rhymes verse, though I prefer prose, it's less constrictive. Like the track "Rambling " by Ornette Coleman, or Wayne Shorters "Foot Steps", or John Coltrane's "A Love Supreme", which is supposed to be a free-form mantra, I just get on a theme, or let a theme work itself out through me, via the pen or the laptop key-board. This is how I've fused Eastern Sufism with Western Depth Psychology, via Black Urban counter culture, for myself. It allows me to unravel all my loose wool, sort out the knots and tangles, and knit something more suitable to where I've arrived at by now.

Pop's Youth.

Pop starts to tell me a bit more about his family, and as I suddenly realise it's also my family as well. He starts by telling me about Make. "Make Golden was your Grand Pop".
"Make ?" I asked, thinking I'd misheard Pop.
"Yep... Make Golden. Nobody knows where he got the name Make from, but that was his name son. Old Make was one mean sonafabitch, old Make was meaner than a rattle snake".
"Make" I mused to myself. So that's how Pop got to be as mean as a rattler, when he was vexed. I have read that many African names have survived, amongst the African-Americans of the South, and one of those names that I came across, was Make. According to my research, I placed it's origins as Senegalese, but I didn't share this with Pop. He wouldn't have been interested in me doing anything, other than startin' into cussing-out old Make right along side him. Childhood hadn't been good for Pop, to hear Pop talk Make had been cruel, abusive, and a troubled soul. "Make drank, and he made your Grand Ma, Eva-May's life hell. She was a good woman. He was a no good evil sonofabitch. As a child. I was afraid to speak around Make in case I got a whoopin'. I was timid, and introverted as a boy. I was a scared kid. I did a lot of thinking. I was a loner. Only in later life did I become a lover." Pop's choice of words made me smile. He had a way with words, if it wasn't a rhyme it was an alliteration. "A bit like me", I thought but for different reasons.

Pop was sentimental, kind, loving, and generous to a fault, but he was also bitter about a lot of things from the past. I was beginning to see why. We were so much the same people, it was truly remarkable for me to witness it first hand. The good, the bad, and the ugly of it. Make Golden was pensioned off after the First World War, after being mustard-gassed over in France, during the allied invasion. His lungs had been damaged, and they'd never fully recovered. He was only 18 years old at the time. Pop showed me a photo of him. He looked like Elvin Jones, John Coltrane's drummer, but a bit shorter and thinner in build. It seemed like it had been more of a relief, when Make had died and left Pop, and his Sister Grace Fatherless.

Pop was a mere sixteen years of age. Pop was close to his Sister Grace, again it reminded me of how close I am with our Tracie, and especially so after Mom had died. Pop told me straight up, "I was a street boy after that, sleeping in pool halls, picking up stubs from the side walk... Bible in me, never begged, or stole !". Pastor Ruby F. Hall of the First Pentecostal Church put the Bible into Pop. Pop was struck a deadly blow to the heart, when his beloved Sister Grace died from cancer. She played piano. Pop had never mastered any musical instrument, he was the word smith, and the troubadour, and Auntie Grace was the other half of his song writing team. "She had strong Mohawk features, and she went to the De-Witty School, and she played piano", Pop said as if he looked up to her, and was proud of her for that. "When Grace died I was trying to get back from Japan". I figured that this was about the time that I got the birthday card from Okinawa. The same time that Mom got the letter on the silky green paper, superimposed with palm trees, and "I love You", written in Japanese Calligraphy, down the side by Pop, along with the translation, and transliteration, exactly like something that I would do, or would have done years ago. Pop continued his story, "I was trying to get back from Japan for Grace's funeral, and I got stranded on Wake Island in the middle of the Pacific Ocean for three days. Eventually from there I got me a plane to San Diego, then another plane to Colorado, and by the time I gets to Colorado it's the day of the funeral, and I ain't got nothin' but forty dollars which was just enough for a ticket to Austin from Colorado. Two hours later I touch down in Austin, and I arrive at the Church just on time for Grace's funeral. It was touch and go, just like that. But as for Make. He wasn't worth the powder and shot it woulda took to kill him." That was my Pop.

We both wear corduroy, and tartan shirts, and jeans. We both have a bad habit of spitting out, and forgetting things, and he doesn't even smoke weed. Once he smoked two packs of Pall Mall Red a day, so that's where my Mom picked that up,

I remember cartons of Pall Mall Red being something I always associated with America ever since I could cognate. But he's never been a big fan of drinking, probably got put off it by being around good old Granpappy Make, as a kid. As a bell-hop, he used to collect all the half drunk bottles of bourbon, and brandy from the hotel rooms, and take them over the pool hall for his crew. Now one of the Deacons, Brother De Shay phones Pop every night, and they pray together over the phone. I try to imagine my Pop homeless at 16, working as a bell-hop, sleeping in pool halls, and not drinking. It hurts. Only this year Summer 2021, my nephew Malik was attacked by three local thugs he'd had beef with. The three of them came in, one with a knife, while he was in the barbers getting his hair cut. He knocked one of them out, the one with the knife ran out and stabbed the tires on his car, and the third one picked up the cut-throat razor that is always laying about some where, and slashed at his kneck, just missing his jugular vein by a fraction. He has a massive scar down the side of his face, and kneck. It was all caught on camera, but the police didn't take any notice, despite the evidence they just ignored it. It's hard to believe I know, but it's true. And Allah is The Knower. This is what we are up against with the police. If Malik had been White it would have been all over the news, "Three nasty niggas attempted murder on innocent White boy in barbers". All we can do is leave it to Allah, and Judgement Day.

Scrap Book.

That evening Pop hands me My Grand Ma, Eva-May's scrap book. It turns out my Grand-Mother Eva-May Crump, the Mohawk lady, was famous in the Black Community as a local historian it kinda runs in the family. I was so privileged to be holding her scrapbook. It went way-way back, almost as far back as Slavery. She'd met the Brown Bomber, Lightnin' Hopkins, Paul Robeson, Muhammad Ali, she had a picture of Malcolm X and Martin Luther King shaking hands. She had a lot of local Black-

American history preserved in a meticulous collection of old news paper cuttings, and Southern Baptists newsletters, documenting local history, and Black achievement. A "Home Owned" news paper, was a euphemism for a Black news papers back in the day. Grand-Ma Eva May used to write for the Capital City Argus: " A Responsible Voice in the Black Community", as it was known. Nowadays it's more up front, I notice as I browse up, and down through the treasure chest of family history, and roots memorabilia. Now you have papers like Black Talk: "The Black News paper of The Capital of Texas", as it's known, or even more in line with 1999: Black Texas.com with their motto "What's Up Black!" Eve-May Crump was born Eva-May Hemphill, of 1908-B, East 18th Street, Austin Texas, 21 December 1904, in St Mary's Colony, the only child of Mr Newton Hemphill and miss Buelah Harden. Grand-Ma professed Faith at an early age with the Church of The Living God, under the leadership of the late Reverend R.H. Hawkins, where she served faithfully by all accounts. She graduated from high school, and furthered her education at Tillotson College. She united in marriage to my Grand- Pop, Make Golden. To this union two children were born, my Poppa, and his Sister Grace who died of cancer. She later married J.D. Crump, who like my Aunty Grace, preceded her in death. She had a warm smile, and had one of those eternally youthful, and forever fun loving personalities, that all inspired artists seem to possess. She had collected a wealth of historical memoirs in her life time, and in 1990 celebrating her 85th birthday, she was recognised for her, "Contributions of historical events for the State of Texas", by Governor William P. Clements Jnr. Eva-May left behind her to cherish her legacy, one son of Austin Texas, one daughter of Austin Texas, two grandson's one of Austin, Texas, and one of Liverpool, England, three granddaughters of Austin Texas, and one grand daughter of Florida, and one other, as of yet grand daughter of Spain, if my suspicions are true. She left three half-sisters, and two half-brothers of Dallas, Texas, ten great grand children, and four great-great grand children. A list which includes myself and some other family members, that I didn't even know about at the time. Rebecca my daughter and my Grand-sons Levi, and Rudi, but we'll get to that.

Grand Ma, Eva-May was known to be very political during the Civil Rights era, but ironically, she didn't like Mexicans, and is always remembered for saying, "Those chicken-shit Mexicans". I guess no one's perfect. Apparently she didn't get on with Mexicans, even though her son Gary married a Mexican woman. Gary's wife being Mexican would make my Cousin Ginger half Mexican, and there were other Mexican Family members in the reunion photo's that the girls had showed me. In fact there were quite a few Mexicans in the Family, but she used to cuss them out all the time none the less. "She used to cuss like hell", Pop told me. Just like my Mom, just like Pop, a little bit like me, I muse to myself. Her Grand Mother was Emma-Jane Hardin she died in 1940, at the age of 97. Ada Hardin was Eva May's Mother, she lived to 108. Gran-Ma Eva-May married the Gospel Minister Fred Douglas Hemphill. She was known as Big Momma, like the old wise-woman in the film "Beloved" who preaches in the clearing, "Let the children laugh, and the men dance". She is described in her orbituary as a wit, and an endless, and often rambling talker, an actress, a spiritual drifter, and an all round bit of a character. I found stuff in her scrap book from the NAACP, and RAM the Revolutionary Action Movement. She had correspondence from groups like CORE, The Black Panthers, Jesse Jackson, and a host of lesser known Civil Rights activists from back in the day. This was way back when the Dewitty school, used to be the head quarters for the NAACP, and it was at that time that Eva-May won the Dewitty Civil Rights Award. The Dewitty School was now an elementary school where li'l Diamond went. Eva-May had collected a heap of press cuttings from the local papers, some of which commemorated her meetings with people liked Lightning Hopkins, Joe Louis The Brown Bomber, Muhammad Ali, and Martin Luther King.

She was a big fan of Louis Armstrong, at a time when he was not so popular in Texas due to certain Black fanatics criticising him over the song "Shine". A song that my Mom taught me as a kid back in Liverpool, as an article of faith, and a corner stone of my child-hood identity. "The Shines" are what we 'Mixed Race' people, used to be called when I was growing up back in the day ironically enough. It never had a negative connotation to us. "Shine", is also a song I would discover, that acted as part of my Pop's, very own path towards self- hood. At the time though Brother Louis was getting lamb-basted for writing, and singing it, by the more shallower Black radical types. Eva-May was celebrating the song with Pop, almost like my Mom had done with me, as an affirmation. Grand-Mom, Eva-May also had cuttings, and write ups on Jesse Owens at the notorious Nazi Olympics, Tommy Smith and John Carlos at the infamous Black-Power Olympics, Malcolm X, and Muhammad Ali, and a curious head line about Jesse Jackson that read, "What We Gonna do With This Preaching Nigger !" As I scan the pages of the ubiquitous scrap-book, I'm surprised to see an article on the poet Robert Frost. One of my heros of English poetry. She had clippings about LBJ, another Texan, called in one article the "Outlaw from Texas", Texas being known traditionally as Outlaw Country. The article in question was actually written by H. Rap Brown, now known as Imam Jamil Alamien, one of my seminal influences growing up, and a major push towards, my becoming a "Rap-Panther". The caption says, "Rap it to 'em Baby !". Imam Jamil was also the Amir to some of the Liverpool Brothers, on one of their trips to Mecca, for the Haj pilgrimage, the World really is a small place, and history is a spiral.

Eva-May was a prolific cultural historian, she wrote for local Black owned papers like the Capital City Argus, a "Home-Owned" weekly, coming out of the Greater Zion Hill Baptist Church at 15 cents a shot. In an article that she wrote on Muhammad Ali, she shows an understanding of Islam, that many Baptists in America today have apparently lost. In her own words, she was a big boxing fan, and the said article was published in her church news letter, by the Greater Mount Zion Baptist Church, on Chestnut Street. In it she writes seemingly in defence of Muhammad Ali, after her subsequent interview with him, and in response to some bad press that his visit to Austin had received in other papers. As evidence for this, next to the cutting of her article, are a couple of cuttings from around that time, relating unfavourably to Muhammad Ali's conversion. One article dated July 3rd, 1967, is accusing him of becoming a, "Symbol of Black Militancy in the USA", by "taking up the mantle of Malcolm X". Another one is an earlier piece from the Austin based paper, American Statesman, dated February 28th, 1964, it just says "Cassius Clay admits he is a Black Muslim". There is other stuff like; "What is Cassius Clay ? Charlatan or hoax ? Fighter or Fake ?". I wondered if Pastor Reeves had written that article. Eva-May's article in the "Austin Argus", was short but sweet and to the point. It read: "What Muslims have done is recognise that the Negro in America was facing various, and peculiar problems that were unique, and different from those of any other group. The founders saw many reasons to pattern their religion after that of Muhammad of Arabia, and his traditions. From the Koran the Muslim has learned that a great nation was formed by welding together widely scattered, and multi-racial peoples through preaching the Unity of God, the condemnation of idol worship, the brotherhood of Man, and the necessity for a virtuous life." I think to myself as my eyes eagerly scan the pages of my Grand Ma's scrap book, "I fit in over here, more than I could have ever imagined." Next to the news cuttings I saw some writing, she'd written, "Welcome to Austin Muhammad. We need you there's work to be done." I got a lump in my throat when I saw this, my eyes welled up with tears. This is my Mohawk-Grand Ma, Eva-May Crump. "Big Momma", or "Biggie" as she was also known. It's as if she was talking directly to me. As if she was showing me who I am, and that I'm OK to be who I am. As the Arab's say "Makhtub !", it is written. The quote is dated Thursday, February 23rd, 1967. I would have been eight years old when she wrote that. The synchronicity has me in tears, my Muslim name is Muhammad, it's the name I answer to mostly these days. The Way is compassionate, and is there for the needy, and God's always in the plan.

In her scrap book I found a cutting from The Houston Post August 5th 1962, it read, "Lizzie Borden took an axe and gave her Mother forty wacks. When she saw what she had done, she gave her father Forty One", Texas Oral Tradition. I pondered whether that was an Eva-May role model of sorts. It lay next to an article on drill surveys in oil country. There was other stuff interspersed with quotes from the Bible like, "Create in me a clean heart, God, and renew a right Spirit within me", Psalms 51: 19. Written underneath this was, "Church of the Living God". Every now and then she'd scribble stuff like, "You can't hold a good man down, without staying down with him", Booker T. Washington, or "As I would not be a slave. so I would not be a master", Abe Lincoln. Her church's motto was "Keep Cool", and in good ole' Texas rhyming tradition she'd written, " Keep Cool. I suppose it's difficult for the young to realise, that one may be old without being a fool." There was a small obituary, that must have been one of our relatives, it read, "Car Crash Victim Augusta Hardin, 74 years old". Another one that said, "Sammi Davis plans mixed marriage."

Eva-May was racially aware, but not a racist, according to Pop Eva-May had a lot of White friends. She was also hooked up to the Abyssinian Baptist Church, up in Harlem, where I've visited myself once when up them ways. She's written a note in her scrap-book, "Abyssinian Baptist Church, Harlem, founded by free slaves, and Ethiopian merchants in 1850. Eva-May departed quietly Wednesday, April 4th, 1996. The hymn was "What a friend in Jesus". Her favour song was, "His eye is on the sparrow".

Gaby and Mo's.

On hearing that I was a performance-poet, itching to show off for them, three of my four Sisters, Wanda- Jean, Pamela, Grace, took me to a Poetry Slam at Gaby and Mo's, up on Manor Road, East Austin, not far from Pop's place. Sheila was coming down at the week end, cos she was up at Fort Hood with her Husband Will. It was a good feeling driving up Manor Road, in the car with my Sisters. I was eager to strut my stuff, do my "thang", and represent for the Brother's back in Liverpool. Gaby and Mo's is a sort of layed back, organic eating place, with a Caribeanesque veranda outside with tables, and fairy lights. Like in the Tapper Zuki song, "We jussa satta over yonder de pon Chachi's veranda, and smoke marijuana, and dhe whole yoots come overs ayah!". Except there was no marijauna. Gaby and Mo'st had kind of a resort atmosphere to it, festive, maybe cos it was coming up to Christmas, or maybe cos it was Slam night. It was staffed by polite plaid shirted, denim legged Country Rock types. Populated by an assortment of Folk-Rock-Grunge-head, studenty types, and older, bearded, thick sweatered, Beatnik members of the local litterati. Who looked like University lecturers, folk singers, and general middle-class anorak types. Post Slam you got the odd Black, or Mexican act as entertainment. No chittlings for me, grits are OK.

"Breath in Texas Wide Open Spaces", "Keep Texas Wild", and "Don't Mess With Texas". Various slogans from the current anti-litter-ecology campaigns, splashed around on stickers. They had a lazily seductive, sunken lounge area, where you can select from the range of CD's what you want to play, just like being at home chillin'. Gaby and Mo's played a good Texas Headneck flavour, on a portable CD player, contemporary versions of the band America's song "Horse with No Name", one of my all time, mystical-feel-good tunes. A cool easy-vibin' place, that served excellent flap-jacks, and other real healthy food, and did a lovely Chai massallai, which I associate with iftar, breaking fast time at sunset, during Ramadhan. Alhamdulillah.

You could tell most people were regulars, or part of a clique of local slam heros. The presence of so many students in East Austin on the Black side, showed just how, what was being called the gentrification of East Austin, was, as is the case in the Black Ghetto in South Liverpool, a euphemism for the slowly, but surely encroaching spread of The University of Texas, and White property speculators, onto traditionally Ghetto land. A Martin Luther King Junior statue, that once heralded the beginning of the Ghetto, is now firmly surrounded by University buildings, squarely set within what is now the University of Texas Campus. Another ironic symbol of this local issue of displacement. The demographic mix if not the ambience, in Gaby and Mo's reminded me of the old Everyman Bistro in Liverpool, or even the old Casablanca back in the day, when it was a sleazy dive of a place run by, heretic Somali's, mostly ex-merchant seaman, who drank, and gambled, but still went the mosque to pray five times a day. The old Casablanca was also on the cusp of the Ghetto, and the University, and attracted a similar mix of students, ethnics, scallies, and bohemians alike. An infamous hang out for poets, artists, and writers like The Dead Good Poets Society, and members of The Everyman Theatre. The main difference was, and it was a big difference, was that the Boho element in Gaby and Mo's had a sort of a students meet the Slacker-Headneck Vibe. Where as the equivalent vibe in the Casablanca back in the day, was more of a students meet the Crusty-Scally-Druggy vibe that passed as Bohemian in Liverpool.

Tea with hot milk, cheese cake, flapjacks, cookies. I put my name down for the poetry slam. There's one sheepish undercover brother avoiding my gaze. The Poetry Slam begins. Round one. "I've always been a boxer", said the lean youth shadow boxing with the mic-stand, and bringing up images of Simon and Garfunkle in my mind. A more mature looking guy with a beard, and spectacles, a university lecturer type, tells us in his Beat styled prose poem, how he longed to live in a cave, and run wild, and be free. He seemed like the sort of Romantic-Primitive type, that often start to emerge in their early fifties, as a rebellion against cotton-bud suburbia. He compares Doctor Martin Luther King Jnr to Tupac. I don't get it, other than they were both Black, both got shot, but totally for unrelated reasons. "Or was it ?", I guess the poem was trying to say. He challenges middle-class complacency. Not that far from where the Martin Luther King statue points towards the Ghetto, he gesticulates his point, from the comfortable security of the Texas University Campus, on behalf of the Wild Frontier, that is Martin Luther King Avenue and East Austin. In Liverpool some students call Upper Parliament Street the Wild Frontier, as it marks a line between the now gentrified Georgian Quarter, where I live, and the start of the Ghetto.

A fattish one armed guy in his mid-forties, in a short sleeved Summer shirt, shorts, white socks, and sneakers, does a poem about Austin's kitsch anti-hero Mike Nesmith. A younger Slacker did a poem about, his pee turning a weird colour after taking too many vitamin pills. A really cool guy called Villon, who later on said to me, "Hey man I really dig your stuff. You were awesome. Liverpool huh !". He did a poem that reminded me of a younger, more Countrified version of the late-great Bill Hicks, who was an native of Austin. I'm buzzing, on a natural high just being in here, just fascinated by everyone that gets up to read. I can see a definite Austin Slam style taking form. It's a sort of Jazz prose, Beatnik, story-telling for the Suburban rebel. A slender young blonde woman with ice blue eyes, and as graceful as a bird, performed a poem that could have been written in Leeds, by Akwa, an ex-girl friend of mine, who was a Buddhist, artist/writer/performer, and student of Wing Chun. A Hippy woman dances next to me, then in front of me. She is a shy but sensual dancer, a slow burner. My Sisters are watching everything. Watching out for me, I'm touched. A guy called Elgin won the fifty dollars prize money, he was in fact a Slam Champion, and he was good. Despite my inner anxieties, I like it at the Slam Night. It has a nice friendly "place to be" feel to it. I felt so at home here, after the Ruda Maya experience, that I entered the Slam, as I said. Not a mistake in itself, because the Texans are as loud, and gregarious as Scousers. One thing I noticed was that the noise factor after each performance, was decibels higher than my genteel, modest Church going Sisters could handle. God Bless them sweet angelic things. No, entering the Austin Poetry Slam was not the mistake. The mistake was more in my choice of material. I should have known better than to be performing my poem "Slavepool". At least not in the Deepest Deep South, Deep in the Heart of Texas, home of the Notorious Texas Rangers, Night Riders, and the Ku Klux Klan. Bringing up Slavery, even if it is my most celebrated poem, was a definite faux-pas, and to add insult to injury. I also ran way over my allotted three minutes of time. I was on for ages don't really know how long, I lost track. After a while I forgot it was a Slam, and I was on one. I mean I was just outrageously showing off in front of my three Sisters. In fact I indelicately talked about, a whole Range of other subjects, that I maybe shouldn't have, or at least not in such an irreverent Scouse manner, and certainly not in Texas, at the Austin Poetry Slam. As wild and as wooly as the West is supposed to be. I rapped "Slavepool" as rakishly, and as acerbically, as I would have in the Unity Theatre, or The Tollpuddle Matyrs Bar, The Zanzibar, or The Harlem Bush Club in Leeds. I slagged the "Yanks". Talked with a certain nonchalance about the Beatles. A cardinal sin in Austin, or anywhere outside of Liverpool. Mocked some one who asked me, "What kind of British do you speak ? Is it the King's British ?" I told him he meant the Queens English, and confused him by telling him that the Queen wasn't actually English she was German, and that Prince Philip was a Greek, and that the Prince of Wales was a half-caste. The Texas crowd were gob-smacked, stun-gunned. I felt like I was at Home. So I continued. Lets subject this evidence to the most rigorous stand-up investigation. The word on the street back in Shakespeare's day was that, anybody with the name Black, Blackamoor, or Moor is in fact descended from African Ancient Brits, i.e. Richie Blackmoor is a Negro by default. Ipso fact. In fact Calypso facto, that authentic symbol of aristocratic English Sophistication Roger Moore's ancestors were probably Black man. We even had a Black Queen once upon a time called Queen Charlotte. I was on a roll, this was all old tired, worn out material for Liverpool audiences that I'd been doing for years, but tonight it was landing on fresh ears. Each word exploded like dynamite, in the liberal psyches of the Austin intelligencia. "Hey-hey I'm a signifying monkey, and people say I monkey around, but I'm too busy singing to put anybody down. I'm just trying to be friendly...", I thought to myself. Famous last words. I was on "One", as we say in Liverpool. I smiled at the crowd, flashed my mad grin, all teeth, and shining eyes, like Jack Nicholson. Exit stage left, and as I left the stage I ordered more tea from the mic, "English Breakfast tea please, if you have it?". I go into my English tea ceremony, to calm my post-gig adrenaline rush. Needless to say I didn't make the second round of the Slam, my Scouse sense of humour, was lost on most of them, but like "Hey!" who cares. I'd just Rocked 'em in Austin, live music Capital of the World.

Chillin' Like a Villain.

Texans in general are a strange mix of the outrageously gregarious, and those more concerned with being down home, and hospitable. And then the down-right hostile. In general the Gaby and Mo crowd, are a very polite bunch of people. As such a lot of people seem to like my stuff, but I get a sense that people like Bensley, the chief adjudicator is dubious as to the content. He's a marker as to how my Slavery material, and my Hip-Hop-Punky irreverence, could have gone down elsewhere in Austin, shall we say, on not such a jolly, balmy evening, in somewhere like the Ruta Maya Peruvian Coffee House. Wild as they seemed to be with their applause, I could tell performing the rap-poem "Slavepool", hadn't been a good idea. Not that night, not any night, not in Texas. I could tell I was really messing with the Texas sense of racial order, religious order, and their "Order" in general, by even touching on the subject of "Slavery". They didn't like it. Even if I'd have told them that, Liverpool was the only place in the World to have a Confederate Embassy, it would have not been a good idea. I make the resolve to be more pleasantly English to anyone that may have been offended during my performance. I often do this to compensate for my Scouse brashness.

"Your raw Eugene !", said Wanda-Jean.

"Eugene your so raw ", said Pamela.

I grinned in modesty, no teeth this time.

"You were just like Pop up on that stage. You even sounded like him at times. The way you presented yourself to the audience was just like Pop preaching".

That pleased me beyond belief. I sounded, and moved like him on stage, that felt good. I don't even know why, it just did.

After I chat to a few folks, indulging in some post-gig-post-morteming. Pamela and Grace realising that there wasn't probably going to be a lynching that evening leave. Wand-Jean and myself stay and watch the band. A really excellent act actually that have just turned up, and started setting up on the stage, getting ready to perform once the Slam's done.

"There's a party coming out of his mouth", one young lady in a cowboy hat remarks all bright eyed, and bushy tailed, talking to Wanda about me.

"Ya'll rock !", she said to me. I thought she was going to kiss me. "Hey dude ! Way to go!", comments another young Slacker dude in a bib, and brace, and a lilac paisley bandanna. I'm sitting there with my eldest Sister Wanda- Jean, drinking tea, and waving to Texans who are telling me, "Hey Man ! You rock !" I'm talking to a young woman who is telling me about her recent visit to Europe, and what she thought of England, and next to me sweet Wanda-Jean is being embarrassed, by this dizzy New Orleans, strawberry-blonde's innuendoes. Dizzy seems to be making obvious advances towards me. Hinting at whether or not I like a good toke on a spliff of weed. She's stoned, all giggles, and wiggles as she hands me her card. She thrusts it into my hand, by way of invitation to New Orleans. The card reads: "Jacinta La Soire/Catalyst For Fun. New Orleans." Miss La Soire goads Wanda-Jean with, "Come on down to the session, there's a great organ player man he really gets down. It's like Church." The penny drops, this chicks trying to wind Wanda-Jean up. I feel for Wanda. I think of a Mexican Evangelist cartoon that I'd seen on cable that morning, "Bible Man", a Christian super hero.

I can just hear him saying to the very mischievous Catalyst For Fun: "As long as there are Gringos like you, there will always be a guy in purple spandex like me !" The wildly flirtatious, New Orleans lush suggests to Wanda-Jean once again, in a mocking, probing sort of way that, "It sounds good. Just like church". Then she is cut off by a more serious looking woman, who hands me a card with a Polish sounding name on it, and a message that says, "Anya Stazja: Poet and Chocolate Lover. Will Work For Extra Bitter Gourmet Chocolate. Will Work For Artist's Rights And A World Without Oppression". I mention that I'm a Muslim. She imagines Farakhan or the nation or some sort of extremist Anti-White type often the stereo-type in the States... I can tell because... She wobbles slightly, and it's only 1999, the pre-9/11 era.

D-Madness, the band are sound-checking, getting ready to do their set. It's getting more difficult to talk. I discover that Anya and I have a mutual acquaintance back in England. When I was in Huddersfield at the Huddersfield Poetry Festival once, Huddersfield is the poetry capitol, and the experimental music capitol of the UK. I was working with sax player, and poet, Keith Jafrate of the Wordhoard, headlining was a Polish-Yorkshire woman, Gosia, doing a lot of poetry about her recent whistle-stop tour of Texas. She was there as part of the Bradford writers group. I remember her talking a lot about Cowboy poetry,and driving back to a ranch with a Cowboy for a one-night stand, and him cooking fried vegetables for breakfast the next morning. The Polish-Texan was a poetry connection to Gosia, the woman back in Huddersfield. She did workshops in hospice's, and I would have liked to have got to know Anya, more, and maybe done some voluntary workshops if I'd been there longer. As fate would have it, I phoned neither of them while I was there, especially the sleazy New Orleans Fun lover, hung up over the Scouse accent, or was it my rapping.

"It's like Church", the mischievous minx had said having a dig at Wanda-Jean, that was just rude. I smiled along with her not realising it the first time. But that night despite, all the groupies, and the Slam hype, rumours of the Raw Rappin' Englishman, from Liverpool, the Scouser that talks about Slavery, and pokes fun at the Yanks, The Queen, and the Beatles, had already gone round, and some seeds had been sown, and would precede me on my second visit to the Ruda Maya. A place I would return to. Although I was also unaware of that at this point. It was January, 2005, when I decided to read a " Diverse Arts and Culture" magazine called, "Austin Arts : Downtown". It was the article on the Sun Ra Arkestra, written by Rasha Amen, that I was interested in reviewing. As I was scanning the contents, under the features subheading I notice an article by Anya Stazja entitled, "Slam:The World Sport". The magazine was dated November, 1999. I couldn't believe how tunnel-visioned I'd been, to have had this magazine for over five years, and not noticed this important piece. She opened up with the Austin Chronicle's definition of a Slam Poet as, "The bastard step-children of theatre and literature mixed together". Anya Stazja gave me a good insight into the history of Slammin' in Austin, and the key personnel that called the shots. The only names I recognised were Villon's, and Baron's. Apparently a cat named Wammo started the Slam-Jam going in Austin after visiting New York in 1994. Hmm... that's about ten years after I started Slammin' in Manchester, in the Night & Day Bar, and also down at The Café Largo Corner of Seel Street just up from where the legendary Pun Club used to be. As a slammer I'm ten years ahead, I thought as I read on. A lot of key people were named, Bill Easter was another name I remembered, because the Bristol woman behind the poetry tent at Glastonbury, is named Kath Easter, and then of course who could forget the illustriously labelled Helen K. Cleopatra De Winters-Millet. Apparently, 1998 saw the Austin Slam rock like a hurricane, according to Spike Penry, the guy being interviewed by Anya Stazja. That year Austin hosted the National Poetry Slam, and broke the mould. They sold out the Paramount Theatre, got CNN coverage, and was the largest National Poetry Slam in history. Mike admits in the interview that the scene is very much a clique, but that all you need to do to join is, "Show up, and love poetry". I guess I can validate that, after digging one of their Thursday night sessions at Gaby and Mo's, what intrigued me though was the picture of the Slam Inner Council, that accompanied the article. There were a selection of about eight Slam Elite Core members, in a photo taken at the Electric Lounge. The two guys in the front, Spike Penry and Blammo, had computer generated messages, superimposed across their t-shirts. Darling Spike's t- shirt had "Austin Poetry Slam" written on it, and Pioneer Poetry Pal Blammo's t-shirt read "Don't Move Here". Being paranoid of course I though it was a message to me, but not seeing it until five years after the event, and having only fond memories of everyone, and every thing that happened, the good of it and the bad of it. I wasn't hurt in the slightest. It was a nice poetic moment. A beautiful moment. A fitting moment. A Zen moment. Ironic, in a mystical, poetic, retrospective sort of way.

Fambo.

It's Tuesday 1st December the lights are going up all over town. There's over a million lights on 37th Street, it's on tv telling us about the grid-lock, due to the elongated traffic jams for Austin's most blinged out avenue. I'm browsing through an arts magazine, there's a potential open mic session, at Ivanhoe's Inner Circle. It's a lot cooler today, but it's still fairly mellow for December, just a bit of breeze. I'm amazed at how fast the e-mail thing, has become a part of the media over here. Adverts with e-mail addresses like, "Font- Freaks, and "Fonts'n'Things", are totally a new thing for me, like mico-waved tea, but I'm adapting quickly. I live a pretty primitive life-style in Liverpool really, a push bike, no car, land-line, but no mobile phone. The Married One, gave me her old mobile phone. Probably to keep tabs on me. I had it six months, and never got it hooked up. In that time she'd lost two, and had one stolen, so I gave it to her back unused. It took me years before I ever bought a video, and I've only got a

DVD now, because Wes bought me one, because I was depressed, and he feared that I might top myself, like his mate down in Oxford had done. The company of a few good friends, that's all you need to get through this life sometimes, in one piece. I haven't heard from my girl-friend, the Married One, for days. I'm sort of thinking about her, with much more fondness than I imagined that I would. Wanda-Jean, my eldest sister, the sensible one, is picking me up today. I think Grace, and Pam are gonna be there. It'll be nice to just hang together, with my new Step-Mom Doris, and some of my other Sisters. Doris, their Mom, is so cool she rhymes things all the time, like most Texans. She's a sprightly Step-Mom, a fly gal at seventy-seven. "That's low down Blues", she'd say with a hip sparkle in her eye, and she'd chuckle with the cutest smile that any octagenarian I know, ever had. A lovely, warm, person, and what a cook. I don't know why Pop would wanna go astray, but then I'm not him, and come to think of it, people have said that about me, on more than one occasion. Wanda-Jean works for the Texas Department of Human Sciences, as an information systems analyst. Wanda's place is out at Round Rock, an upmarket housing estate, just on the outskirts of Austin. There's a town near by called Cherokee, where I'll wager you'd have a hard time trying to find one real live Cherokee. There's a lot of Otoe Indian tractors about though, nice logo. I'm beginning to recognise the run out to Round Rock, it's the same Mopac 35 route Pop and I use to get to the Mall. We get some food from the Chinese on the way there. It's a veritable feast of affection. A movie is also on the menu. My new found Fambo, are educating me into their way of life. One of the keys to passing on, those all important Family Values, both sides of the Pond, seems to be the Family photo albums. Wanda takes me through her photo albums, shows me photos of my Nieces wedding, and photo's of her other two kids. Two sons. The oldest one living away from home, and the younger one ready to fly the coop more or less by the sounds of things. She lets me keep a couple of shots of the wedding, and one of Cousin Kaye, and some other Cousins that I haven't met. Kaye is looking spruce in a tangerine jacket, over a richly exotic floral dress. The words, "fruit- cocktail", come to mind, with some freshly ground cocoa nut.

Family events like Sunday dinner, days out, and eating together in general, act as a cohesive force that binds people together. Certain movies that emphasise family reunions, and Human values, like "Soul Food", and "Beloved", are another agent of social cohesion. As I've noted with Evelyn, and her Grand-Momma-work with Diamond. There seems to be a celluloid-canon of Certain Black movies, that say it all for them, movies that a lot of people identify with. Black stories captured on film, that seem to make up articles of Faith, on their personal, and collective Shrines of Selfhood. "Soul Food" is all of my Sister's, and their Mom Doris's, number one movie. It's also the favourite film of my Sister Tracie back in Liverpool, and a lot of Black women that I know locally. There is a saying in Africa, "God made man, because he loved to hear stories". He must have made Woman, because he wanted to hear better, more compassionate stories. Wanda shows me around her new house, it's an amazing place, with a beautiful garden. It has an open-plan kitchen, spaciously designed, great walk in ward robes with mirrors, like an actors changing room in the main bed-room. As we eat our Chinese, I sit through a commentated reading of the film, "Soul Food", with Doris, and my three Sisters. It's a great big Family hug, from my Sisters and their Momma. Wanda invites me to stay over before I go back, to give me a break from Pop, but in the end I don't make it. I didn't really need a break, it was all good to me. Wanda is so sweet, she looks dinky next to me, but she's every bit the big Sister, the Elder Sister. "Remember Yesterday, dream of tomorrow bur today live every minute like you mean it", she says. She's definitely next in line for the role of, "Big Momma", in the Golden-Family-Matriarchy.

Wanda, the girls and Doris, discuss Pop's way's with me, and test the water to see what I make of his cussing, and his bad temper. They just seemed worried about me. I tell them about our little confrontation, down at the store, and reassure them that I'm not a boy named "Sue", and I'm not likely to start rolling around in the dust, fighting with my Old Man. I've got more respect than that, and as for the cussing, well they aint heard me get started yet. They seemed to have a hard time being brought up by Pop, only the youngest Sheila, ever really talked to him now. They said I was probably better off being raised by my Mom. It made me think about a lot of stuff. Since becoming a one-parent family, following Mom's death, I'd been rewriting my own cosmology, based around Sufism being the Matriarchal aspect of Islam, with Orthodoxy as the Patriarchal pole, as it where. I'd come across a Sufi concept of the "Angel Zamyat". The Angel Zamyat being, a Sufi symbol for the Eternal femininity of the Earth. This led to discover an old hadith that states that, when the Prophet Muhammad (saws), was clearing out the idols from the Kaaba at Mecca, he came across a portrait of the Virgin Mary and the Infant Jesus, and threw his cloak over it, and said, "Destroy everything except this. Save this." I would have loved to have seen that painting, was it an Ethiopian painting, I wonder.   A Rasta brother of mine, Kif, had a painting of the story of Solomon and Sheba, from the Ethiopian Kebra Negast. I imagined it to be in that style, as it was Surah Maryam, or the Chapter of Mary, that won over the heart of the Negus, and in effect saved the first Muslim refugees when they fled to Ethiopia. It's how the Jungian, and the Sufism knit together, into a nice woolly tartan scarf for those long, cold nights of the Soul. I'm talking about experiencing the Self, not as it appears outwardly, clothed in the veils of the material, the cultural, and social, but the path as it appears veiled. Moment to moment, veiled in these changing lights of our inner-experiences. The upper-left quadrant if your hip to Wilbers Integral philosophy. I often drift off into reverie, when in company. My ex-wife Henna calls it, "Planet Muhammad", She reckons I may have a slight case of autism, it's like a Condor moment. It was happening as we sat watching the movie "Soul Food".

Americana.

My Mother would always dress me like a toy Yank, in stay-press shirts and KD's, Converse baseball boots, or sneakers. She liked using American words that she'd picked up from Pop. She'd explain to me how the Yanks called an umbrella, a bumbershoot, how they called pump, sneakers, and lemonade, soda pop, sweets, candy, stuff like that. The whole Americana thing had become her thing, a kind of cultural escape route in times of romantic reverie, longing, and melancholy, but always underlined with the sounds of Bluesy, black eye-liner. Billie Holiday, Sarah Vaughn, Nina Simone, Billie Eckstein and Paul Robeson. Until this trip, this journey, until now, I had basically given up writing. At least I hadn't wrote much, for the past three years or so. This was mostly due to being bored, with my own head-space, and having nothing I thought worth saying, that hasn't already been said. Such are the stifling effects of orthodoxy, and dogmatic, tired, worn out, routine stereo-typical ideas of self, or self-concepts that have passed their sell-by date. At the risk of sounding vain I remember Walt Whitman's words, "Great poetry requires a great audience". Now I have a reason to re-think, and a validation of that thinking process, which has given me a renewed sense of purpose. Now I have a new reason to write, there is no stopping me. My humble effort has been to try and, carve some sense, out of my mountain of Nubianesque mystical notebooks. As one Sufi sage said, "Pebbles maketh the mountain".

We leave Wanda's about dusk and head back to Pop's. On the way back to Pop's we pass by Wanda's church the Mount Zion Heights, darkness is settling in for the night, there's a chill in the air now, as if the weather's decided to try and get cold in time for Christmas, I muse to myself. I 'm checking out Mount Zion Heights, it's a much bigger, and grander affair than Pop's church, at St John's Bible College. She hands me to her Pastor for a chat on her mobile, Pastor Chester D Baldwin, he seems like a nice guy. She gives me video of a massive rally-come-service , and CD of their choir, with Chester singing lead. It's quite incredible. I'm still taking it all in. The amazing Gospel tradition, that is part of my heritage, it's a roots and culture extravaganza for me. This whole journey was beginning to slot so much into place for me, and it was only just beginning in a sense. We pull out from the car park, drive down hill towards Pop's place on Singleton. As we're driving along, we commence back to our game, of judging whose got the best Christmas lights up outside their house. Christmas lights in Austin make the Blackpool illuminations look like a glimmer in comparison. As we career into Martin Luther King Boulevard Doris points to the right and exclaims in a youthful, gleeful voice, "That's Miss Rights lights." We all laugh, and agree. A thousand and one fairy-lights were shimmering in the crucible of my imagination, and as it distilled into the wine-gourd of my heart, I sipped it slowly, savouring the flavour. I liked the taste of me own unique blend of English Breakfast Tea. It is the light of Tauhid, Unity of Being. As I sit and contemplate the syncretic nature of Human creativity, down on Singleton Avenue, East Austin, Travis County, Texas. It's hard to fit non- duality into a nutshell, it's like the sound of one hand clapping, what it is? Is what it is, and it's like that, cos that's the way it is.

Barton Spring.

I'm sat eating breakfast with Evelyn before she goes to work, then college straight from work in the evening. She explains to me her plans. She seems to be saving up to move on. That's the impression I get. Diamond is showing me some new books Evelyn's bought for her, and some new additions to her video collection. Evelyn's movie school I call this project. We've watched Toni Morrison's "Beloved", "Anaconda", because Ice Cube was in it, "Wild West" with Will Smith, and "Seraphina". We all particularly liked the scene in "Beloved" in the forest, where the slaves are listening to the old wise woman preaching, and everyone starts dancing, and jumping. That scene left it's mark on my Soul, watching it with my kin folks in a plank-house with a porch, way down South where the children used to play. It was like being in situ, like once when Levi and I were passing through Mildenhall US Air Base to visit Levi's in-laws Jackie, and Jerome who was from Texas. We were on our way back from a gig at the Africa Centre down in London. Jerome decides to show his favourite film of all time, "Apocalypse Now !" Being on a US Air Base at the time, seemed to bring it all home.

Evelyn gives me a fresh cup of Texas, micro-waved tea, and then I'm introduced to some of the characters from Diamond's books. Mary Mcleod Bethnie, and James Pierson Beckworth, adopted Crow Indian, Chief , warrior, mountain man, started a school in Daytona Beach Florida, on one dollar fifty. Jean Baptiste Poite Du Sable, Haitian polyglot, artist, and pioneer, founded something in Chicago. There's a story on Cochise versus the US military, and a story about Geronimo giving his real name as "Koyaku", "One Who Yawns". It's all enriching my experience of Texas, all filling in little details of where I've come from, and how I got to be here now. The TV sells dry cleaning by pitching clean clothes as an investment. The guy reminds me of one the Ferengis from Star Treck. He's all about money, and acquisition, it's as if everything is subtly aimed at conformity to the American Dream, which is Capitalism. Pop chips in, in a matter of factual way with, "I know people all too well. That's the problem", as if mirroring my thoughts. Sheila phones about doing brunch tomorrow, Pop hands me the phone, and then lectures me on commitment while I'm trying to listen to what Sheila's got to say. He quotes Goethe, "This is a little couplet I picked up around 1951 son, 'Whatever you can do, or dream you can... begin it. Boldness has genius, power, and magic in it." Sheila is telling Pop, about Wanda's new car, and her new house, up at Round Rock. Wanda-Jean is there with her. They're telling me about the Bombay Bicycle Shop, and we arrange an evening when we can all go out together. I'm looking forward to it. I'm beginning to really like my Sisters.

Texas TV.

The TV is talking about, "Bodies found on ranches near El Paso." The Cuidad Juarez Cartel, and Federal Police drug assassins are mentioned. The spokesperson calls it a "ten million dollar violent business." Two graves were found containing twenty two Americans, and drug-dealers in uniforms. Also an array of trucks and vans, all loaded up with cardboard boxes, and blocks of stuff wrapped in cellophane and taped up. Drug plane, Mary-Jane, plane crash in Mexico. Apparently demonstrators over-run Seattle. Pop is reaching some parable about "Town of Mess and Town of Neat", and "Hindsight is twenty-twenty". Pop cusses a lot, but he has his Japanese Tea Ceremony, and his poetry. Like me tea drinking, and thinking about thinking. It's early and my mind is still in the Barzakh. I've been reading a book called "Arabesque" that I picked up at the Dobey Mall down the Drag. It's about a person sitting out the war in Beirut, with no visible means of support. The news runs on to something more interesting to me right now. Eight million Muslims in the US, and thirty two million in Europe.

After Diamond is dropped off at school, Evelyn, Pop and I take a drive over to Barton Springs, in the Barton Creek Green Belt area, Zilkher Metropolitan Park, South of the CIrado River. Barton Springs are fed by the Edwards Aquifer, which pumps thirty two million gallons of cold, crystal clear water into the open air swimming pool there. Barton Springs is where the Philosophers' Rock is. We stroll through the sandy, prairie parklands, surrounding the Springs. Pop and Evelyn are acting friendly with each other for a change. It's nice to see them behaving like a couple. Pop is naming trees. "This is what we call a Lime Oak. " "It doesn't look like an oak tree", I say, thinking of an English oak, and my little pocket book of trees that I used to carry around with me, everywhere. He stops to check with

110

this old guy in a straw trilby, and a golf jacket that's sat on a bench about six foot away from us. The brother confirms it. "Yep ! That's a Lime Oak", the old guy confirms. "You see, over here son, that's a Lime Oak, and this one, that's what we call a Mesquite, and this... This is a Cedar Ash". I'm impressed. Pop's trying to tempt the squirrels with morsel's of food. It provides an opportunity for a mini sermon, "That squirrel's done out-smarted me..." He ponders then continues... "God provides for everything. He provides for everyone and everything". Solomon the Wise, had many wives, because like all the Prophet's and Holy men in general, there seems to be a correlation between Virility, and Spirituality. This is where I see Pop as a Malami Ghost Warrior, because he accepts his shadow, and lives with it quite comfortably. Only when we realise that all claims of piety are hypocrisy, and everyone is blameworthy, only then can we confront our own crude, instinctive, survival mechanisms. Only then do we become Allah's Humble Lions, only then is it easy for us to avoid acting out our lustful, and vengeful drives, and desires. All praise being due to Allah, at the end of the day, Rumi, Ibn Araby, Al Ghazali, Lao Tze, Chang Tze, Sigmund Freud, Ken Wilber, and Carl Jung. :-)

We reach the Philosopher's Rock. It's been converted into a piece of public art that incorporates bronze statues of Frank Dobie, Roy Bedichuk, and Walter Prescot- Webb. Three of Texas's most famous philosophers. I'd never heard of any of them. I make a mental note of their names, with the intention of researching a bit more information about them, when I get the chance. Evelyn is all sunny, and bright today. She tries really hard, but Pop is a bit of a cruel bastard to live with. I sympathise with her. We stroll through the trees, the three of us, just feeling the feeling of, being together, out in the fresh air, a step closer to nature. A step closer to our inner natures. This is good therapy in itself. I'm discovering that I need to lower my expectations in the outside World, but it's took me to a middle-age crisis point to do it. Jungian's and Sufi's both start sorting out the folly of youth around forty, so I suppose this is just par for the course. Maybe that's all there is to it.

Pop, and I seem to share an affinity with the Religion of the Birds, as the Native Americans, and the Sufi's both say. We leave the Philosophers Rock at Barton's Creek, it's been a reflective day, a quite day, a day of taking into account. On the way back from Zilker Park Evelyn and Pop point out Threadgills, a famous place for bands, a lot of people have played there when they've passed through Austin. People like Janis Jopplin, Zappa, Beefheart, Van Morrison, The Clash, Waylon Jennings, Bruce Springsteen, it's almost as well known as the Armadillo World Head Quarters, and Hippy Hollow, where all the nude bathing goes on in Austin. It looks like the kind of diner that I like. There is a menu outside that reads, "Biscuits and Gravy, local Devil's Rope (whatever that is), and Armadillo, (surely not) I think to myself. I'm curious to get out and walk around one of the trailer parks, doing my pseudo anthropologist routine. Pop says, "Not a good idea son. Keep away from those Peckerwoods. They're dangerous." When we get in Evelyn makes me a nice cup of Texas micro-waved tea, and cooks up a whole mess of Soul Food, meatloaf, corn bread, and collard greens, Louisiana hot sauce, sweet corn, yams, sweet potatoes. I've always wanted to try meatloaf, it was good, but corn bread reminds me more of Madeira cake, nice though, but with custard, not meat gravy.

A Quiet Night In.

It's another quiet evening at home, we've all been playing "Candy Bears" with Diamond. Board games are great for family bonding rituals. Pop and Evelyn actually seemed to be enjoying each other's company, or at least having fun competing against each other. The fun that's what's drifted out of their relationship. Diamond won, despite my efforts, now Pop's trying to pack li'l Diamond off to bed for school tomorrow. But before Diamond gets ready for bed, she decides that she wants to start sharing a lesson on Buffalo Soldiers, something she's picked up from school that day. Then she sings us the song they learned the "Poo Ying" song. Evelyn's off out somewhere's, Diamond's stalling for time, trying to stay up till Evelyn comes in to see what she'll bring her. Sometimes she brings in a bucket of craw fish from Popeye's Ocean Emporium, it's a bit like scampi in the basket. Pop gets drawn into the Jack move, and starts to sing along with her. "Take a peach take a plum take a stick of bubble gum". He's got the beginnings of a cold. The nights are getting a bit chilly, and we were standing out on the corner talking till it got dark tonight. Diamond's in bed now, fast asleep at last. Pop and me are having a cup of tea as we just sit around the kitchen table. "Where your Step-mother at ?" Pop asks rhetorically referring to Evelyn. So now I have two Step- Mom's. "I'll put a fire-cracker on that woman's ass", Pop says in his killing joke sorta way. "You wouldn't think she was in the military for twelve years", Pop snarls like Muttley, then laughs "Sorry Son, I seldom swear for real. When I'm mad really I'm just having fun. We puzzle our minds, but God already got things worked out". "Sho' nuff Pop", I say falling into my Southern drawl. The TV is on in the background just for the ambience, 150 channels and we can't find anything to watch. "Wheel of Fortune", with catch phrases that relate to Yanks only. I'm at a loss. Pop likes, "The Price is Right, baseball, basketball, American football, Comedy Fox 7, the Lottery to check his numbers, and of course the news. He's got me making tea in the microwave, a cup at a time, but I have him drinking it by the gallon. It's good for the colon, reduces the risk of cancer. I do pick up some Texan slang words for Tri-Racial. "The Neapolitan Race" is one, meaning one scoop of strawberry, one scoop of Vanilla, and one scoop of chocolate, or just plain ole' "Ice-Cream Combo". It's all good to me, it's what I need to see, what I need to hear. It validates me against all the anti-mixed race attitudes I have often had to face in England, both from Black people and White people. There's a ring at the door. Pop goes to see who it is. I go into my room to get something, and I can see Pop through the window talking to this traffic cop, on the whittling porch out front. All I can hear is a general Huckle Berry hound sound, of Texans mumbling. Pop seems irate. I consider going out to see what's going on, and then remember where I am, and my eyes fall on the young Cop's holster, and gun. I think if I go out, Pop's gonna say, "And this is my son he's Mooslim", and it's gonna spook this Cop, and somebodies gonna end up shot. So I just watch. Pop sees the Cop off down the garden path, and comes in shaking off the evening's chill. We sit around Pop's table, drinking tea, and talking about what the Cop wanted. Apparently he'd come to issue Pop with a summons to appear in court. After cussing the guy out, real mean and ornery. Pop starts to explain a few more of the darker things to me. Pop starts telling how he got, "Thirty days in the can for pulling a gun on Evelyn". It didn't surprise me. This is Texas, and he is my Pops, and it doesn't surprise me at all. Just like Brother James Brown, I thought. "You see Son... I told that darn woman not to be hitting on Diamond like she does, but she didn't listen to me", Pop emphasised the point with his index finger. "I caught her one day shouting, and cussing at li'l Diamond, and then she just ups and smacks her across the head. Now that's the one place that your not supposed to hit a child. You can paddle their butts, but don't ever hit a child across the head, cos it can give 'em brain damage, and it can even kill in some cases." That's the one thing I don't like about the States in general, the guns are everywhere.

Pop's Guns.

A lot of Pop's anger seem to come from righteous indignation. Pop continues his confession, "So I gets one of my guns from my office. I keep two guns, I always have done since I was 14 years old. I keep 'em wrapped up in socks, in the top draw of the bureau in my office. One time I was real low on money, and I pawned those two guns. That night I walked into the pool hall where all my buddies hung out, and some guy from out of town took a dislike to me over something, either that, or he mistook me for somebody else. Next thing I know, he came at me with this cut-throat razor, and cut me right across the side of my kneck. It just missed my jugular vein. I could've died". Allah is closer to you than your jugular vein, these words ran through my mind as I thought about our Malik's encounter with a cut-throat razor. Like the song by War says, "Don't you know that it's true, that for me and for you the World is a Ghetto". Pop's still talking about his guns. "Since then! I've never let them out of my reach. That is until those Redneck-Honky police broke into my office and took 'em." Most of the stuff he talked about was stuff that riled him, and so it wouldn't be long after getting into a story, before he got to riling himself up over it. I worried about his heart condition. And I worried about the fact that, I was exactly like that myself. Pop continued to explain, "The thing was, I didn't even really pull the gun on her. It was still in the sock, and I had turned away from her, with the handle pointing at her, and I just poked her in the ribs with the handle. But then one of those two shit-kicking Grand-sons of hers from Oklahoma City, ran out into the street hollering like a pig on a fence, "He's got a gun ! He's got a gun !" Pop imitated a pathetic, squeaky-sounding sort of voice, to emphasise his contempt. I laughed along with him. Feeling my empathy, his mood lightens, and he segue's into, "If it wasn't for her I'd get us a couple of shake dancers in. Women that shake their butt", he laughed his mischievous laugh. All teeth and gaps, with grinning eyes. I thought "Wow !", my Poppa's into shake dancers. He'd like the Married One's Belly Dance routine. He pauses, sighs, looks into the distance to reflect back at the gun incident, and then adds, "So that's how come they got me up in court tomorrow." "Wow !", I thought, "Pop's up in court for pulling a gun on his woman. Just like, Brother James Brown". He continues his tirade, "You see that Redneck cop broke the God- darn law... Broke into my office took my guns. That shit's illegal". Pop explains his constitutional rights. Recites extracts from the Bill of Rights from memory, the First Amendment and stuff like that. Shows me how the cop broke the law. "It's like Jim Crow law son. I tried to do 'em for burglary, cos technically that's what it was. But they wouldn't even take the charge on board. Damn sonsabitches", he spat the words out like something bitter in the mouth, but sort of matter of factual. Bitter was normal, just par for the course.

Pop was raw like one of Rumi's chic peas, cooking in the Creator's pot. Reflecting with Pop, always brought up parallels in my mind. I've had my house bugged, and burgled by the police repeatedly. They'd be in and out of my place when ever I'd go out. They had me under observation because some lying, privileged, elitist, told them I'd threatened him with a gun. I hadn't of course, but racial profiling won them over. I was subjected to Psi-Ops, and all sorts of shady tactics in the process. Still they'd leave stuff in my flat, books, CD's, DVD's, postcards, all with intended cryptic messages, that were supposed to spook me. The thing was I had no idea what any of the missives actually meant. It was all just part of their typically monological gaze. What I learned from it was that I was on a level, beyond their understanding. Their parochial narrowness just seriously annoyed me. Nobody ever asked me my side of the story. I remember someone saying to Clint Eastwood in a cowboy movie once, "You scare people, and that's dangerous". Clint's answer was, "It's not me they're scared of, it's what's in their own heads". Xenophobia is the biggest cause of violence towards the 'Other'. That makes it tough when to the monological mind set, your always going to be the 'Other'.

Hill Country.

Wanda-Jean and Sheila pick me up early, it's another sunny December, Texas morning. The lights kind of salmon pink in Austin today. We drive over to Grace's for breakfast. Grace lives in a duplex, it's a sort of semi- detached. Cousin Kaye lives in the other half of Grace's duplex. Their area is quite swish, a sort of up-market version of Doris's, not as up market as Wand-

Jean's, but way up market compared to where Pop lives on Singleton Avenue. All my sisters have MA's, they're all in good jobs, and they're all middle-class, by UK standards. When we got to Grace's house Will was there, Sheila's husband from the Air Force. They are stationed at Fort Hood. I wondered if Fort Hood was all Black, with a name like that. Grace had more ornaments than my Mother. Lots of Afrocentric ceramics, and statuettes, and some nice art pieces, inter-mingled with the African-American kitsch. She showed me around the place, it was full of her personal Ju-Ju, collections of photos, and memorabilia. Grace told me a little bit about her husband, who was in Lagos, Nigeria. It was almost a full house, Pop, Grace, Kaye, Sheila, Will, Pamela, and Grace's daughter Sante Fé. They had bought turkey bacon especially so as I could have a halal egg and bacon breakfast. Needless to say breakfast was exquisite.

Will was keen to learn about cricket. I sketched out the basic pitch for him in my note book, and then draw the shape of a cricket bat, pointing out the obvious difference between a Base-ball bat, and a cricket bats more sophisticated shape. I tried to illustrate how the bevelled back was good for slicing, and the flat front for defensive moves etc. I loose him when it comes to the scoring rules. He can't work out runs, and overs, maiden-overs, and ducks loose him totally. We abandon the project after a while, but it was a good ice-breaker. Sante Fé, Grace's daughter, and my niece, is a pretty Black-Mohawk, with a ginger streak bleached into her fringe, fairly shy. Her Pop's Nigerian. She looks about seventeen. "I'm twenty two", she tells me. Wanda-Jean is getting stick from the other's cos she's wearing white ankle socks, they keep saying that she looks like a Piny-Wood cracker. I think me being here has taken her back to her youth in some way. I know it's been like that for me. She seems to be playing her big sister role, that she maybe played before everyone grew up, and got kids of there own. The other Sisters can see it, I can't, but I can tell that something's going on. She's giddy, and all little girlie, in a fun, and excited sort of way. I've been pestering them for a trip into Hill Billy Country, they seem reluctant to go. I get the impression it could be dangerous.

In the end after breakfast is done, Pam, Grace and Sheila take me on a trip upto the Highland Mall, up into the Hill Country. We go in Pam's Space Bus. The girls are playing Purcell in the car. Wanda asks if I like it, she says that she listens to it all the time. It's that, "It's classical, so it must be culture, kind of deference that Momma used to have", but it's a lovely gesture, and I am actually quite fond of Purcell. I think they're playing it just for me, as a sort of English thing. They're so sweet. It's nice having a day out with all four of them together. We pass through Clarkesville, and they explain it's history to me. Clarkesville is historically the oldest African-American community in Austin, and one of the oldest existing communities in Austin. In 1871 a freedman, it says in the brochure, Charles Clark, purchased two acres of land in an effort to build a settlement for former slaves. No longer exclusively Black, the centre piece of the area is the Sweet Home Missionary Baptist Church, founded by the Rev. Jacob Fontaine in 1880. It's an attractive part of town, it reminds of New Orleans French quarter a bit. Probably from the same period, it's got that Old South feel to it. I'm just checking all the sign-posts, and logos, as we career along the Free Way. I'm a big fan of Otoe Indian tractors, just through the logo design. Dairy Queen Ice Cream, has a tempting design, certain combinations of colour, and image draw you in.

I was thinking about my mother, wishing she'd still been alive to share it with me. I was thinking about Day's Out in Wales, and I mention it to the girls. "We have an equivalent to the Hill Country, near Liverpool, it's where people go for Sunday drives, and weekend retreats and stuff. It's called Wales". As the words leave my mouth I glance out the window to my left, and there right before my eyes is the Welsh flag, fluttering in the breeze. I point it out to them. Of course we were zooming along the Freeway at the time, and by the time I pointed the coincidence out to the others, we were a half mile past it. They ask if I want to go back and see it, but that wasn't the point, so I just let it go. It was synchronicity. During all the time I was in

Texas, I saw a lorra Old Glory's, a lorra Texas flags, and Mexican flags, but that was all. And then while we were driving in the Hill Country, I just happen to mention that we used to go to a place called Wales on Sundays, and that was kinda like our Hill Country, and as I looked out of the left-hand window there's a Welsh flag blowing in the wind, at the side of the freeway.

This is what it's been like. I started doing large amounts of Jung, informally, as a sort of extra-curriculum activity, instead of getting sloshed and going to discos, during my Youth Counselling training, back in Wales circa 1979-1981, so the whole synchronicity thing surrounding this whole trip, was totally awesome for me.

We are all a little bit giddy. We stop on the Free Way to visit a futuristic looking Church, built on a ridge with a view that spills out of a vast window inside the main chapel, and flows right down the Colorado River valley. It's a magnificent view, a great place to inspire worship. I can see how proud my four Sisters are of their Southern Baptist, Christian heritage. It's a beautiful thing to see, a beautiful thing to be apart of. I feel so privileged. My Sister's have their things they want me to see. I love it. It's what I need to know, it's my roots, and it's how we do what we do as Goldens. It's all so wonderful, and I'm just so overwhelmed that I love them all. We arrive at the Highland mall, the view over Austin from the car park is panoramic. I'm spell bound for a while, taking in the city scape below me, that is by now bathed in a sort of golden light. We find somewhere to park, and swan around the Mall until we find somewhere to eat. I get a Philadelphia Cheese steak sandwich, or something similar. They don't have any chilli sauce. The Mexican kids serving me, seem amused that I should ask for chilli. I get the impression, that there's some kind of racial politics attached to eating chilli with everything.

The advert for the Arboretum, about the therapy session with the two compulsive shopping disorder sufferers, came to life, when Grace and Pamela disappeared into a clothes shop, and asked me not to tell Doris that Pamela had bought anything. I followed them into the store, and Pam was promising to give Grace a top that she had bought brand new, and had not worn, so she could buy this newer one, and not feel guilty. I buzzed when they told me that Pamela has a slight compulsive shopping disorder, what I once called a " shopping-mall-malady", in one of my satirical poems. Grace said that if she wanted to please her Momma, and deal with it properly, she wasn't supposed to be even in the Mall. Poor Pam seemed like the Black sheep of the family. She was the only one who smoked cigarettes. The only one unmarried, and who had gotten herself pregnant by a GI in Madrid, while Pop was stationed in Spain, and busy himself making some Spanish woman called Maria, pregnant with our Spanish Sister over there, and she was the only one still living at home with her Momma Doris. We laughed about it, the more I found out about them, I just loved them. As we left the Mall, I saw a woman at the Highland Mall in a sort of Heidi out fit, all in red, green, and white. It looked Bavarian, or Austrian. I though maybe it's a leading up to Christmas thing, but it looked more like a lederhosen thing, than anything else. As she was in her fifties, I imagined that she was probably from Fredriksberg. I read that some of them had a penchant for traditional German folk costumes, up that way, and this is the USA, so anything is possible. I bought an Austin version of the game Monopoly, some American footballs, and catchers mits for my nephews.

Sun Ra.

It's about six in the evening. I'm in my room waiting for Wanda-Jean. She's gonna take me with her to the place where she edits her Gospel programmes for Community Access TV. I used to hang-out with, a dynamic Jazz-Dub duo, Gerry and Yvonne Kenny, from up by Burtonwood, the old US Air Base just outside Liverpool, and once the biggest US supply dump in Europe. Gerry and Brenda, had got me homing in on, an unknown to me at the time legacy of Jazz as Spiritual journeying, through people like Pharaoh Sanders, John Coltrane, Archie Schepp, Yusef Latif, Ahmed Jamal, Don Cherry, Idris Muhammad, Rashid Ali, Roland Kirk, onto Sun Ra's mythocratic meanderings, and all of that Eastern-orientated-Afro-Jazz school of experimental, holistic-ritualistic, Soul exploratory stuff. This coincided with the time I left College in Wales, and helped set up Delado: School of Africa, in the Rialto Community centre, in the same year as the Toxteth Riotous Uprisings. Around that time there had been an epidemic of Dutch Elm disease all down Prince's Boulevarde that had decimated the Dutch Elm population. Tree surgeons had left piles of Dutch Elm logs of various sizes up and down the Boulevarde. As part of the Delado project we were working with a guy called Dave Shade who lived in Jermyne Street at the bottom of Granby, five minutes from the Boulevarde. Dave was an antique furniture, and musical instrument repairer, in short he was a master craftsman when it came to working with wood. In his basement he had lathes, band saws, vices, and all the wood work and metal work tools we'd need, to turn the Dutch Elm logs into African drums. So under Dave's excellent, and skilled tuition, that's exactly what we did. It felt good to be playing drums made from recycled dead trees, from the neighbourhood. That made them a bit special.

As Cecil Taylor states, "Music is an attitude, a group of symbols of a way of life, whether your conscious of it or not."

Wand-Jean shows up and the door-bell rouses me from my reverie. Wanda's brought me a copy of the Mount Sinai's new CD, starring their Pastor Chester T. Baldwin, it's complete with a video taken from a massive gathering of united Baptists Churchs from across Austin. We're sitting at the table in the kitchen and I'm sipping my freshly micro-waved cuppa, and check this for a piece of synchronicity. I see in the local paper one evening while over in Austin, that Sun Ra's band have been running mass percussion workshops in town, and I come across an add for a Su-Ra video that I've been after for ages also. The store that sells it is on Guadeloupe just past the main drag for the University, known as The Drag. I ask Wanda- Jean, my eldest Sister if she knew how to get there, she said, "Yeah ! I'll take you there tomorrow!" So we leave Pop's house for the Community TV Studio where Wanda-Jean is editing the TV programme that her Ministry puts out on Cable TV, it's called "The Mount", and it's the flag ship of the Mount Sinai Missionary Baptist Church, Ministry for Mankind. She edits the programme for cable TV, twice a week, every Tuesday and Friday, and as she gets into the car, and I get in the passenger seat. Wanda-Jean turns the ignition key, and the radio comes on automatically. It's a Jazz station KAZR 88.7 that she always has it tuned into, no big thing, except that the title of the video I'm seeking is called, "The Sound of Joy". It's named after a Sun Ra track that I had actually written some lyrics for in Vocalese, and as the ignition switches on the power the radio kicks in automatically, and it's that very same record I have in mind that is playing. Not half-way through, or near the end, but the very first opening notes of the introduction. "Bahhm ! Bahhm ! Bahhhmm !", the brass glides in so smooth, and was timed so immaculately that you couldn't have set it up, even if you had tried. I mean of all the records played on all the Jazz radio shows broadcasting that evening, what are the odds of that happening. Wanda-Jean didn't even know the tune so she wasn't as amazed as I was. Never the less it was as if the Spirit of Sun Ra was with us in the car at that moment. Who knows? As Pop said when I explained it to him, "When ever that happens son you know God's in the plan."

We drive off into the balmy Texas evening to the Austin Community Access Centre, where Wanda's gonna be editing one of The Mount Zion bi-weekly cable broadcasts. Wanda brings joy, her answer machine message says it all, "Have a blessed day !" We arrive at the The Austin Community Access TV Centre, it's like a Community Centre would look like, and it's not far South from Pop's, deeper into the Ghetto, on into Mexican territory. The Way is full of Isharah, synchronicity, or Divine hints.The most important thing I've learned from hanging with the big Sheikhs is that, "I know Nothing !"

The Bombay Bicycle.

It's later on that same day, "Saturday the 5th of December, and it's still warm and mellow in the early evening here in lazy Austin, Capital of the Lone Star State", I think to myself sounding like a local DJ already. Grace and Sheila are taking me out to the Bombay Bicycle Shop downtown Austin. It's kinda of a small chance to see some more of them just before I leave to go back to Blighty. Wanda, the oldest Sister was tired, and Pam had a bad leg, her leg was in plaster during the Mall drive, she'd damaged her knee or something. So I went out with Grace the next to oldest one, and Sheila the youngest of the four, who lives on Fort Hood Base with her husband Will, who being a cool, mellow guy, warm, friendly, dude from Denver, CIrado, stayed in to mind baby Melissa. "We're going to the Bombay Bicycle Shop" said Grace. "Is it an Asian place ?" I ask. "No, that's just what it's called", Grace and Sheila are amused. We pull up in the car park just out side as we are getting out of the Space Cruiser, five Asians, two men and three women are walking out of the Bombay Bicycle Shop, I look at Grace and Sheila. "I thought you said it wasn't an Asian place", I say bemused. They both Laugh. The Bombay Bicycle is a sort of diner-come- karioka-bar. The karioka was wild ! It was rockin' in there. I mean the place was ram-tam, chokka-block. It's down town Austin, on a sultry Texas evening, and the place is full up of Cowboy and Cow girl couples, Mexicans, ordinary family Black folks, G's from the Hood, Blue Indians, Asians, and petite but very polite waitresses, who micro-waved the tea. There were Cowboy hats, feathers, and bottles of beer being held high in the air everywhere you looked. People were celebrating Saturday night out in fine Texas style. The punters had performance names like Copperhead, La Quintas, Julia After-Dinner Minter, Eagle and Cougar. The quality of the vocals was beyond anything I'd ever experienced in the UK, on a karioka night. Whether it was a Cowboy couple in Stetsons, Cowboy boots, jeans, gingham shirts, necker-chiefs, doing a country duet, or a Gospel Momma in austere navy blue, singing the Blues.

From Rap to R&B you name it, people be just tearing it up with pure talent, every time they got hold of the mic. The atmosphere was hyped, mega-charged up, and pumping like a carnival out of control. The air was heaving with whoops, and hollers, and yells, and screams, and Brother-dogs barking, not just after each act, but even during the song. Most people just like to make noise in Texas. All the people, whatever clur, they make a lorra noise when they're out enjoying themselves. "Come early ! Be Loud ! Stay late ! This is Texas tradition."

We order tea, and when the waitress brings it to pour it out, she asks if we want anything else.

I ask, "Could you just leave the tea-pot please?" She looks at me weird. "He's English", Sheila says.

The waitress looks at me again, curiously this time, with a hint of disbelief.

"You don't look English", she says.

"I know it's along story." I smile.

I also ordered blackened cat-fish and Cajun dirty-rice. The girls didn't eat. They were surprised at the way I can literally drink Tabasco, and Louisiana hot sauce "like it aint no thang." The girls order tea aswell. We all drink tea and talk openly. There seems to be no barriers. Just a lorra warmth, and a lorra love. Our experiences overlap. Everything they talk about ties into something that I know about, or triggers some past experience that I've had. Grace confides in me that her husband, who is Nigerian was deported for possession of cocaine, and sent back to Nigeria. And now he's stuck there in Lagos. I think back to a guy I met in St Vincent, only a few months earlier. He'd been deported from New York for cocaine. He was telling me, "I was there man, and I was living large brother, had fine clothes, fine women, fine car, and then... Wham !" And he'd look to the side wistfully remembering former glories. "Now I'm just making the rounds", he'd say, and he'd walk off for another one of his daily walks around the block. Everyday he musta did that walk about thirty or more times, and Kalliaqua's, St Vincent is a small place. It musta been doing his head in having once tasted the freedom of New York, then loosing it. He didn't seem down though, he seemed kinda reconciled to his barefoot, ripped tea-shirt and shorts existence. I remember visiting a poet friend of mine Winston I-Farrel, in Barbados once, and he'd travelled World wide, and was working with some Senior Citizens on a play about Christmas in Barbados, past and present. There was a lorra parodying of Bajans who'd lived in England, or the US for a while, then returned home expecting everybody back-a-yard to be impressed with them. He was doing some constructive work with his art, but he had the wander lust. He described being stuck in Barbados, like being imprisoned in Paradise. To me as I later described in a poem... "The palm trees in Barbados - Swayed like Samba dancers In the cozy Caribbean breeze - Their frayed serated leaves - Like a Steel pan man's frilly sleaves - Maracas, bongos, cabassas, congas - Coco nuts, mangos, and purple passion fruits - Palm trees like Calypsonians - In exotic carnival suits - Limbo dancing in the hot Bajan wind - My friend perused inside the antique shack - I stayed outside and grinned."

It was all falling into place for me as a poet, the whole post-Trans-Atlantic Slavery diaspora thing. It was a massive legacy, an enormous heritage, and far from being cut off from it back in England, I had actually tapped into it, in places that most African-Americans had only just began to tap into really. And it had happened for me through identifying with what Paul Gilroy described as a Black Atlantic diasporan sense of self, that combined Africa, Europe, and The New World of The Americas. The more I travelled the more it was gelling in an experiential, and existential way.

The breaks in the Sacred Hoop were well on the mend. We drank tea, talked from our hearts, enjoyed the electric atmosphere of the Bombay Bicycle Shop, and we laughed and we joked a lot. Sheila is really funny. You can tell she's the baby of the four. Grace is more serious, she's sad thinking about her guy back in Africa. Grace tells me that he used to smoke weed aswell. They kinda know that I've been into weed, cos they saw me do my stand-up routine in Gaby and Mo's. But I don't say nothing, cos I don't wanna play up my one vice, that I've been off for a month, or so already, and I'm thinking when I get back this could be it. I kicked it for five years once, I've only been back smoking a while, maybe this could be my last effort. So I begin to see myself as a none smoker.

It's easy in this environment, where I live it's more like Holland, everybody smokes, people's parents, Gran-parents, and Great-Gran-parents smoked. It's just normal. It's considered a Black thing, or nowadays a Scouse thing. Sheila and me discuss Country music, I'm aware that I'm rambling, and I close myself down. I worry that my manner may be too abrupt for Austin. Sheila's tone signals something that makes me worry about my etiquette, but I can't put my finger on it. Maybe I'm too ofay with the drug scene, that she suspects that I'm a bit more of a Scally than I'm letting on to them. It's not important, I'm over sensitive sometimes, especially when I'm hungry for approval.

Heartical Vibes.

Grace seems dead set on joining her long lost lover in Nigeria. Synchronicity pops up again. As we'd just had a series of, fly on the wall programmes based around Lagos airport, running on TV back in the UK, I had to give the low down. Allah works in strange ways. He brings people together for his own purposes.

We discussed Pop and Evelyn's sitch. They agreed with my analysis, and didn't seem surprised that I'd sussed out the dynamics of the relationship, and we all agreed that the whole affair was turning out to be unhealthy for Pop, and Evelyn, but most of all it wasn't much good for Diamond. I verified their suspicions that we more than likely had a Sister called Maria, somewhere in Madrid. From Pop's term in Spain. One song of his that he played me was apparently about her, to her Mother. Pop had seemed embarrassed when I listened to it, and he'd said that it was to my mother, and he'd had to disguise it. But it didn't matter. I understand his motives. And as a Muslim it's not a problem in my mind, him having a woman in each country. That was only three, he was due one more according to my tradition. Me and the girls talked about the fact that we should try and contact Maria at some point, just to say that she's our Sister, and we wanna know her. We all ended up crying. It was a healing. A truth saying. A cleansing. A reconfiguration of my identity, that was all part of the epic history of the post-slavery, trans-Atlantic hybrid known as the Diasporan.

Islamophobia.

I was studying to teach English to speakers of foreign languages working voluntary with Somali and Yemeni refugees and immigrants of various ethnicities. After my mother died, my girl friend of ten years left me, about six months later. So I was feeling doubly bereaved. I was one parent family trying to look after my foster sister Tanya Khalifa, whose mother Yasmin was Arab. My Mother had fostered them both before she died. As Yazmin was in Styal Women's prison at the time, I promised my mother I would try and look after Tanya. As the first Christmas approached following my Mother's death the sadness only increased. I took my little sister to the cinema to see Santa Clause the Movie, we both sat there trying to be brave, trying to pretend everything was alright in paradise. It wasn't.

We had a flat on the top floor of a big old Edwardian town house set back from the road behind railings. I'd get up to take the kid to school and set of for work at the ESOL Centre on Windsor Street and as I'd open the flat door the stench of pig urine and pig excrement would hit me full in the nostrils. I'd take a quick glance down and close the door, and usher my ward back into the front room while I got the bleach, disinfectant, mop and a bucket of hot water. All down the two flights of stairs leading up to our flat door someone had spilled buckets of pig faeces and piss all down the stairs. Once they left a big notice saying, "Burn in Hell".

It was at that time I realized where the expression "Thick as pig shit" came from. Sometimes the persecutors would leave messages on the answer phone like "You Arab bastard!" or "You dirty stinking Arab!". I wasn't Arab but the nine year old already traumatized child was, and I realized eventually that they really meant Muslim. This was back in 1983, pre the rise in Islamophobia, it was just plain old Redkneck Ismschism.

All I could do was stay calm and carry on. I'd check the answer machine regularly to save the kid from any hate messages, and always check the stairs before I let her out of the flat. Never the less my little Arab Princess got straight A's in her first year as my ward, probably due to my just as much to my good neighbors and friends, as to my penchant for education. Years later when the Iraq war was on, my pals who started a city farm in Walton had one of there pigs beheaded. The head turned up the door of a Yemeni corner shop. Sounds like the same tactics, if that's not terrorism I don't know what is. It started for me as soon as I came out as a Muslim way back in the early Eighties, and it just got worse in the post 9/11 era. The fact that I can still feel love, write creatively, laugh at my self and my crazy life means I must have survived the worst of their sorcery though, but at what cost to my sense well being I'll never know for sure. But I am obligated to wish for the perpetrators of such heinous crimes, only what they would wish for me.

Confession.

I told my Sisters about the Married One. They seemed all ears. I began with how it started and stuff, "You see it was a veritable Summer of Carnivals. I'd done Carnival in about four or five different cities around England and in the Caribbean, that year as part of my work, and also just socialising. I was on a bit of a Dionysian odyssey. We'd been at the Swansea Carnival knees up, it was a balmy mid-August sea-side evening, and so the Married One and me slunk off for a quiet moon-lit walk along the beach." Grace and Sheila seemed cautionary as I slowly revealed some of the sordid details. "We had a spliff on the beach, and stared out into the coal black waves off the West coast of Wales. After a while we walked some more. I noticed that you could see the B&B were I was staying upon the brow, about ten minutes from where we were strolling. I pointed to where it was, and we some how eventually ended up back there and in bed together. The next morning when we woke up, and we were just laying there talking I said, "Well I don't know what your sitch is, but I'm single, at the moment so I don't have any problem with last night." She said, "Hi ! I'm married, but actually I don't have any problem with it if you don't." Apparently she was from Munich, her family was quite rich, her husband collected antique cars, and was at least twenty years her senior. She was into searching for her lost sense of Soul within the world of cultural tourism, WOMAD, World Folk Music, belly dancing, trade craft, carnival, and the occasional fling on the side. Apparently her hubby didn't mind. I was even invited to her home in Surrey to meet him, she insisted he didn't mind, and it would be totally cool, but I thought that was going just a tad too far. Or was she just allowed to go a tad too far, preferably ethnic, if not Black, at least Irish, or something rugged, and rampant in a rustic sort of way. Lady Chatterley came to mind.

I explained to Grace and Sheila that the affair between the Married one and myself, wasn't just about sex. It was two star crossed seekers of life's higher truths, co-dependently dredging through, the culturally diverse, postmodernist universe, of art-culture, middle class guilt-working class angst-World music, politics, religion, philosophy-ecology, and all generally during Festival Seasons, and Carnival week-ends, or less festive more furtive week-ends in seedy little B&B's deep within some metropolis somewhere, or on some remote coast line over looking the sea. Some times as a pair of lost seekers of the Soul's purpose, other times as mere members of a larger group of mutual friends, and revellers from the Festival-Carnival, community arts world.

What started out as a Summer fling, became a bit an addiction to the, co-counselling aspects of the relationship, for the both of us really. It's like Lou Reed put it, in his song, "I like Girls, your someone I can talk to, and I like to look at you." And not necessarily want to have sex with all the time, I thought of adding just to make the point. "That's how it is some times", I said, "Especially as you get older. Things like mind's, and hearts, and companionship become more valuable to you". They were listening intently, "Once a door is opened. You gotta walk through it", said Sheila sounding a lot like Pop. I explained that, "The main problem for me, despite the slight moral dilemma, is really that I'm still kinda on my own most of the time, and I know it aint gonna go anywhere. A woman aint gonna give up a mansion in the country, and a yatch in the South of France for a singing, joking, story-telling Carnival Negro drifting from town to town". They smiled as I started to sound like an old John Lee Hooker, or Little Walter number. The Truth is I don't want it to go anywhere... I guess I just get lonely some time, and I'm looking for love as much as anybody else is, truth be known". I made a note of the advice that they gave me, concerning the whole affair with the Married One. It was, "Put it back in the bag, bury it in the yard, and never speak of it again". It reminded of the lyrics from a Country and Western song, that they'd been playing a lot on KASE 101, during Scarlet's Country Kitchen: "I'm gonna bury your drawers in my back yard", and something about, whatever it takes to drive you out of my heart. It was like a healing, confessing to my Sisters. It's much easier to speak from your Feminine side, in the company of Women. I think my Sisters think that I may be gay. That happens a lot, and if I was I wouldn't have a problem stating my preference.

Casa De Luz.

A while after I got back from Austin, I did an hour long interview on film, with some students from The Liverpool School of Performing Arts. Afterwards I felt sorted. They had their questions already worked out but I just freestyled through them, and eventually I'd answered them all. Their final question was, "How do you view yourself?" My closing statement, "I teach creativity, creativity is the path towards Spirituality, and self-healing so I'm an animateur, an enabler, and like Malcolm I'm a wounded healer, basically that's it." That was the trip I was into at the time of the turn of the millenium. Y2K saw me at home alone memorising Qur'an. I stopped at midnight to look out the window and enjoy the vibes with my neighbours, take in the fireworks, and listen to the jollity, then I was back into memorising Juzz' Amaa. It felt good not being carried away with all the pre-Y2K hype.

I micro-waved some tea, and commenced to whittling down my thoughts, at the hearth stone. Talking with my new found Sister's, took me back to my old Family home back in the day. Just me and my sisters, and cousins in Fazakerley, our Tracie, and Yasmin, and my cousins Halima, Soraya, Helen, Tina, Miriam, Margaret, Florence, Lillian, and Little Ena, as opposed to Big Aunty Ena her Mother, all girls and just me. Always some one to make me a cup of tea.

Yep! Pop's got me into Country music. I never thought I'd see the day when I could really say that I dug Country, but I'm actually taping Scarlet's Country Kitchen at this very moment. It's cos I'm feeling kind sad, and Country has started to mean something to me. Me being here, and being half Texan... Country is starting to affect my mood, that's when I knew I was feeling it. It started to sound like sadness, simmering in the Texas sunshine. I could hear the loneliness of the wide open spaces. Evelyn shows me a poem about "mean spiritedness". "Generous but Mean Spirited", it's called. As I'm reading it I'm hearing a

Country tune about burning bridges called "Then What ?", the tune has a steel pan in the chorus. My buddy General Akhipongo, from St Vincent in the Caribbean, is the island's top steel pan man, him, and his outfit " Potential."

"Potential" where over in Texas once performing, so it shouldn't surprise me. The World's a lot smaller than you think once you get ot there. It doesn't in fact surprise me. One of my trajectories as always been to seek out that which is Living inexistence, despite, and "Beyond the Sterotype." It really does help blow away any preconceived notions, and ideas I might have once held about Country music. Once there was just a label "Redneck Country", sealed away in a little Black box some where, in a corner of my mind, but now there's Outlaw Country, Kool Kowboy's, Cosmic Cowboys, Headknecks, Slackers, Beatniks, Red Blues, and a Black-Mohawk from Bitter Creek's music, and it's all a kinda Country. It's the Tuesday, the 7th of December, I phone Nigel at long last, he's a senior software developer for Triple Eye International. Austin has a Silicon Valley, it's internet city. Everything on TV has an e-mail address over here, it's only early days in the UK for the Internet, but I've gotta get on-line soon, God Willing.

I meet Nigel six pm, at the Ruda Maya. He suggest it cos it's a known cool place for poetry, and acoustic music, and tonight is a special night for open mic and stuff. I tell him about my feelings towards the place. He tells me it's not that sort of a place. I think, "Not for you my sweet and innocent brother, cos your White my mate. No disrespect my brother, but it's different pour moi. Je suis tres desolé, c'est n'est pas my faux." But I don't labour the point, I don't want to fall out with him, so I just go with the flow, and avoid the "faux pas". We meet there as planned, and have a cup of tea. It's seems OK. The poet Abraham, leader of Express Bus, and Erin another cool poet from Gaby and Mo's, the Slam Champion. In fact, are sitting outside on the steps that lead up from the dusty street onto the board walk, about four or five-feet high up from street level. I stop and talk to them and introduce them to Nigel. Abraham says he's coming to Liverpool for Hogmanay, and we exchange contact numbers. Nigel and I have a quick cuppa and then leave about 6.30. Nigel has an excellent itinerary planned for the rest of evening. He assures me, he's such a really nice person, but then so are his Fambo back in Liverpool. Assuring me, to my dismay, that we will return to the Ruta Maya before the nights out. I feel uneasy about it, but he knows the ropes. As we cross the street the Juice Head Baby, a music connection, waves to me, "I'll be back !", I say in an Arnold Schwarzenegger voice. Abraham and Erin, smile, ominously.

Years later when I eventually take the time to study Spanish I will realise that this means "House of Light". I will also notice that "Luz", the word for "Light", is used a lot in Spanish in ways we wouldn't concieve of in English. Some quite beautiful ways. Ways a lot similar to how it's used in Islam. And I can see in this the remnants of a Moorish influence in the Spanish mind set. As well as the presence of over 5,000 words of Arabic origin. Hebrew, Arabic, Aramaic, and Ethiopian Amharic all being closely related on a Semetic level, something I learned about from my buddy Sam Zussaman, who was a Jewish linguist, and a cantor in both oriental, and oxidental styles of Torah recital. Who taught me a lot about Judaism during my time at Brahma Kumaris University of World Spirtuality, on Pound Lane, in Willesden, North London. Don't you just love the hybrid syncretic nature of reality. On any level you look at it, on all levels, everything blends into a Human oneness. We are truly all related. Mitakuye Oyasin, as the Native Americans say.

Ruta Maya Revisted.

Nigel and Patricia take me for a stroll down 6th Street.Sixth Street is to Austin's legendary musical heritage,what Bourbon Street is to New Orleans, or what Matthew Street is to Liverpool at least once a year during the Beatles Festival. Sounds fuse into each other as you walk down Sixth Street. Some Blues vocals coming out of the sunken garden of a club ahead of me on my right, blend beautifully as they are blown about Sixth Street on the breeze with a more Jazzy feel from the open court yard of an open air jam session, in a Jazz joint just across the road. It's not until I'm parallel to them both, that I realise it's two different bands. The whole street is a veritable kaleidoscope, of inter-textual sights and sounds. We turn the corner of Sixth Street, and I realise we're right on top of the Ruta Maya. "Oh well it's been OK so far", I tell myself as I step forward to face my fear. Never dreaming for an instant that anybody in there might be expecting me, or even expecting a lynching

Second time around the Ruda Maya loomed up at me like an Aztec grave, complete with death metal vampires straight,from the set of a Tarantino movie. Dusk till Dawn was Sesame Street compared to this place after dark. I reckon word had well reached the Good Ole' Boys, about the set I did at Gaby & Mo's. I could tell once I was inside. Moving through that crowd was like, walking through "Hell with gasoline drawers on", as Pop would say. At the Poetry Slam at Gaby & Mo's, to all intent and purpose, I had spoken from within the shadow of veiled knowledge. I had delivered a poem on Slavery, in a disenfranchised tongue, wet with savouring the concentrated taste of strategic melodic flavours. Yes my Scouse accent had threw them a bit, but not as much as my subject matter, "the Trans- Atlantic Slave Trade." I realised something in this little epiphany. I actually think it hurt some of them hearing me speak irreverently of England, and Europe, their ancestral home, in an English accent that was genuine, authentic, beyond their imagination. Beyond even their imitation. Beyond the Sterotype. Some of the White folks present at the time, were seeing Red. They were so in need of their European ancestral link, and they knew it, and I knew it, and they knew that I knew it. It hurt them primarily because I was a 'Nigger', and secondly because I had something they could only stand in deference to, an English accent, and it was mine, all mine. Some folks at the Slam, hadn't heard any thing like my Northern brand of English before, but, it was English non-the less. And of an authentic regional form, acquired naturally. I had been my old brash Scouse self, and out brashed the brashest Yanks in brassy Christendom, the Texans.

It's around teatime on a mellowed out Austin evening. Tonight I'm back at the Ruda Maya and the Posse's laying in wait. The place is ram-tam-chockabloc by the time we arrive. The first face I see as I step through the door, is the Gollum character in the white woolen hat, that I had mistaken for a Muslim on my first day in Austin. His eyes are glazed, slightly fearful, but there's is a territorial defiance, and a slight uneasiness about his potential hatred. "No Chics, No Bucks, No Cocynuts, me Blanco amigo", I think to myself. He sees me, and sort of slithers along the bench he's sitting on. Seemingly repulsed by me, but more out of fear it seems, as he tries to melt further into the corner he's lurking in. The look in those slow brooding red eyes. White pain glowing darkest bright. I'm not alone this time, and the word has obviously gone around that I'm a poet, and not unknown back in England. I'm big in Huddersfield, poetry capital of the UK. ;-) Even in Gaby and Mo's somebody had heard of me via their Yorkshire poetry connections. So I'm not as easy a target for him this time around. Gaby and Mo's is actually a friendlier place, cos it's situated East Side in Ghetto land, the Ruda Maya is West Side, smack dab in good ole' Redkneck territory. So I also suspect there is a certain amount of guilt knocking around, inside this place right now.

There was a guy setting up equipment on stage, the base-ball cap he was wearing, with the word "Honky", emblazoned across a yellow rose of Texas, said it all. It didn't take me long to piece it all together. The Slavepool poem actually had impacted more than I'd imagined. And I'd imagined a lot. But now I could feel some of the fall out. This definately wasn't England. It definately wasn't Liverpool. It was Austin, Texas. Yeeea Hahhh! I didn't care, I was Shangoed up like Django, and I knew I was an anathema to some of these guys. So what's new. There was nothing else in their experiential world, that they could relate me to. The only response they knew was one of intimidation. And as I looked at myself in the mirror I realised, that the hood of my sweat suite top said it all, as it lay across my shoulders. I pulled it up over my head, and I noticed me in a new world. My world but a different configuration. My best features shaded by the black hood of the sweat-suit top, rising up from inside, the upturned pointed collar of a black leather jacket.

Dervish Robin. Robin of the Hood. Cold eyes over my shoulder scolding with their heated gaze, at my sneering coolness. Jeering at my own naivité, my stupidity, my touristic, Homeboy, Rebel-Rock, Northern Soul openness, and ebullience. Ignorance the true shackles of their serfdom. We push through the punter's that are rapidly piling into the place, as show time swiftly approaches. We hit the bar, aquire our poisons, seek seats. Nigel, Patricia, and I find a table near the front with our cup's of coffee, and tea. On the table next to us is a character known as the Enigma. I would see him on TV back in England years later, in a program about Goths, piercing, tatoos, and surgical implants. He is covered from head to toe in a jig-saw puzzle design, and he has two bone implants grafted onto his head, that look like horns. His girl friend also has some pretty awesome customisation. A likely candidate for cosmetic female circumcision. The gold sleeper type. They smile pleasantly, they seem like nice people. Maybe I'm just paranoid about this place, maybe it aint that bad in here. Nigel seems convinced it's a cool place, but again he isn't a tactless pickaninny poet, at a potential picnic.

The first part of the night was like an acoustic poetry session. A grungey looking, first time singer/song-writer called Louise does a turn. She's mellow, Joni Mitchellish, but she seems depressed. A sort of Country-Grundge dude sings a song about, "I smoked fifteen bongs sitting on my porch... Fell asleep in the bath... Pulled on my britches ran into town..." Then there was a pumpkin faced Hill Billy boy, who sang what he called a Hill Billy love song on an African marimba, with one of his arms all bandaged up like it was in a splint. He sang a song called, "When am I gonna learn." I got the distinct feeling it was aimed at me. As he passed our table he stared me straight in the eye. His friendly, beaming, watery-glazed eyes told me, "I'm on your side, but it's kinda rough around here, and you need to know that pardner." I was getting the picture. A friendly warning, "Don't Mess with Texas", or at least the West Side of Austin, anyways.

Now, here in what could very easily be Hell's Mouth. I sedately sipped sweet tea, of the English Breakfast variety. As my potential enemies delicately dipped their arrows in it's venom. My Church of England up bringing hidden in the darkness of the Dervish hood, pulled over my cowered head. The next act up seemed to confirm for me the fact, that some people in there were a little upset with me. The guy with the Honky-hat, was the lead singer with a band who called themselves, for the evening at least, "The Demon- Strators". The Demon-Strator's set seemed to coincide with current affairs, in a number of ways,and on a number of levels. They had put together a special number to commemorate the Battle in Seattle called, "Beating a Horse to Death." Although they seemed, apparently Left Wing, I wasn't that convinced. I'd seen, and experienced, White Supremacist socialism back home, on more than one occasion. It wasn't hard to imagine some of these good old boys morphing into a lynch mob. Like the wiley coyote in the white Islamic topi, that had greeted me with "No Chics, No Bucks, No Cocy-nuts", on my first day. They could have been either spoilt middle-class wannabees, or just out-right poor-White-trailer park trash, with a grudge against Society, Jews, Niggers, and Yankees, and not necessarily in any particular order. I've seen so many well meaning middle-class Liberals, and So-called Socialist workers turn into Right-wing knee-jerk reactionaries, when the subject of Racism, or Race-relations comes up on the agenda. It's a kind of denial. One of them stared me out with an evil fixed gaze, right throughout the number. I sat there sipping my tea, vibing back as cool, and as English as a Blackman can get. Like I usually do when I'm abroad, especially when I'm in the States. I endured the totally unrestrained vengeful nature of their onslaught, that was a cross between the Texas Chain-Saw Massacre, and Captain Beef Heart on bad-acid. Their whole demeanor left me in no doubt, they were friends of, and some of them I think were actually from amongst the guys I had run into on the first day. This was their patch, and mouthy Negroes were not at all welcome. I could feel it more than anything else. The saving grace as always was, that there were mixed feelings towards me, and surrounding me in there that night. I scanned the crowd before sitting down, I'd clocked Noah, Elgin, Villon, and a few of the more liberal, literary types. I was slightly perturbed, but not disturbed, as I felt that a lot of what I was getting from these guys, was more a psychodrama based around them saving face. They didn't really know me, their hostility was aimed more at an unknown, plain speaking Black entity. I was a Scouse entity that had unwittingly made them blow their own cool, by just being a talking Blues poet, when they didn't even know it. To most folks like the Enigma, and his girl for example, I was just another piece of life's puzzle. Nigel was feeling the intensity of the music, but seemed oblivious to the subtexts that I was deciphering. What I realised more than anything is that, over here I was from East Austin. I was from the Hood.

Black Urban Life-histories evolved from a rhythm different from those regulated by their symbiosis with the central placenta. The absent centre. Truth versus 'Reale Politique, my Shadow awareness sneers. Watches me. Inner Consciousness. Studies. Assesses. Guards psychological territory. An English poet producing meaningful shapes, amidst the abstract palimpsests of systematic negation, omission, misrecognition, and inappropriate definitions of the other. I still kinda felt like, as musicians, and would be Outsiders, these guys were still my Brothers. I understood them, their poor-White trash anger. I forgave them. I loved them. Identity is a time based art, it shifts as it moves through the greenwood, light speckling it's environment with the dust of evolution. Our cultural history in today's UK a living narrative. Liquid. Flowing. Fluid. Like water, sparkling, with the soulful shimmer of an expanding, morphic resonance. A story to be sung. Our Trans-World. Pan-Global. Black-Atlantic culture. A Something spoken. Not found. Sculptured soul welded from retold histories. Unsolved mysteries located in the future. Hayakul Nur. The shape of Light.

After the Demon Strators had raised Cain from the dead, in an effort to straighten out a couple of demons of their own, or even mine, if that was the case. It was like a Jumbie Jamboree, a night of the zombies. Nigel suggested that we move on. I can't say that I wasn't relieved. The band play some thing funky as we're leaving. I dance cooly, and funky to their next number, in my Kangol, just outside the saloon doors. I'm eyeballing the menacing musicians, but with a smug grin, as if to say, "Peace! And I'm outa here!" Nigel and Patricia say their farewells to some people that they know, and we split the scene.

We depart from the Ruta Maya, anti-diluvian, coffee house that opens out onto one of those wooden walkways that you see in Cowboy movies. We descend some steps to cross the street. A White guy, with reedy-blonde hair, in his forties, bent over with humiliation, approaches us asking for money. "I don't drink sir, and I'm looking for work, but it's hard, and I got kids, but I'll work if I can. Could you spare some change". I gave him five dollars. That's a lot apparently. Maybe to them, but to me it's only about two fifty in terms of Pounds Sterling. His humility touched my heart. He was a humble lion of a man. I'm soft like that. I feel for people. No matter what colour, creed, or class they are. It's a weakness of mine. But it's also what makes me a Dervish. Nigel and Patricia just look at me. He wasn't a conman, I could feel it from him, and I felt for him. I know what it's like when you need money to feed your kids. It hurts. It hurts deep down inside of you. It's hurting my Pop right now, with him not being able to show me around like he'd like to. I can see how hard it is for an ex-veteran, turned Roots and Culture teacher in the ghetto. I've been there in my own sort of way.

Theme Park Ethnics.

139

At first I hated having a Scouse accent. It wasn't Black enough for me at the time. There ws no Black in the Union Jack. Years later I would explain to Melvin Bragg on Radio Four, how in the seventies when Dub poets were all the rage, having a Scouse accent meant you wasn't Black enough. Of course now it's more of an 'And/Also', you can be British and also Black, without there being a contradiction, so these days Black's with regional accents are coming into their own a bit more. The BBC programme with Melvin Bragg, 'The Routes of English', portrayed and validated this point of fact, much to my reassurance and delight.

My main gripe at this point in time was how easy Black culture was becoming commodified, and appropriated under so called 'Multi-culturalism'. Representation of Black images, and available role models in the media, had flourished from scarcity to a deluge, and with that deluge came the gross manipulation of Blackness, and Black identity by the media. Marketing strategies and PR people began trying to control Black identity, or water it down, everyone trying to fix it in line with their own agenda. Black Islamophobes saying Malcolm was a Socialist, Malcolm was a Nationalist, everything but what he was, a Muslim. The pressure was on to assimilate into some sort of theme park ethnicity.

I rebelled in my own magnificently obsessive way, Geronimo to the bone. Racism, and cultural awareness saturated everything I did, essays, shorts stories, plays, poems, songs, stand-up comedy routines. And always the same themes kept popping up, like the incident when I was warned to stay away from my daughter's Mother. I could assess how much that had impacted on me when I was making a video tape, and collecting some books of poetry, and recorded memorabilia together for my long lost daughter. As I was sifting through the printed word, and the hours of video footage of talks, workshops, interviews, performances, carnivals and gigs, I could see the pattern of how often, certain things that still caused me pain had cropped up in my material. How over the years, how many times I'd referred to not being able to marry a White man's daughter. I'm still taking a stock of the damage, each reference a hint at the mental scar tissue that hides beneath the surface, each disfunctional attitude the sear of an open wound. You can't be a Dog Soldier and not incur wounds, and that was how I'd become, kamikaze, like the Cheyenne Dog Soldiers whose habit was to wear a long sash that trailed the ground, and carry a scared arrow. In a conflict situation they would pin the sash to the Earth with the sacred arrow, and stand their ground till the victory or death.   Having said that, in a relative sense I was becoming more reasonable than I had been. Just accepting that I was damaged goods was a step ahead of where I had been. I had less need for pride for a start, but I did need my dignity. There's a diference between humility and humiliation. There didn't seem like there was any place where Black people could own their own feelings, and actualise their fully aware selves without becoming termed radical, or negative. It seemed to me that once "White" folks had cottoned onto the fact that we were using culture to redefine our selves, in our own image, and not in relation to the conditions of worth laid on us by "Massa", they also realised that that could mean trouble, especially after the Black uprisings of the early eighties. I always liked Stewart Hall's comment about, who we think we are being largely shaped by what people project onto us, and how that limits our notion of our identity.

The Calabash.

We walk down to where Nigel's parked the car. Nigel and Patricia drove me back to Singleton Avenue on the East Side. Pop came to door in his dressing gown and slippers. He'd been waiting up for me worried that his English son might come unstuck amidst Austin's night life. He was nearly right. He waved down the path to Nigel who was driving away, as I did. He had a big smile on his face as he studied Nigel's face smiling from the car window. I could see him pondering who my friend from England might be. As Nigel drove off, I gave one final wave, and a thank you, as I walked down the garden path towards Pop.

When we got in I put a cup of water in the micro-wave to make a cup of tea.

Pop said something like, "You sure get on fine with those White folks son."

I said, "So do you Pop, that's how I got here remember."

Touché! He looked at me stunned at my cheek. But who else could have said such a thing back to him other than me. My Sisters couldn't. In fact considering some of the evenings less savoury possibilities, there was more than just a tad of irony in Pop's remark, in my reposte. In fact that there was so much irony surrounding that remark that you could have picked it up with a magnet.

The next day me and Pop are out and about in the Lincoln. I can sort of feel that the journey is closing to an end. This is probably the last time I'll visit this Mall with Pop that is, unless I can make it back to Texas again. Maybe that's what's making me melancholy, this could be the one and only time I ever see my old Pop, in my entire life. I'm enjoying cruising the Mall with Pop. I find a cool sports shop, and buy some American footballs for my nephews. I get them the customised ones, with the Texas Longhorns logo embossed in rubber. One each for Ashur and Malik. For Akeem I buy an Austin-based game of Monopoly. I see some rattlesnake heads, made into various things like key-rings and stuff, so I buy one for my friend Karla. Her Mutha's a mix of Irish and German, and her Father was a half African-American, half Cherokee GI. We have a lot in common, so she's sort of like a Soul Sister, and I know she'll like it. We stroll around the Mall, just people-watching. I see a guy with four stripes down each cheek, like tribal marks. He reminds me of a guy in Liverpool that we used to call One-one-eleven.

We're driving back to Pop's in the beat-up old, Boot Strapper Mobile. I'm flicking channels on the radio. Some Country music sounds like Soul, some like Blues, some like Motown, some stuff sounds like contemporary R'n'B, and other stuff more like Funk with Blue Grass violins. There's a few seconds of silence and I listen to what comes on, next thing I hear is: "Are you tired of seeing the White Race down trodden," followed by what seems to be a party political broadcast for the Ku Klux Klan. The rhetorical piece is followed by an implied twist, as it's put across as a commercial: "See the controversial new play, The Brotherhood of Hate." For some reason, the twist didn't convince me. I look at Pop and I say: "I can't believe I just heard that." He says: "Believe it, this is Texas, son." Pop starts straight talking: "You see, in Austin, you'll only find Black businesses on 11th, 12th, and 6th street." He points some of them out as we drive past, and tells me with just a hint of cynicism: "Black business around means barbecue pits." An item comes through on the radio news flash concerning Baseball, and corruption in betting on sports, followed by more stuff on the Seattle riots, now being called the "Battle in Seattle". The report tells us that, Senate and the House of Representatives, are concerned at the number of divergent groups involved, and that they have come under severe public criticism. Pop chips in: "We elected them and voted them in, so we should just trust."

We cruise along for spell, Pop starts to sing the "Lords' Prayer," in a Black Gospel styly. I join in with him on the harmonies, but I'm competing with him in melodic runs, and flourishes. I mean, we did a mean-routine as we prayed the "Lord's Prayer" together, bussing along the Mopac 35. Hearts alive. I had tears welling up in my eyes. When we finished with full-on, wailing-Gospel cadences, flowing like springs of fresh clear water. We both laughed out loud, cos we'd raised so much joy between us in the process. Pop is enthused. He starts telling me how back in the day, they all used to compete, just like how we was doing right then. "Doowopping on the corner," Pop added, as he looked in his rear view mirror, and snarled: "He's been riding my butt, for a half a mile or so. I'm gonna put my boot so far up his ass, he's gonna think his tongue's made of shoe leather." That's my Pop, he'll switch on you just like that, but I love him for it.

As we hit Manor Road, I notice a sign that reads "Calabash: Caribbean Restaurant". "Let's drop in here Pop, and see what they got. I was in the Caribbean in August." As we approach the Calabash from the car-park, they're playing a kind of Island-muzak, Calypso-ala-The James Last Orchestra. I was expecting it to be a Jamaican place, but it turns out to be Cuban. It's run by a White woman, and her daughter. Even though my Step-Dad, Arturo, was Cuban, I've never quite associated Cuba with the Caribbean. A Black American in a Jamaican base-ball cap, comes from out of the back of the place, as we enter, and sit by the bar. I'm reading one of the electric pink flyers, that I've picked up on the way in, it proclaims proudly: "Voted Best Ethnic". It also says less flamboyantly: "Every Thursday is Dollar Night. One dollar on all domestic beers. Happy hour all day Wednesday." The breezy Calabash is empty except for us, and the security guard, sipping Bacardi. The staff seem curious, and a little nervous, paranoid even. My guess is that they're part of the new insurgence into the Ghetto, we're actually on Manor Road, just up from Gaby and Mo's, where I did the Austin Slam Night. I can see Manor Road becoming an equivalent to what Hope Street represents in Liverpool, a demarcation zone. I'm an alien in the café at the end of my own street at present. It's weird. Pop wouldn't eat. He was either being proud, or just resented eating in this place. This was a journey of a Life Time for me. I was gonna eat Cuban. The woman who cooked, she was the Mother of the place, came over to take my order. She seemed OK, but I don't think she was Cuban, not that it matters. Authenticity is a neo-colonialist notion at best, that often means nothing more than "marketing strategy" for White folks. I ordered jerk shrimp, quesadillas, Cuban black beans and avocado, and something called a Ginger Storm, even if it was Texan-Cuban. As the lady who took my order disappears into the kitchen, Pop says: "She's so ugly she got ugly she ain't used yet." They play a lounge-core Reggae version of "You'll Never Walk Alone". At first, I think it's synchronicity, years later, I worked out a simpler explanation, she must have recognised my accent. The Beatles got their harmonica style from some Texans, Country Boys, who got their thing, from some old time Blues greats. I now play the Blues harp, "Gob-iron," they call it in Liverpool. As the sounds of the Liverpool National Anthem, waft out from the bamboo, and palm frond hidden speakers, I'm sitting with long-lost biological Pop, thinking of my Cuban Step-Dad, Arturo Villada. It all gels in time and space.

After serving me my food, our hostess stands behind the bar, sort of chatting to the guy in the JA base-ball cap, and clocking us at the same time. Pop is busy telling me about the car incident, and how it went in court, that morning. I'd been waiting to get the proper story, of how he felt it went. "The lawyer couldn't tell shiznit from wild honey," he growled. "I wanted to shoot the sonofabitch with forty shit pistols firing at different times." He's telling me how it went, and raving over the original car-crash incident. The guy at the bar shifts uneasily, as Pop raises his voice. "That's not a Blackman; that's a Nigger," Pop says fiercely. "That's a Nigger!", he repeats with added emphasis. The guy in the JA base-ball cap shifts even more nervously. Pop's actually talking about his lawyer, but the poor Bacardi soaked watch-dog don't know that, and his conscience is dealing with him. "Brother Owen recommended the guy;" Pop sneered, talking about the lawyer. "So, I trusted him, but the sucker took me for two thousand five hundred dollars." Pop shook his head in disbelief. "I need forty thousand shit pistols, and I'd leave him on an island with no water, covered in it." He laughed, and shook his head again before saying: "I let this shit warp my mind." He looks around into the distance, there's a short penitent pause, before he continues: "Forty bucks a month! That's not a righteous law. It's just a money-making scheme; that's all it is, it's not justice, it's not democracy." "I don't know what it is?" I say, trying to console him, "But it don't sound good." I add in support. "I'll tell you what it is. That's a bunch of bullshit."
Now, I can see why he has no appetite. The court case this morning must have been a real downer for him. I'm in the same position as I always am. Seeing my loved ones suffer, and

being helpless to do anything substantial to help them. It tears me up. "The muthfeckas be talking about 'Five year-probation'. I'd rather do time!" Pop snorted like a defiant bull. He starts to tell me about all the Police harassment he's been getting since he tried to take the Police to court for burglary. He reckons the car stitch-up was just another aspect of the overall game they've been trying to run on him, since then. I know that dance. "Well, that's my defence for yah. I need to stay in practise. I got no time for dog-assed people." Pop was on a roll with the dozens: "I hope when he's old and a syphilitic wreck, he falls through his ass, and breaks his kneck." He chuckles wickedly and adds: "I said to him, go ahead, make an ass out of yourself, cos you gonna need one to protect the one you think you got." At the time he lost me on that one, but I think I've worked it out since. Pop continued his righteous ranting: "They gonna make a mistake and give me five million dollars. Then I'm get me a White lawyer, and I'm get White arse to kick White arse." The Brother at the bar, and the White lady running the place were all ears by now, as Pop raised his voice to make his final point: "I'm a military man" Pop rasped. "I'm trained in the art of kicking ass! I'd run a ten-cent nail up his dick." I don't know what a ten-cent nail looks like, but it didn't sound too pretty. I hadn't heard from this guy in forty years, and even those first three years are virtually non-existent to me in terms of memory, other than as legend, but if I couldn't have gotten to be any more like him, if I'd followed him all my life studying him. We were both built from the same components, configured by the same regime, White Anglo Saxon Protestantism.

In my repertoire of Frog-songs, I have a song called, "Wild Frontier Blues", and another entitled "Ghost Dance Blues", and in there lies the rub. It was happening here, in Austin. I could see it. I could feel it. I was living it along with my Poppa. Forty years on and Cowboys and Indians, are still a potent leitmotif that runs throughout my work. Still as useful for explaining the relationship between the World's elites, and everyone else on the planet, as anything else.

"You better pick up your little sack, and put it on your back," Pop says as were leaving, reminding me not to forget my rucksack, which is slung over the back of the chair I'm sitting.

When we get back, it's about two in the afternoon, I decide to do the Japanese Tea Ceremony meditation. It reminds me a lot of poems I used to perform with a Jazz trio, called, "The Japanese Garden", about a garden in Calderstones Park in Liverpool, that I used to visit with my girlfriend on Sundays to catch the diffusion of light at sunset. The sweet scent of roses on the warm gentle breeze, the melodic tinkling of wind chimes, a stone Babette laid out like stepping-stones amidst a fresh sea of flowers, and fragrant herbs. A miniature stone temple, that doubles as a fountain, "Cascade mouth", "Taka Guchi" in Japanese. We have so much in common, my Pop and I, it's amazing me. I shouldn't be, but I am.

Gary shows up. I've heard a lot about him, Pop said he was gonna call over to see me before I went back. Gary E. Smith is my cousin, Pop's Sister Grace's son. Cousin Gary was a lineman for the county, a job that he used to do in the Forces. He's wearing his lineman dungarees, a tartan shirt, and an old sweaty, grey and blue, Dallas Cowboy's baseball cap. Gary's come over straight from work especially to see me. He takes his hat off and says, "I ain't got nothing with me to give yah, cos I just come straight over here from work, but take this," and he takes the hat off his head and gives it to me. I'm deeply moved. It needs a wash, but I'll treasure it for the rest of my days. That's the type of sentimental old fool I am. I chew the fat with Cousin Gary, and say my good byes. I'm glad I got to see him before I go back, even it was only short and sweet. Evelyn comes home from work. We eat a wholesome down-home meal, the vibes are good, Diamond's happy. Evelyn and Pop are in truce, it would seem. Maybe Pop's giving it a shot at being civil cos I'm getting ready to go back to Liverpool. It happens that way sometimes.

Slavepool.

So here I am in the now, but before I leave you to ponder my story, or dismiss it as you will, I have one final tale to tell, probably the most important one for me personally. One of the best responses I got from performing the poem "Slavepool", was when I performed it when I hosted the opening dinner entertainment's at The Collegium of African American Research conference,nin the Adelphi Hotel Liverpool, where I met many top scholars of African-American history from around The World, amongst them Henry Louis Gates Jr, one of the foremost in his field, someone I'd read a lot of during my university days. A consequence of that performance a copy was requested by the English Departments, of Pace University New York, New York State University, also The Shonberg Museum and Archives of African American History in Harlem, and a copy shares the honoured position of being one of three poems framed, and hanging on the wall of the Head of African American Studies in The University of Laguna, Canary Isles. I Googled my name once and it came up next to the poem in so many diverse contexts, that I filled ten pages with references to where it had been used, quoted, or published in parts, but the Collegium of African American Research, for me tops them all. So for the curious among you this is the poem:

Slavepool.

"A seaport sprang from the blood of slaves
In the pool of Life a macabre parade
Human marketplace Black flesh for trade
I'm talking African people held in chains.

Cargo bought and sold on the cotton exchange
With the gum and the rum and the sugar cane
Branded like beast who feel no pain
And all for Ye Merrye Olde Englande's gain.

But things are changing rearranging,

Only we can clear our name, growing knowing, trade winds
blowing. Reciting The Most Beautiful Names.
Things'll never be the same.

Pirates auctioned and pitched / Parliament pitted their wits
The church sold out our soul for gold that's how come the church
got rich /With the capital they carved a cosy niche
For the cotton industry and the nouveau riche.

Excuse me I don't mean to preach
But Black blood sweat and tears
Toiled and slaved for years
to create all the wealth interest free
Banking shipping industry.

Black poverty paved the way to prosperity
John Bull cashed in on our posterity
With legitimised robbery of Afrikan property
A legacy of history we still can see.

But history changing rearranging
Cos only we can clear our name Growing, knowing, Faces
glowing. Reciting The Most Beautiful Names.
Thing's never e the same.

Our real contribution dismissed and forgotten
By delusions of grandeur corrupted and rotten.
Slave ship to the cotton picking slave plantation
Sold down the Swannee to dehumanisation.
Jump down turn around pick a bail of nuthin'
But a bullwhip noose or a gun or somthin' .

Imports exports holiday resorts
The imput was largely ours of course.
The worlds largest ever unpaid workforce
With the most abundant source of natural resources
And we didn't profit one iota more is the worse.

Our mineral rich land time energy and pain
Help to build an Empire that ruled in shame
Now dismissed go collective claims for credit
Or a share in the wealth of that direct debit.

Just 400 years of shackles and chains
Attitudes slander media campaigns
And outrageous claims that retard our aims
By the trivialisation of Racist games.

But People changing rearranging
Cos only we can clear our name
Growing knowing, waters flowing.
Reciting The Most Beautiful Names.
Thing's never be the same.

If you've ever been on the dole or without a home
You'll realise what I'm saying that it all began
By a way of life that carries on
By keeping masses of innocent people down.

City in a society built on a truth that's cruel
Once upon a time you were the nation's jewel.
Now discarded like a worn out industrial tool
With redundant rhetoric and bourgeois rules.

Used and abused like the slaves of old
That's how the Beatles were Blues-born
From a Blackman's Soul.
Some say they understand. And I guess that's kool,
But the song remains the same Slavepool !
And it's like that cos that's the way it is!"

Valkyrie.

My Mother Flo, or Doey as she was sometimes called,

because of her doe eyes, was never a battle-axe, but she could wield a fire axe. My Mom used to sometimes try to get in between me and my girl friends as I was growing up. No one seemed good enough by her standards, but it wasn't always my Mother who came between me and my girl friends. If I had a penny, a nickel, or a silver sixpence, for the amount of girls that would tell you out straight that they didn't want their parents knowing that they were seeing a Black boy, I'd be a multi-millionaire. Such rejection was par for the course, it was how it was. The only time it ever really impacted dramatically on my life, beyond the realm of mere heart-break, which was also par for the course , the only time it came back to haunt me, was when Lorna's father and older brother came up to my Mother's in Fazakerley, and warned me away from the girl I was planning to marry. I was sitting on the couch watching tele, combing out my hair with an Angela Davis Afro-pick, a rare commodity In those days. I was just sitting there peacefully watching "Get Smart" and I saw their Brylcreamed heads bobbing up and down above the higgledy-piggledy Hilly-Billy fence, that marked out the forgotten wilderness that we called our front garden. Then the knock at the door and I knew they'd come on the bounce. I studied their faces, I knew why they'd come. Lorna's brother had old Pop Gillard's face, so did their Glenda, but Lorna didn't. Old Pop Gillard, Lorna's Dad, had basically said we were too young to be seriously courting. We were both about seventeen, going on eighteen, we were planning to get engaged. It hadn't been a problem with Spooney, Lorna's ex. I said straight out, "You only want me to stay away from Lorna cos I'm a Nigger !" To which Lorna's Dad had replied, "Your not even a Nigger son, your an Half-Chat." Give me a man whose not afraid to call a spade a spade, when he means Nigger. I went into a Shotokan Karate stance. My Mother had been ear-wigging and jumped out with my German Grand-Dad's rusty, but trustworthy, old fireman's axe, and said, "Don't you call my son a Half-Chat. I'll take your head from your shoulders. Now get!" (a favourite shout of hers, as I fondly remember). And they went. And that was that.

After that Lorna and I saw each other whenever we could, but she had cousins in Fazakerley, and whenever she was spotted anywhere on Longmoore Lane, never mind Haven Road it was assumed that she was hanging around Fazakerley to see me, so the country cousin grassed her up to her folks and she'd be grounded. Not long after the warning visit. I caught an eye infection, went blind in one eye, and semi opaque in the other one. I went into St Paul's eye hospital for two weeks, and by the time I'd came out, it was all over bar the pouting.

Lorna.

Lorna was Spanish-Irish, she had blue eyes, and she was olive skinned, with jet black wavy hair. Lorna Doone me Mutha used to call her, from a story about Britain's first Black settlers, the Picts. A stunner of a girl in white embroidery Anglaise , destined to be a heart breaker. Once when she came back from her holidays in Spain she was darker than me, and she looked even more exotic. She'd had an affair with a Spanish waiter, and I'd had a pre-emptive dream about it. My teenage jealousy was so intense, I'd sensed it. It was an abstract vision, but I had understood what it meant. Paella everywhere.

Lorna worked in Chelsea Girl, and dressed like a model. I was crazy about her in her navy and yellow Jersey midi-skirt and matching bolero. We were both very much in love, and we were engaged to be married. We were both only seventeen and a half at the time, but the half made all the difference. Yes they called it 'puppy love'.

We all knew that the real reason Lorna and me never happened was the fact that, her Father was a Racist, and at the time so was her older brother. Although ironically the brother would end up with a Black woman, the sister of my two old Rasta mates. He's a really cool guy now. We get on ok, he's my daughter's Uncle after all. At the time I guess he was like everyone else he knew in Walton. Life is so short when you look back. That was fourty years ago. At the time I was a definite No-No, and that's the way it went. I had to live with it. So did Lorna. After two weeks in the St Paul's Eye Hospital, where I had a whale of a time actually, but that's another story, I never saw the incredibly whistful Lorna, as a girl friend ever again. I would see her once as the wife of an old friend, over ten years later, at Sunday lunch at me Mother's. She had married an old buddy of mine, a guy we called White-T, cos his name was Tony, and there was a Black one, a Mixed race one, and a White one in the crew.   He became White Tony, or White-T, in much the same way that Ghanaan Dan became African Dan, Black Sammy became Sammy Black, or Berkley Janet became Yankee Janet. When I'd known Tony he'd been living with a Black transgender person known as Derek Hazel, but who we all called Dee, or Dee Hazel.

Me Mutha had met Tony and Lorna in town, knowing both of them already, she'd invited them for one of her legendary Sunday dinners. She also invited me and my steady girl Pat Manning from around that time, also a friend of White-T's from our Splurge days. It was for a kind of reunion. As we ate a hearty Sunday Dinner, and caught up with each other's lives, Lorna had a secret that she'd shared with Tony, but not with me. I think Momma X knew something, and was hoping it might come out during the evocative, and unfolding ritual of carving the Sunday roast. I wasn't to find out what the secret was for another eighteen years. Even though at the time Tony had urged her to tell me, apparently. She just wouldn't.

How I eventually found out, was when our daughter Rebecca, eventually traced me on the internet, via The Windows Project, a Poetry based Community Arts organisation based in Bold Street. I got a call from Dave Ward, my mate, and the guy behind Windows, saying that a woman named Lorna Hughes, wanted my number, and should he give it to her. I sort of knew who it would be, and what it was about. There was noone else with that name that I'd ever known, and there could only be one reason why she would want to talk to me after twenty eight years. I had heard a rumour back then off her friend Susan, Kif's ex-babe, and so I sort of knew, but not for certain, because noone had ever really confirmed the fact that I had a daughter to Lorna, it was just rumour. And false rumours abounded.

She hadn't mentioned it ten years later at the Sunday Dinner, so I was half in denial about the whole affair for most of my life, but there were moments when I recognised the possibility of there being somewhere, the existence of a child that belonged to Lorna and myself. I sorta knew, even when I eventually traced my Poppa to Austin Texas, after forty years, the first thing he'd asked me was, did he have any grand-children. I told him, "I think I may have a daughter from when I was seventeen. Her names Rebecca". I had also told my sisters about Rebecca when we went out one evening to the Bombay Bicycle Shop, an eclectic karioka bar in down town Austin. So before I'd had it confirmed, before I'd knew for sure that Rebecca existed. I had received the possibility, and there were times that I sort of boasted about my possible daughter. I wanted to believe that she existed, even though I never really knew for sure.

Sure, it's true that I had fostered our Tanya, after my Mother's death, that was a bit like being a one-parent family, although Tan was more like a little sister to me. And then there was my step-daughter Tammy. Tammy who was Margie's daughter had called me Dad since she was born literally, and I love them both very much, but to have no actual biological offspring apart from a rumour, then discover the rumour has flesh and bones. After tracing my long-lost GI Father, who I never thought I would ever meet in my life. Now I was about to recieve blessing number two, I was about to discover another missing piece of the Sacred Hoop. I phoned Lorna as soon as I could. The first thing she said before I even opened my mouth after she told me was ,"She is yours Gene ". I never doubted it for one instant. She filled me in about what had happened.

Lorna told me how Rebecca had been taken off her all those years ago against her will, and put into fostering and then adopted. She told me how her Mother and her had wanted to keep her, but how her Father wouldn't allow it. I learned how Rebecca had traced her Mother only three years previous to tracing me. The line that had been so callously drawn under our past connections had suddenly been erased. Lorna kept assuring me she was mine. I said "I know", and I never doubted it for one cotton-picking minute. I did know, somewhere deep down in my Soul. I could just feel it in my bones. That's what I'm like, intuitive, mystical even.

Lorna and her Mother had wanted to keep Rebecca, but her Dad had made her get her adopted. When I got the full story from Lorna it killed me to know that our child had been fostered to a couple in Fazakerley. She could have passed me, pushed in a pram right in front of my eyes and I wouldn't have known it. We had a big Foster Family, there was no reason why we couldn't have raised Rebecca in our Family. I couldn't help thinking how much it would have meant to me Mutha to have known that she had a Grand Daughter before she died. Now our child Rebecca was fully grown, and married, and I had a Grand-son L'il Levi who wrote poetry, and a really cool son in law Phil, who surfed, and climbed mountains to make money for kids in need. But I hadn't met any of them. My head spun, and my heart pounded. Lorna's mild mannered voice whispered down the phone. "She wants to meet you Gene ".
"I want to meet her Lorna".
"So will you meet her?"
"Of course I will. I can't wait. Honestly I'm over the moon".
"She's coming down to ours with Levi her son, and her fellah Phil.
You can meet her then, she'll be made up that you want to meet her".
"Why wouldn't I ? She's my daughter".
I knew this, somewhere deep down inside of me I always knew it was true. I've had the name Rebecca floating around in my head for over thirty years. I knew. "Honestly Lorn, I'm made up".

I thought it was best to meet Lorna first, and catch up with what had been going on, in the three years that she'd been in touch with our long lost child. We arrange to meet. Probably just to sort out any pre-match nerves. I put the phone down, my landline was still on at the time. I needed to tell my new found Pop, my sisters, my mates, Tracie everyone, just everyone, the whole wide World.

Today the sky is grey, it reminds me of England, purple Welsh slate rooves, red brick Georgian houses, yellow waistcoats, Harris tweed, and James Joyce. Joyce once said that during the day, we walk through a multitude of characters, each a subtle aspect of undifferentiated inner potential. The good, the bad and the undecided, all accompany us on our Earthly sojourn.

Cheltenham Cathedral.

The Married One phoned yesterday and left a message, while we were at the Mall. I've had trouble getting through to her, she's stilt fishing in Sri Lanka. I'm trying to return the call, and I eventually manage to get through, but the phone goes dead. Then it rings. I think it's the illusive operator, and to my surprise it's the Married One, phoning me back again. It's good to hear her voice. I must be getting attached to her. I didn't mean to, it was only meant to be a fling.
"How is your Father ?"
"Pretty good, yuh know, he's OK".
"How's Texas ?"
"Nothing like I imagine stilt fishing in Sri Lanka to be".
We chat some small talk. I avoid the "L" word. I sorta feel something, but it's a big word, and it's hard to measure it actually, and even if the emotion measured up, the situation is unworthy. It sounds like England herself is calling me.

We would eventually end the fling in Cheltenham, one sunny Summer weekend, the following year. I had been involved in a week long residency in Essex, as part of a month long Black & Asian literature festival, and The Married One had drove over to spend the weekend with me. We wandered around

Cheltenham town centre on Saturday afternoon exploring, and taking in the sights, and we came across Cheltenham Cathedral, so naturally I wanted to see inside it. The nave was almost empty, except for a small group of senior citizens sitting in a huddle near the apse. They were all listening attentively to a woman, who looked to be in her sixties giving a talk. She was a missionary in a cosy looking, home-knitted cardigan, tweed skirt, pearl necklace, gold rimmed glasses, and silver permed hairdo. I noticed some Black faces sat off to side, next to the conservative, silver haired speaker. They were Africans straight off the boat, by the blank mystified looks on their faces. So we both sat in the huddle to hear what the motherly missionary women had to say.

She was discussing how Africans have interpreted the Bible totally different to the Europen interpretation. She mentioned that nowhere in the Bible was there an mention of shame and guilt, and yet European Christianity was based largely on shame, guilt, and fear. She quoted how mny times the Bible urged people to 'be of good cheer', and how often it spoke of 'Joy', and how often it urged people to make a 'Joyful noise'. She brought a few Africans back with her to prove the point. Apparently Joy is mentioned 430 times in the Bible. All of this intrigued me, because it was actually what my analysis of Black Southern Gospel churchs had concluded. It's all about the 'Joy' not the judgement. As we left the cathedral I noticed one of the stain-glass windows in the narthex was dedicated to the American Airmen who had been stationed in Cheltenham during WW2. I took a photo of it just to capture the moment of synchronicity. Life is full of surprises.

Pop's Flack Jacket.

I take in the room I'm in. It doesn't take me long to settle, and adapt to a new environment. I scan the clothes rack. See the green flack-jacket. I try it on again. "The Bongo Veteran's jacket",

I think to myself. It's become a symbol of something, like the word "Bongo". What ? I'm not quite sure. I've been doing a lot of reflecting, the kind of outside looking in reflection that distance, and travel, alone afford you.

Pop has a tasty calendar on his kitchen wall just above the micro-wave. It's produced by "Running Strong For American Indian Youth", a project for Christian Relief Services In New Mexico. It's an organisation started in 1975, after the Indian Self Determination and Education Act was enacted. What was interesting for me about the calendar, were the colour plates of atmospheric paintings of scenes from Native American life, painted during the early 1900's. I could have sworn that some of those same paintings were in my Indian book, way back when I used to retreat to my own little wig-wam at the age of five. Another useful thing about the calendar was the way that each day, were applicable, it would have information on a point of Native-American history relative to that date. As it was December, and it was running out anyway, so I rolled it up and brought it back with me. Most of Pop's appointments like choir practise, Veterans admin, means test, and court and stuff, had all passed. It was like two historical documents in one. It's like I've found a key to my past visiting Texas to see Pop, and it's opened up doors that have been closed for decades.

It's all Blues. Low down Blues. But I have my own spin on the Blues, one that I picked up from travelling the World seeking knowledge. It was about time I added it to my story telling repertoire while I was in Austin, and pass it over to li'l Diamond. Next time she went to visit her Momma in the State Pen, she could tell it to her, and her Momma could pass it onto her inmates, cos there are always lots of Muslims, in jail, and always lots of people becoming Muslim while they're inside. Teach them in a language they understand the Prophet told his followers, peace be upon him. So I tell her my favourite Bilal story.

"There's a saying in Africa, "God made Man because he likes to hear stories." Diamond giggled with glee at the thought of God liking to hear stories. "I'll tell you a Muslim story from

Africa, that you can tell your Momma, next time you go to Georgia to visit her in the penitentiatry."

"Yeah ! Yeah ! Yeah !" L'il Diamond was hopping up and down, like a Mexican jumping bean.

So I began to tell her the story of Bilal that I learned from the Gnoua's of Marrakech. I tell it in my classical Sufi storytelling manner, putting in the relevant etiquette's of "sallahu alihi wa salem", "Peace be upon him" after the mentioning of a Prophet, and the "Radiallu-anhum", "May Allah be pleased with them" for when one of his family, wives , or companions are mentioned. In a traditional group majlis, or storytelling session, the etiquette's are echoed by the listeners, and add a "call and response" effect, that makes the ritual more of a collective event, and more sociable for family gatherings.

"When I was in Morocco, in Africa, back in 1981, nearly twenty years ago, I met some wandering musicians called Gnawoua. They recounted to me an oral history, a story, a very old story, and a very important story for musicians, Muslims, and Africans alike. It's a story that tells of how Fatima Zohra (ra), the favourite daughter of Rasul-Ullah Sayyidina Muhammad, The Messenger of Allah (saws), who was as a rule usually bright as a button, and full of beans, was on one particularly darkened day, particularly downcast, gloomy, and very-very depressed.

The Prophet (saws) was quite upset, for, Makhtub ! It is written ! that he (sawas) said to his companions (ra): "Fatima is a piece of me. What hurts her hurts me. What pleases her pleases me." The dark cloud that cast it's shadow over Fatima's Soul seemed to linger for days. The Prophet (saws) became worried, very worried indeed. He was so eager to see his little daughter smile again, that he offered to grant the wish of any person who could make his (saws) favourite daughter (ra) smile. Many specialists came from far and wide, bearing lovely gifts of frankincense and myrrh, jewellery,and precious gems from far off Cathay. Some were skilled in singing, some at speaking gentle words,other's excelled at telling amusing tales, and exciting stories, but none succeeded in lifting the dark cloud that had

159

descended over the blessed Soulof Fatimah Zorah (ra), the most beloved daughter of the Prophet Muhammad (saws).

One day Bilal Ibn Rabah (ra), the close companion of the Prophet Muhammad (saws), dressed himself up in a cIurful African robe, that he'd decorated himself by sewing cowry shells all over it, Habashi fashion. Bilal (ra) then put on his carnival robe, and danced through the streets to the music of the two large wooden castanets that he (ra) carried in his hands. On his head Bilal wore a red felt hat, like a fez, that he'd decorated with white cowry shells. On top of his hat he sewed a black silk tassel, that he (ra) spun around and around, as he (ra) danced along and swung his (ra) head, clowning for the people of Medina, all the way to the Prophet Muhammad's (saws) house. As Bilal (ra) danced through the streets of ancient Medina, people cheered him for he was well loved, and everybody loved the sound of his call to prayer, which sounded like the voice that you like from the tape, the voice that recites "The Most Beautiful Names." As he danced he sang, and he laughed to the rhythm he was playing. Fatima Zohra (ra), the daughter of the Prophet Muhammad (saws), was drawn to the window by all the noise, and when she (ra) saw Bilal (ra) dancing joyfully down the street, in his red topi with the black silk tassel spinning around on top his head, she smiled and then she (ra) laughed. She laughed heartily, so much so that you could see all of her back teeth.

Makhtub! It is written! that some of the people of Medina, who were present that day looked up at the daughter (ra) of the Prophet (saws), and were heard to remark; "What beautiful teeth hath the daughter of the Prophet, and what Sakina/Serenity descends from the radiance of her smile." And the more Bilal (ra) danced and clowned, the more Fatima laughed (ra), and the more the darkness and gloom that had enshrouded her heart evaporated. The people of Medina Munawara, the City of Lights, were gob-smacked with wonderment (Ajeeb). The Messenger of God (saws) was so overjoyed that he (saws) vowed to ask Allah (swt), to grant Bilal (ra) his very own wish on the spot. Bilal (ra) thought about it for a while then he (ra) said; " Oh Messenger of

Allah. I wish only that anyone who plays this music should like me, be able by the Grace of Allah, to cleanse the darkness of the Soul, and remove the shadows from people's Hearts, and in the same way bring happiness to others, and riches to themselves."

By the end of the story, Evelyn and Pop are an eager part of the audience. Evelyn's pleased to see Diamond showing an interest in her Mother's religion. Pop is silently impressed with the Islamic element, and happy to see Diamond showing an interest in religion. If there was a moral to the story, then it was probably more relevant to the adults, than to Diamond. Loa Tzu comes to mind, "Live life like a poem. Arrange things s if they are in a painting". Like Muhammad said, "If you have to go to China to seek knowledge, then go for it is reputed that there is wisdom there." Loa Tzu's Momma was a Black Woman, by the way. She was a Nakhis, a Black Chinese from the South of China. How come ? you may ask. And I may answer in the words of that other famous Chinese "breed", as he was known, Kwai Chang Kane, " Who can say ?"

Purity is a construct. Everything is a mixture of everything else if you dig deep enough. "Creole" is King. Origins ? File under "belonging to everybody". Having said that, I'm also aware that some definitions of "Creole" ring synonymous with corrupted, bastardised, tainted, polluted, suspect, unwanted, and rejected. Never the less the vibe was mellow, seemed like we were all set for another Sunday, just up the road from Pleasant Valley.

Pop & Eve.

It's evening time, I'm busy listening to the sounds of dusk. I've been out and about, and I ended up catching a cab home. I give the cab driver who says he's from Denver originally, a four dollar tip. That's insanity over here, "It's an English thing", I tell him. He's impressed. Money, and generosity with money impresses Americans a lot. "What bed have your boots been under", Pop smirks. "None", I say smiling at Pop's jest. Despite my Poppa's bravado, there's a strange atmosphere, it's as if everyone's subdued. I'm not wrong. Apparently while I was out Pop had a bad fall. "Oh no !", I think. I look at Pop he seems weakened by the fall. All of a sudden I become aware of how frail Pop is, under his macho front. I've known this guy a week, and I'm mortified by his accident, all of a sudden I find myself worrying about his imminent mortality."Wow !", I never expected that I'd ever feel like this. The news hit me quite hard.   Pop looked pale for a Black man. What my Mother would describe as, 'the colour of boiled shite'. His spirit's at a low ebb. Evelyn seems genuinely concerned. The Deacon phones Pop, like he does each evening, and they pray together, but tonight it's a little more emotive. Pop's shook up by the fall. Pop has taught me to pray properly again. It's not about formulae, rituals, dogma, or rhetoric. It's all about that "Rootical" vibe. It has to come from the heart, not merely the sound of your voice. I like the spontaneous acts of beauty. I had the idea for a Sufi jam session, based on the idea of "Spontaneous Universal Faith Improvisations". You can get to be over formal, too orthodox, it's like Mom used to say, "It's nice to be nice but it's not nice to be too nice." Pop would make a good Sufi.

After preaching his quota to me for the day, Pop prays with Brother De Shay, then we all play Candy Bears with Diamond. Evelyn's showing me some of the films, and educational books that she's bought for Diamond. Evelyn has her own cultural programme for her Grand daughter that consists of a lot of Black history books, and films that compliment them. We watch Beloved. Pop nods off with Diamond on his knee. Evelyn packs them both off to bed. She comes back into the kitchen, where the only working TV is, except for Diamonds portable one, that lives in her bed room. She starts to cook-up my supper, as I was out late and missed supper time. She 's talking about how, "Pop shouldn't get himself all worked up, cos he's had one heart attack already, and his heart aint gonna take it." I agree with her, but I know it's easier said than done. So much has surfaced in me through just being here. Echoes of former selves, younger selves, memories that needed recalling, and ghosts that needed laying to rest. Spectres rising up from the uncharted depths. I felt like I was witnessing the end of an era, in more ways than one, and for Father aswell as for Son. Evelyn seems over attentive this evening. She lifts up my feet and places a pouf underneath them, then she places a cushion under them, and passes me the paper. There's a photo of the Washington World Trade Centre, and an article on the Seattle demonstration, it was televised, and caused sympathetic demo's in Austin. It's refreshing to see some sort of collective statement coming from the people. I can feel Evelyn being extra nice to me. I almost expect her to whip out a pipe, and some slippers. I'm suspicious. It always makes me uneasy when people fuss around me. People waiting on me, and calling me "Sir", for example always makes me feel humbled, but in an uneasy sort of way. As she placed a tea-towel on my lap, and laid a tray full of Country goodness on top of it, I felt like Evelyn was making a move on me. Maybe she was also worried about Pop's mortality, maybe she was sizing me up for her Muslim daughter in the Georgia state pen. Later she starts telling me that, "I put up half the money for this house, your Pop knows that." This come out of the blue to me, all I could assume was that she must have heard Pop offering me the house. He told me it was his Aunt's, who died, and that I could take it over when he died. I reassured her that I had no intention of staying on in Austin, and that I didn't come there seeking anything material. I came in search of my roots, my origins, my Pop. She seemed at ease with that, but she did seem to be playing Hoochie-Momma upto me. I didn't have to make any overt rejection of the move though, my Spirit, or my eyes, or my voice, or body language, or a combination of all of it seem to tell her how I was feeling. Blood was thicker, and Pop was my "Sang Reale", my mission as a "Grail Knight", and my loyalty in that cause was unfaltering. To even contemplate such base treachery, would have been an abomination to me. She sensed it was so, and bade me "Good night!", before shuffling off to bed.

Evelyn fussing around my feet, and putting them up on a cushion, had flashed me back to Pop's shoe- shine story. My first job at the age of fourteen, was a window cleaner. I reflected on Pop's shoe-shine ritual, and the many meanings of the word "Shine". Mom had taught me the song, as a good thing, because it was the anthem of the local mixed race community back in her day. In a poem of mine called "Soul On Ice", there's a few lines that say, "And together as Brother Sisters We make a joyful noise to the Creator and together we Shine!", and I'd chant that last phrase over and over again like "We Shine ! We Shine ! We Shine ! " Ju-Ju Priestess, Sister Ebony and I used to have a private joke whenever we were gigging together, and we'd be the only Shines there. She'd be in the audience, and when that bit came up for the chant, we'd get eye contact with each other, and she'd chant with me "We Shine ! We Shine ! We Shine !" Only we knew what we meant. Women have been some of my most important role models, both in terms of vocalists, and as Spiritual entities. Matriarchy rules in our family, both sides of the Pond. We used to have a place in the Ghetto called the Gallery, it was started by a brother called Joe, who was the elder brother of my younger foster brother Jimmi, as I said Liverpool family connections are complicated. The Gallery was a cool place for creatives, it was based on an idea from New Orleans called the Neighbourhood Gallery. One of the associated projects was a cultural exchange in which a number of people from a variety of disciplines, and creative backgrounds came over and stayed, and did a series of talks and workshops in local Community Centres, and Community Arts venues. As part of their introductory talk which was held in the Black Church, a big centre for Black Awareness during the Seventies, they chatted about their influences. They touched on Afrocentricity, and Black art in general amongst their community over in New Orleans. A couple of them were Seminole, a mixture of Black, and Native American. They cited the Black Arts movement of the Seventies, and made a big point of vilifying the use of the word "Shine", in a very dogmatic manner, and filled us in as to their take on the word. When I told them the history of the word locally, and how it was used as a badge of honour, they couldn't handle it. I just wrote into my own personal take on it now.

Knowing that Eva-May had loved Satchmo, despite her being a member of the NAACP, and that song, even when his peers had slammed him for it, I reckon it was her that passed it onto Pop, and Pop that had passed it onto Mom, then my White Momma X, had taught it to me, along with it's cultural significance, which has stayed with me right up until today. I went to bed that night thinking of shoe-shines, shines, and shoes, and the low down Texas Blues, and how poor folks World wide be still paying dues. Whittling away in my mind as that lonesome freight trains whistling on down the line. Snap shots of past incarnations running through my imagination, with a soundtrack to suite each place , and each time.

The remembrances, like the memories, encoded in the music somehow, someway. In pubs, and bars, clubs, and cars, house, flats, and tenement yards, during street parties, church halls, and carnival parades, a beat for every occasion. The incidental music to my life, now taking on a transcendental function. Pop never stops singing, neither do I come to think of it, neither did Mom. The language of the birds. Every breath a precious jewel that we can only spend once. I seem to spend mine dramatising, and romanticising, those things that other's might consider best placed where they belong, amongst life's mundanities, like for example my failed career as a poet. If ignorance is bliss, then awareness must be the unpleasant bit. I keep having to relearn that point, over and over again. I've been praying for Sabre and Shukr, that is Patience and Gratitude, but I keep getting the words Simplicity and Appropriacy, buzzing around in my head. Maybe they are related concepts. So much to think about before going back to Blighty. So much of the past, bum-rushing the present, and the big Y2K "Future" looms heavily on the horizon. As time passes, the folly of youth becomes just that,"folly".

Diamond.

I am now back in my room, and merely staring out of the window watching clouds drift. I'm aware of a figure standing in the doorway watching me. "Everytime I come in here something smells good." It's l'il Diamond. She's sneaked in whilst I was distracted. She's so curious about Islam, because her Mother's a Muslim, and is now locked away n the state pen. It's like it's the one thing that connects her to her Mother, that and the sound of the Quran, captured in the recitation of "The Most Beautiful Names of Allah." I smile a knowing smile,"Thats probably 'attar' that you can smell, baby. It's Muslim perfume.They say if you eat garlic, or onions before you pray the angels will stand far back from you and they won't hear your prayers properly, but if you wear perfume, they draw near to you, and they hear everything that you say, and carry the correct prayers back to God."
Diamond's face lights up, she is so bright, and she is so eager to learn about Islam, she reminds me of myself as a child. "You wear it so that when you pray the angels draw near", she says with wonderment. I decide that the "Elders Moot" has adjourned.

It's like it's time for Sunday School duty. I continue with the story of attar, for Diamond's sake. "In the mosque in Liverpool, back in the day, everybody would sitting around on the floor like me, facing East, and an old man would come around and rub perfumed oil on everyone's hand before they prayed. She held out her hand, "Like this", and I showed her with my little roll-on bottle of attar that you buy in mosques, reciting, "Lailaha illallahu", as the old man would have. "It means . 'There is no God but the One God'. He says it and you say it, and then you rub the backs of your hands together, and smudge some oil on your beard." She repeats the Kalima.
"I don't got a beard", Diamond says giggling.
"Well just rub it on your chin."
She rubs her chin, and giggles again, imagining herself with a

beard. Diamond has had my Walkman, and my tape of "The Most Beautiful Names", all week. I think she gets a lot of comfort from it, so I'm letting her have it. She shows me were she's up to with her recital of the" Ninety Nine Most Beautiful Names". She's good. She's memorised the first five or so, but she can recite most of them in clear Arabic, just like on the tape. Children pick up new languages quickly. My friend back in Liverpool, Yusuf, plays Quran as he's driving around and his kids have picked it up, and can recite much more clearly than either of us adults can. "I wanna show my Momma, what I'm learning next time we visit her, cos she's Muslim." Diamond has her own agenda sorted out already. I could tell it had something to do with her Mom whose in jail. Poor Diamond. I can see now why she's so studious with the tape, she wants to impress her Mother, next time Evelyn takes her to visit her in the Georgia State Penintentiary. Pop and Evelyn are always arguing about how much they care about Diamond, and who cares the most. They seem to miss the fact that all Diamond really wants, is to be with her own biological Mother.

Gladys Street.

It was a grey, dull, hang-over sort of, Sunday afternoon. All slate rooves, Edwardian brickwork, and cobblestones. Liverpool after the rain. My thoughts went back to me Mutha's, and the old Orange Lodge days living in Everton. I got out of the taxi on Gladys Street, and saw the purple Welsh slate roof tops, and the familiar Georgian brick-work it all started to come back to me. "Keep the odds mate", I said to the cabby as I disembarked from the classic Black Hackney, and scanned the rain-dampened street, flanked on one side by Everton Football Clubs ground. Walton's streets are all like Coronation Street, all the same type of terraced houses. Some neighbours were standing, jangling on the doorstep as I stepped out of the cab. I could almost hear them saying, "There he is Rebecca's Father after twenty eight years." My eyes scanned the rest of the street. As I approached the door young Anthony, Tony's eldest son came out to greet me. "Your Eugene, Rebecca's Dad", he said, his face lit up with a warm welcoming smile. He was the image of "White-T". I felt old. "Rebecca's Dad", he'd called me. It was so strange to hear it, it made me feel like I'd been, denied part of my life, twenty eight years of my life as a father. "Me Mother's at the shops, she'll be back soon. Come in." As I went into the front room , I could see a large photo in a frame of an Indian looking girl on the mantlepiece. She was wearing a flowing white satin and lace wedding dress. It was Rebecca. I could see the resemblance to our Tracie.

I couldn't even see Lorna's family in her, all I could see was my sister's face. I just kept praising God, and thanking God. It was a religious experience. Lorna came back from the shops clutching some cigarettes. She looked just the same. She was older of course, but she had the same flashing eyes, and the same feminine allure, the same voice. It was so-so strange, but it was good to see her. I didn't even know why. After a cup of tea, Lorna and I took a walke through Stanley Park, and talked about some of the stuff she'd been through. We hadn't seen each other, or spoken for nearly eighteen years, and that was only the once over Sunday Dinner. Since then much had transpired, but there was hardly any distance between us as people. She felt more like an ex wife, even though we'd only been together from 17 to 18. Just a year, but I felt incredibly bonded to her. My own wife Henna was in New York at the time, and had been for a couple of months, her Mother, two Sister, two Aunties, two Uncles, and a load of her Nephews and Nieces live over there, and she has lots of friends there, and her Sister was about to have a baby.

Henna my wife at the time, who died of cancer, (Innallahu wa inalayhi rajiuun), would be also visiting her Muslims Sisters in Flatbussh, Brooklyn, and some Sufi Brother's and Sister's down in Philly, she would read a poem at the Million Woman March with her friend Betty Shabazz, Malcolm X's Wife, and Sheikhs Zaid Shakur,and Hamza Yusuf, then she would take a trip with her Aunt to Pensylvania to visit the Hamish people. She was a friend of Betty Shabbaz, Malcolm's wife. She brought a present from Aaliyah, Malcolm's daughter. It was a signed copy of her book "Growing Up X". I'd been thinking about Henna a lot, and now all of a sudden I'm here, almost thirty years back in the past.

It's so strange when the past catches up on you. All you can do is surrender to Life's endless mysteries. We sat-off on a bench in Stanley Park both dressed in black like we'd just been to a funeral, and we talked basically. Studying each other intensely. "What's your Muslim name now ?"

"Muhammad ?"

"I prefer Eugene. You don't mind if I still call you Eugene do you ?"

"It doesn't matter really, people still call me both. It's still my name, it's all me don't worry about it.".

"What made you become a Muslim ?", Lorna asked me as most people do.

"It's a long-long story at the end of day. God probably !"

"I don't believe in God anymore", Lorna's tone was painfully emotive.

"Why not ?", I asked her.

"Because He never answered my prayers!"

I knew what she meant. Her words hit me deep in depths of our heart felt shared past. Her eyes have a habit of widening involuntarily. It's like a twitch. I'd forgotten she did that. It was all coming back to me.

"I'm just so angry with Him ", her face was wrought with dark memories.

"You must still believe then. You can't be angry with someone you don't believe in."

"Nah... If he exists why does He let so many bad things happen."

"I don't know, but I still believe."

"I can't Gene. I prayed and I prayed and He did nothing."

We just sat for while still, silent. I don't even remember hearing any birds tweeting. A guy in a black leather jacket, that looked like a bouncer from town walked past and eyed me suspiciously. Probably one of those police tails that you can spot a mile away. They had spooks on me everywhere I went. You get used to it. I took in the once familiar scene. I'd knew Stanley Park quite well as a youth. I played football here when I was at school. Today it was desolated. Just Lorna, myself and the Spooky surveillance dude.

Eventually we left the park, and walked back down towards Gladys Street. Lorna, her Mother, and her daughter to Tony, Ruth, all lived within a minute of each other. Lorna took me to meet her daughter to White-T, in Dane Street literally a minute away. I met Ruth, and her fellah, they seemed cool enough. The guy was a musician a bit older than Ruth, we chatted guitar talk.

Then Lorna took me around to meet her Mother, Grand-Ma Becks, literally half-a-minute away in Nimrod Street. I realised only there and then that Rebecca had been named after Lorna's mother. Years ago when I was forbidden to see her, never mind enter their street, I had visited Lorna's family house once when her folks where at the British Legion. I remember having to flee over the back yard wall when they arrived back unexpected. Lorna's father had passed over now. It was so long ago I had no hard feelings towards anyone. I was too traumatised.

The impact of travelling through time so rapidly was creeping up on me ever so subtly, bit by bit as it dawned on me how real my unknown daughter was. There were pictures of Rebecca's wedding everywhere. Lorna and her Mother had attended the wedding, and they were also on the photo's. All that was missing was Moi, Pop's the Pre-Nuptial Pirate. Gran-Ma Becks kept staring at me, studying my face. I knew she could see her Grand-daughter in me, my intuition told me that much. She studied my face, my manner, my earings, my beard, my clothes, weighing me up, like my mutha used to with my old girl-friends. I had a tie on, a white shirt, black jacket, and my silver-grey suit keks. I was being Mr Phd. Literature & Cultural History. Sipping my tea, and nibbling at my biscuits, on my usual good behaviour for a Sunday afternoon. I did mention rather mischievously that I'd seditiously been invited around there once about thirty years ago, and that Lorna had sneaked me in, one cold and wet Saturday evening.

"We must have been on holiday" Granma Becks , growled indignantly.

"You were at the British Legion just around the corner on County Road actually."

My churlish remark didn't go down too well. Lorna told me not to wind her Mother up, so I didn't. I felt sorry for her, she reminded me of me own Mother. I could feel that she knew somewhere deep within herself, that Old Pop Gillard had made a mistake back then. An error that would forever be irreconcilable. Or maybe that's my vanity again.

The place was full of ornaments, and lace doylies, and the walls full of gilt-framed family photos just like me Mother's. A lonely place on a Sunday afternoon now, apart from the photos and the ghosts of the past. "You can't change the past", said Ma Gillard as if arranging a picture, or dusting off a piece of Capo de Monté. I was glad that I'd been officially received into her home, by her personally, as L'il Beck's Dad, father of her much loved Grand-Daughter. I could feel that she was proud for Lorna, that her love-child's Father at least knew how to behave civilised on a Sunday, and sit and have tea and bickies, and could speak educated if he wanted to, and was respectful towards her and her daughter, still after all these years. And I was proud to prove to her for Lorna's sake, that her daughter had good taste back then when our prospective life together had been so self-righteously written off.

It was a healing in a lot of ways meeting Lorna's Mother, it was a sad moment in many ways, but there was closure in it for both of us. Like my Pop said when I caught up with him, "A love childs better than no child son." He was right of course. He was so right.

Once I realised that there were so many questions that

my long lost daughter Rebecca wanted to know about me, and my life, and those lost twenty eight years, I started to get some memorabilia together from the hundreds of hours of film footage that various people had collected of me over the years. I wanted to relive my whole life all over again for my long lost, long denied daughter Rebecca, so we could live it together. I scanned through a load of videos, and poems, and comedy sketches that I'd had published, or that I'd performed and recorded on video. I was reliving big chunks of my life. The whole affair had knocked me for six. As I retraced my way back through CD's, booklets, video footage, and old photos', collecting examples of my work from various friends and associates from up and down the country. During the process I even came across some super eight from the 1972 Granby Festival that had Kif Higgins and myself DJing from the back of the Play on Wheels truck. And as I sifted through my personal archive of material I became more, and more aware, of how much the whole incident of being separated from Lorna against my will had scarred me.

The fact that being a Black lad equated to not good enough to marry a "White man's daughter", kept raising it's ugly head time and time again in my writing and in my improvs. Of course mixed marriages were actually illegal in some States when I was born, but whether it's the US, or the UK, it amounts to the same thing, an unspoken, not so subtle form of oppression.You could see traces of it in my stand-up material, in dramatic pieces that I'd written, in songs, poems like "Checkmate Othello".

It had damaged me ever so subtly in ways that I had not even noticed until now. It had been par for the course up until now. Normal for people of cIur. As I sifted through the mountain of memorabilia before me, I became aware that there had always been a lot of unresolved anger and pain surrounding the incident. I could see it clearly now, as I retrospectively culled the cream of my past obsessions captured on the page, tapes of rehearsals, live gigs, studio recordings, videos, films, radio and tv interviews, and various forms of creative expression that I've

Shamanically, and even manically used as sutures for my torn psyche.

I could see the theme recurring, again and again, "Not good enough for the Whiteman's daughter." Maybe now I could sing a new song to cure the Blues of that particular wound. That old-old hereditary pain of separation, and dispersal. That Slavery aint over feeling. The Diasporan Blues. I spent hours editing my own taylor made eight hour version of "This is Your Pop's Life", for Rebecca to peruse, and she'd be so keen to learn about my work, and read her Dad's poetry, when we'd eventually meet.

Shine.

Back at the ranch in Austin Texas, getting ready for the St John's Farewell, with Pop's getting ready for Church. I follow him into his lair, thinking about the green flack-jacket from Pop's old Air Force days. I saw it in the wardrobe in the room that I'm staying in. I've been waiting for a chance to ask for it. "We puzzle our minds, but God's already got things worked out", Pop chirps as if reading my thoughts, as he does. Pop had a new pair of shoes in his hands. A brand new pair of unworn black leather shoes. He polishes them, like he does everyday. It's his own little personal ritual of Self. Pop likes polishing his shoes with a rag, and some water in the lid of the polish tin. He'd smudge some polish onto the rag then dip it in the water. "That's the origins of the term 'spit and polish' son", he smiles at me. I asked him why, expecting a story, expecting it to be an ex-Airman's sort of thing. To my surprise Pop told me how he used to be a shoe shine boy, and how he got to be real good at it. He sat and bulled his brand new, unworn shoes to shiny black perfection military style. "Don't forget your roots when you didn't have no boots", Pop jives. His rhythm reminds me of a shoe-Black I saw in a low budget, independent documentary about New Orleans Jazz. There was an old Shoe-Shine singing to the rhythm of his own shoe buffing as he swung into his work, like a man on a chain-gang he sang as he shined. The song went kinda like; "Well we shine them shoes like a looking glass. When the water hit it, it roll right off. Shine !", and the brother would improvise rhymes and punctuate each one with the word "Shine !", like an African call and response poem.

Pop started Bluesifying just to keep his hand in, "Always have something that you do consistently everyday son. It's important to have some sort of discipline in your life." I felt like I was in the opening scene of a Tarkovsky movie. "I'm just asserting what we're learning son. When you find a way to do something right you keep right to it. Do like the Hindu do the best you can do", he rapped as he laughed that gummy grin of his. Pop was full of these folkisms. I loved him for it. As I'm pondering his wisdom I think up a name for his tariqah, his path, his school of thought, "The Way of the Shoe Shine". Sounds appropriate enough. I march back to my room, and try to compose myself before my final Sunday Service, at Pop's Church. Some people keep little bits of memorabilia, in an old shoe box. Pop keeps what came in the box, and shines them for remembrance. It inspires a poem from my subconscious.

The Blame Worthy.

Malamatiyya Mystic Knights
Of Ancient Nishapur
Poets of the people's fight
Poverty at their door...

Humble lions of the Soul
Warriors against their-selves
Blameworthy of hypocrisy
Still they beg to delve...

No rhetoric nor dogma
No rituals nor creed
Just a heart that bleeds

Through an open mind
And the lowliness of weeds...

Vain-glorious ambition
A fire fit for the burning
Their temple is an olive grove
It's fruits were born from yearning.

They say; "Nothing we do ever comes from us
We're just the Salt of the Earth
We're the People of Dust..."

Noone to accuse
Just ourselves to reproach
At the Ka'ba of Heaven
No self-righteous approach...

One heroic journey
One invisible road
No outward appearance
Just a chivalrous code...

Within each heart
Of Life and Love and Learning
Where solitude's no heavy load
And emptiness no burden

All free Souls heed
Their silent call
There is only the One
And it Unites us All...

And they say;
"Nothing we do ever comes from us
We're just the Salt of the Earth
We're the People of Dust..."

Good Byes.

It's been just over a week. It feels like a month, everything is so much more intense. Every second carries so much weight, so much import. This has turned out to be a journey and a half. I retire to my room to assemble my thoughts. They line up smartly, ready for inspection. On the way to Church we drop in at Randals. Pop buys Ram-Rod Do Nuts, for the Sunday School youngsters at break time, Mexicans everywhere as usual. They must have a church near by, some of the Mexican Churches are quaint, picturesque, and generally pink, from what I can make out. Maybe it's a neighbourhood thing. I've seen the same White guy begging twice now, on the way to St John's. He's about twenty six, twenty seven with scraggy blonde hair, and a tatty, beard scruffy clothes that he obviously sleeps in. He stands in the isle between the lanes, and walks in and out of the cars asking for change. It never ceases to surprise me for some reason. it's as if I expect everyone to be doing OK over here, especially the White folks, but it's not so in reality. I must remember to look up Psalm 119 : 111. Heritage, that's all the note book says. Church is laid back, people recognise me, but it's no big deal. I'm integrated already. During the service I take a few notes from Pastor Reeves, "Cast your bread on the water it won't come back till it auta", and "He will let the rocks cry out if man slackens off." I don't know why I just liked those lines. Brother Wayman McLamb from the choir gives me a CD, and a smile and a nod that says try and push this for us when you get back to England Brother. I make a mental note about Tingle Thomas a Gospel DJ from Manchester that I know. I got to see the Deacon, Brother De Shay Bling-Bling King of the diamond ring, one more time. He was scrubbed up fine as usual like a Southern gent, Masonic ring, lots of blingery, crisp silk tie, and shiny silk hankey, glamorous hair coiffure, diamond studded tie pins, I was gonna miss this John Lee-Hooker looking-like Brother, a real

Elder from the Moot. After Church we went to Luby's, an eatery out on the Mopac 35. It's kind of a traditional for Black folks, after Church, Sunday dinner, Country Soul Food diner. Lot's of Black people straight from church, all dressed up in their Sunday go the meeting clothes, lot's of young families, and kids in their Sunday best running about the place making a joyful noise. Pop and I get us a mess of that good old down home Country Soul food, and find us a place. I notice that the table mats are stuck to the table, probably to stop the youngsters using them as frisbees. Pop and I are like two lonesome cowboys. Both of us seem to be in a no-win situation, especially where women were concerned. It would have been nice on one level to move over here, and stay with Pop, but I had stuff to sort out back in the UK, and I've learned one thing from this journey, two lions can't share the same den.

Back To Blighty.

It's 12th December Ramadhan begins today, Insha'Allah, and I'm packed into my seat, on the flight back to the UK. On my way back home to Blighty. I knew that I'd fulfilled a part of my destiny going to Texas, I could just feel it. I'm usually scared of flying, especially those long hauls across the Atlantic Ocean. But today I felt no fear. I was too busy absorbing the experiences of the last two weeks. There was some particularly bad turbulence, I thought about the plane going down as I usually do at such times, it didn't bother me. I didn't even care. It felt like it would have been a fitting ending to my life. I was going home, after fulfilling my quest, and if that meant going all the way back home to the Creator then so be it. I was ready. I'd had to go, and I'd gone followed my path, my sulook, my journey. As Pop would say "God was in the plan !"

My dream had come true. I prayed. Then meditated, reflected. And even as I was writing this it all sorta fell into place.

177

Veils were lifting, and I thought maybe Mutha was there in spirit witnessing it all, cos everytime I spoke about her, or thought about her like in the Hill Country, or when I showed anybody her photo, something weird would happen. Yeah... it was my Mutha that had brought me up. A lot of what Pop had been proud of was the product of her tender love and care, her nurturing and guidance. I was feeling elated, chock-full of self knowledge. Knowledge of self as a human being.

Accepting my mortality, and grateful just for the experience of having been given a shot at life. Whatever it brought my way. I was forty three, almost done anyway, or so thought t the time. So far so good, as Gil Scot- Heron would say. I'd been twenty eight when my Mutha had died, it seems a lot younger to me now, looking back, although at the time I'd felt twice as old as I do today. Artura, my step-Dad, having long moved to New York by then, was on the phone. It was funny hearing his voice, his emphesema, his accent, his dutiful concern. He wanted to fly over but I told him I could handle it. I wanted to be left alone to handle it, and he was too ill really, I wouldn't have put him through it. For the twelve months leading up to my Mutha's death, the local GP had been treating her for a migraine. For that whole year she was in so much constant pain, that her features had become distorted with suffering. One day she was rushed to hospital in such severe pain that, the handful of pain killers she was used to eating each day, had become useless. I remember the feeling as we drove along Shaw Street, past Shawry Canyon, on our way to the Royal Infirmary. I was dreading the future. I knew , but I hoped that I was wrong. But I could feel it. The ambulance drove past my old school the Liverpool Collegiate Grammar School for Boys. A line from the school song came into my head: "Vivat haec soldolitas. Decus Esmedunae".

We passed Eastbourne Street. Our old house was gone, knocked down. Only a grassy knoll remained on the corner were nature had reclaimed the wasteland of crumbling bricks, and concrete rubble. Some kids were playing amidst the ruins of what was once my childhood home. I thought of my wigwam. There was freshly fallen snow, and the kids were having a snowball fight, on the very spot were we used to live all those years ago, when Mutha was fit and well. Life went on oblivious to our plight. I knew at this,point that my Mutha would not be coming back from this journey. You just know. I could just feel it.

At the Royal, they informed more or less there and then, as the head of the Family, that she wasn't going to make it. They told me that she had a tumour on the brain, and it had gone too far. I felt that being poor White Trash is what had killed her. If we have had status, or been on BUPA, this wouldn't have been left so late. I could have killed somebody, not just anybody, the doctor, one of my enemies, any two bit punk on the street that crossed me, or gave me an excuse, any nasty John Bull bastard that offended me. I could have killed, killed without remorse, or so I felt at the time. I wanted revenge. That was what made me into the type of angry Black Nigga that makes nice well intentioned White folks say, "I had nothing to do with Slavery", or even more desperately, "I'm a member of the ANC. I think Nelson Mandela is a Sainted man ", or sometimes with their eyes flickering on and off like defective light bulbs, "Do you have to use the word. It sounds so harsh." Black is harsh, and I wanted revenge for my Mutha. Revenge for not being rich enough to take her to see Germany before she died. Revenge for not being able to place her beyond the dependence of an already by then crumbling health service. I wanted revenge on myself for being so complacent about the fact everything would all right. I was full of guilt, and anger, and self-hate. If I'd have had a gun, it would have been a toss up whether I'd have shot someone else, or just turned it on myself. I had a death wish for a long time after that, one that I still haven't fully gotten over.

I remembered returning back to me Mutha's house after the journey to the hospital, the day she went in never to return Home. I looked around the kitchen. Her kitchen, filled with the tools and utensils of her favourite art-form. The pinafore hanging up behind the kitchen door. The cricket ball bottle opener with Ian Botham's signature, and face on it. I still have hanging up in my kitchen, over twenty years later. Her cooking. Her food her pride and joy, her spectacular Sunday Roasts, and always enough for anyone who happened to turn up. The art form that everyone enjoyed that passed through the doors of our house. Her home cooking. The cooking that smelt of security and love. Home be it ever so... humble it was the cooking that smelt of our culture, who we were, what we were as a Family amidst the artificial backdrop of racial essentialism. Soul food, hot, spicey, meaty, food vibes, "Pass the peas" like we used to say. Good vibrations, people vibes, guests, friends and neighbours, sisters and brothers, lovers, others all were welcome, all got invited home to me Mutha for some of her cooking. Magic cooking, Spiritual cooking, Righteous cooking, Spiritual cooking. I wandered into the sitting room, just newly decorated, smelt the new carpet, stared at the pictures of our all the members of our massive Foster Family. Black, White, Asian, Malayan, Arab faces. I looked out the back window at her garden, and the roses she grew, and nurtured so devotedly. Her ornaments from around the World, her display cabinet full of souvenirs, the past cards, and psot cards, my post card from a school camp in CImendy in North Wales, from when I was ten years old. One from my first trip to Morocco. Some sand from the Sahara in a coffee jar, that seems to leak, out even though the lid of the jar is screwed down tight. The fluffy electric green, snake draught excluder. The people who would no longer congregate here, people next door, across the grove, over the road. I sank into the photograph albums all chocked full of memories. Memories that repeat themselves when you least expect them, sharp clear gems that shine so bright sometimes that bring tears to the eyes. Memories that we would all live through again every time we looked at these albums, everyone except my mother.

Florence Annie Lange, I love you so much, that twenty years after your death it's tearing me apart writing this. My eyes fell on her record collection, in the old cumbersome radiogram. Me Mutha was a White Blues singer. She sang at dances in the in the Rialto Ball rooms. She sang Jazz and Soul and Gospel and Rhythm and Blues, and Negro spirituals. I heard Holly Johnson say in an interview that it was Flo who had put him onto Billie Holiday. I remember the Chess label, and it all spelled good news to me, as she would teach me about my culture, Pop's culture, her counter-culture, a Liverpool 8 sub-culture. An organic crosspollination of Human experiences, at a unique moment in World history. As the Prophet said, "Our Mother's are our first Sheikhs, for it is from them we learn compassion, and unconditional love." He, peace be upon him, was asked, "Who should we trust first our Mothers or our Fathers?" He implied that you should trust your Mother three times more than your Father. There was a time when Flo used to play her Nina Simone, and Ella Fitzgerald, and Billy Holiday, Clarence Frogman Henry, and Billy Eckstien records for me, educational times. Down home folksy times, big pans of Scouse, and Hot pepper soup and rice, Sunday Roasts, Curried lamb and chapattis, French stew, and Lancashire Hot Pot.

I remembered that I still had one of her Wes Montgomery records that I'd borrowed to tape, and I'd been about two years bringing it back. I rifled through my mother's LP's, Paul Robeson, Billy Holliday, Nina Simone, Ella Fitzgerald, sarah Vaughm, George Benson, lots of Barry White, most of which I'd bought her as birthday presents, or Christmas presents. Mommas and Poppas, the Beatles "Rubber Soul", my first album, "I'm a believer", The Monkees, my first ever single. Old Soul albums like the Originals, that Uncle Eddie had left for me, when I started growing my Afro, various Motown Chartbusters Compilations, and the older stuff like the Ink Spots album that she gave me, to show me what started her off into Black music. All the seven inch singles on Motown, Stax, Atlantic, Decca, and Polydor, and the Trojan, Camel, Blue Beat, and Tuff Gong, Reggae stuff. I wished my Mutha could have been there, just to make it all tie up neat. I thought maybe she was in Spirit. I played Marvin Gaye's "What's Going On" album, with the arm pulled back on replay, over and over again, "Don't talk about my Father. God is my Friend." I'm sitting on my prayer rug meditating. Doing my own personal version of a vision quest, it's something that I call the "Flying Carpet" meditation. It's more like free association extemporaneous composition, or the cultural-historians equivalent to mental arithmetic.

Brown Babies UK.

As I was finishing off this story, my kneck was aching with sitting over the laptop for too long. So I went into the sitting room to catch a programme on Myths and Legends. I'd been following each week, and this weeks was about "Legends of King Arthur". The presenter visits, Wales, Glastonbury, Shropshire, Ireland, Scotland, Bretton, and Cornwall following the trail of the Grail. He eventually works out, how each community have tried to make the story their own. It's interesting because, just prior to switching on the tv, I'd been waiting for the kettle to boil in order to make a cup of tea to sit down with, and I'd noticed a home-made, Eide card from Fatima, a G.I. Baby from Bristol, who has Native American in her, and is also a Sufi, that I have pinned to my notice board. It has a painting of a Indian sleeping on a giant floating feather, and it's just called "Floating Feather", on the back it has a formidable invocation, "La Hu ! Illa Hu !". Say it as if you were addressing your bodily parts, telling them that only Allah exists, only Allah is real.

As I switch on the TV, and settle down to watch the show, "Who should call ?", but Fatima. I haven't heard from her for about three years. All the way through the programme we're talking, just catching up. Eventually the conversation veers towards, the need to adapt Sufism to the time, and the place, of the community at hand. We get into a sort of post Nine-Eleven, disgusted with fanaticism dialogue. I tell her I'm watching the programme, she tells me she had planned to watch it also. So we hang up, after promising to keep in touch, this time. I can't name all the people who have kept me going, each in their own specific way. Some merely share similar objectives, feelings, or views, but what it adds up to is that, I'm not that alone really. I just feel like I am sometimes. Solitude, and seclusion, this is mostly how I have survived as an artist, and as a person. What heals a wounded heart is the compassion of sincere people towards it, that and your belief in your own sincerity towards them as a Human being. It makes you vulnerable, but whatever helps you grow is good for you.

I found out a lot about my Father from my Mother's memories of who he was, and I found that a lot of it was true when I met him in person. What had been missing from the picture, was how much like my Mother I was. It was Pop that had pointed that out for me, and put the missing piece back in the jig-saw puzzle. Pop kept remarking on how adventurous I was travelling to all the places I'd been, he said I'd got that from my Mother.

I said, "But you were stationed in twenty seven venues around the World? "

And he said, "But yea that's true, but I had the US Air Force with me, you went to these places on your own. That's your Mother in you. I couldn't never have done that on my own. It's not my way. That's your Mother. She was that kinda woman. She wasn't afraid of nuthin' or nobody." He told me that it ran in her family.

Pop told me a story of how Mother, him, and my Auntie May, who was twelve at the time, were coming from the bakery with a big cream cake for Sunday tea- time. A local idiot had called my Pop a Nigger, and my young Auntie May just up and pushed that big 'ole cream cake into the guys face, and started to cussing him out. He said the guy just stood there flabbergasted. He said there was a fearlessness that the Lange women all possessed. I've visited Germany five times, and toured about fourteen cities that side, with The Mojo Dance Floor Jazz Collective, who were based in Hamburg, where The Beatles got their act together. I always thought of my Mother when I was there. Always wished she could have experienced it with me.

Especially when people asked me how come I had a German surname. Maybe she was with me, life extends beyond the body. I know this much from past experiences.

The Married One, often remarked how Germanic I was, and how much I reminded her of a brown version of her own Father. A possible Elektra-thang going on there, but it gave me an insight into a side of me that only she could see, at the time. It took me forty years, to harmonise the polyphonies, and master the myriad melodies, that Life's symphonium had scored for me. On that note, I think I'll end with a brief musical tome, the Pilgrim on the musicians path, is a student of sacred music, he trains both his heart, and his ear to the harmony in life. As Louis Armstrong said, "What we play is life".

My Pops died early December 2004, and although I only ever spent a couple of weeks with him, we kept in touch over the phone. And I loved him very much, he was a great guy, or maybe I just think that cos he was so much like me. I wish I had phoned more often, but then you always wish things like that. L'il Gene they call me in Texas. I'm my Father's son no doubt about that, and I'm also Flo Lange's little boy. I had a feeling Pop knew he was dieing the last time I spoke to him. His words seemed to be telling me something, so I wrote them down on the cover of my Austin 2000 diary that I had handy next to the phone. I'm gonna end this chapter with Pop's last words to me, and I'm gonna make a cup of tea, and I'm gonna weep, and I'm gonna leave it at that. Pop's last words to me were,

"Do what you enjoy... You can be selfish in things... but not in prayer... that's not a sincere prayer... time gonna go by one day at a time. Good days. Bad days. Neither of them belongs to us. Possessions hurt."

That was my Pop when he knew that he might be speaking to me for the last time. And I love, and honour him for it.

Sacred Hoop.

Joy to the World. When I did eventually meet my daughter there was no doubt that she was mine. Her face was my face, and some of our Tracie's. She had my Mohawk nose, Tracie's eyes. Infact for a while, I forgot that her Mother had anything to do with it at all. She was just mine. My daughter. She was so much like me, and my Sister, and other member's of my family. She was also very beautiful like her Mother, but she had my Spirit. I felt this. I could feel my Soul in her, I could see it in her eyes. We related to each other straight away. It was the same when I eventually caught up with my own long lost Poppa, over in Austin, Texas after forty years of wandering the Earth wondering what he looked like, only a mere three years before Rebecca had caught up with me. We just recognised each other straight away. There is no real way of explaining it. She was from the same seed, the same Soul, and I was so happy. Stunned but happy.

I'd known my Pop about the same amount of time that Rebecca had known Lorna. I had had the name Rebecca churning around in my head for nearly thirty years, and Lorna had never confirmed it for me one way or the other. Now I knew for certain, it was like a gift from God. I remember that when I first caught up with my old man, I'd written to him at first, and he'd sent a poem to me with his return letter just a short one, a quatrain, it read ,
"Life is Good / God is Great / Sometimes in Life / The best must wait."

Love hurts, and it's hard to bare your Soul, but when you do it can be such a beautiful experience. It's such a sacred experience, that you just know that, "God's in the plan", as Pop would say.

Rebecca had brought her photo-albums, so I could see what she had been like, as she was growing up. There was one photo of her dressed like Pocahantas, the Mohawk princess, every bit a little Indian girl. My daughter. She pointed it out to me so proudly. She looked so cute, and it suited her. She has the

185

features, the aquiline nose, and the colouration. And wow!... Her middle name is "Joy".

I was so proud. Lorna must have told the Social Services what the babies Father's origins were, and they'd passed the information on to her adopted parents, and they had introduced her to her 'roots', in much the same way as my Mother had to me. It was like history repeating itself. If I ever believed in Destiny, it was then, as I stared at my daughter as a little papoose. I was so proud that she'd been positively identified with her Native roots, my essence. I was so proud that she'd wanted to know me so badly, that she'd traced me all those years later. Remembrance is a celebratory prayer. Memories are mantras. I loved this life so much at that instant that there wasn't anything that anyone could have done to me that could have diminished what I felt in my Soul one iota. God is most great, and that day as Pop would say, "God was in the plan !" That's all I could hear going around and around in my head, "Allahu-akbar ! Allahu-Akbar Lailaha-ilallahu waduhu la sharika la ! Lahul-mulk wa lahul hamd ! Wa howa ala kulli sha'in qadir." Rebecca had managed to trace her Mother three years before she'd found me, and still Lorna had not told her where I could be found. That still puzzled me. I have no resentment about her keeping it from me. I understand that she had so much pain to bare having to give up her baby, and her fiancé, just because their face didn't fit. But as we looked at our daughters life recorded in snap-shots, I felt that now it was as if the Sacred Hoop had been partly completed, and I felt nothing but the deepest affection for Lorna. Not a romantic love, or a sexual desire, something deeper. Something more Spiritual. Something connected to the fact that this woman was my Baby-Mother. The long suffering, mournful Mother, of our long denied daughter Rebecca.

"The sound of the Boogie is a joyful sound, a vibing sound, a nitty-gritty boogie-woogie-jiving sound. Tell it Like it is! Tell it like it is! People! Let the sound of joy ascend high up to the highest height!" Baraah! That's all I kept saying to myself when ever my heart got fit to burst. Poetry and prayers poetry and prayers until their was no distinction between the two.

The first time we all met together as a virtual family, I took them all out to lunch at the Pan-American Bar down the Albert Dock. Lorna, Rebecca, L'il Levi, and Phil. They play Blues and Jazz down there, I wanted to take her somewhere with a cultural flavour that related to her hidden heritage. It was a strange day, a blessed day, it was as if the Creator had placed various member's of Lorna's family, and my family in strategic places just for the day. As we pulled into the car park, Lorna's Aunty and cousin were getting out of the car right next to us. They took one look at our faces and read the story.

We met my Aunty May, with Marley one of our Soraya's kids, and my young cousin Aysha. Aunt May just looked at me, and then at Rebecca and just made some sort of exclamation that denoted recognition and just embraced her, tears in her eyes. No need for any words. It was mystical. In the Pan-American a half-Chinese guy I hadn't seen for thirty years Roy Sam greeted me, unaware that he'd stumbled onto a rare gathering of the clans. Roy was a mutual friend of both Lorna and I from back in the day. He'd thought we'd been an item from way back then continuous sort of. I mean talk about irony. He came down to the area a few weeks later cos we organised a guys reunion in Brother Yusuf's, someone else who Roy had known from back in the day. Roy was telling us about how on the very same day he'd bumped into us at the Albert Dock, that very same night he'd been at a friends of Lorna's brother's girl's, and heard the story of Rebecca from her. He'd heard my name, and realised as the tale unwound that he'd been there right in the middle of it when it was all currently happening, back in the day. Liverpool's a small place news travels fast, what can I say.

After the Albert Dock, and a fine lunch at the Pan-American we went to my sister's house so Rebecca could meet our Tracie. Our Tanya, and Kyle were there, they'd coma over from Birkenhead, and Tanya had her new baby Ethan. That night Lorna's sister Glenda had come over from the Wirral, with her twelve year old daughter. She didn't seem to have changed much although the last time I'd seen Glenda she'd been no more than twelve years old herself. Now she was forty years old, and my daughter's Aunty, that was very wierd. She said I was the vainest person she'd ever met. I said "You were only twelve how could say I was vain." She said, "Believe me I know vain when I see it." We laughed.

Spirits rose and the wine came out, and eventually our Tracie and her crew, along with Lorna and her sister Glenda, ended up getting Rebecca involved in a two day bender, rotten eyed drunk. The noises coming from the back-kitchen sounded like hysteria, I've no idea what they discussed during that time, but a pack of hyenas would have given them a wide-berth. Phil and I stayed clear and we just sort of let it all happen around us and held the fort, while the kids and their mates, all played upstairs on the play stations. By the end of the weekend Rebecca had met various cousins, and nephews and nieces, the word seemed to spread. I heard from someone that, two of my other cousins Helen, and Tina, who work down at the Albert Dock had saw us all together, and put two and two together, and told everyone without even waiting to get it confirmed, just on the strength of their own assumptions. We had looked like a family, if even only for a day. I still give thanks for that, it was more than a special day. Especially for Rebecca. It had been the first time in her life that she'd ever been anywhere with her Mum and her Dad. It was such a basic need, but so profound. My heart was pounding all day long.

I had been so carried away, that I had forgotten when I'd introduced Rebecca to our Tanya, how Tanya's Dad had rejected her when she'd eventually traced him. I felt bad about it. She must have been comparing the two reunions, that hurts me, cos I love our Tanya a lot. I wish it could have turned out better for her. Jimmy's Dad accepted Yasmin, but rejected Jimmy. I know our Jim's never quite got over that, he told us that much last time he was down from Barry, Christmas last. This life can be so harsh, and unpredictable sometimes. What we all need is Love. Womb to the tomb, cradle to the grave. Love is most great.

The second time Rebecca, Phil, and Levi visited us, there were two things going on. The Africa Oyé festival, and Tina's fortieth birthday party. Tina is our Tracie's friend from childhood, friend of the family, and the wife of my friend Yusuf, who is the cousin of Leeroy, the Father of our Tracie's three lads, my three nephews. Yusuf and Tina used to run the Fountain, a Sufi café on Smithdown Road at the time. We all go back a long way. The upshot being there was a big extended Family gathering of Tracie's in-laws, and my friends, and we were all invited. It was a wonderfully warm affair, all the generations playing their roles equally well. Kids being boisterous, old folks being nostalgic.

The Grand-Dad of my three nephews, Ute, short for Uriah, was jamming some half-caste Calypso, all his own lyrics, and strains of the Odie Taylor Combo wafting through, in between shots from his hip-flask. It was funny listening to him sing as he strummed his guitar. I learned where my middle-nephew Malik got all his risqué Calypsonian double entendres from and his Trini-Lopez accent. I joined in, I was jamming on Yusuf's youngest son, Sadiq's, alto-sax. Someone got on the piano, I think it was Alim Yusuf's middle son, and before you could say "La Bamba !" It was rocking, well lilting sort of, with a totally tropical rum-bar taste. I was just so pleased that Rebecca could be there, I felt like folks had done us proud. It's so important for people to get together for occasions other than funerals. It's so important for people to be able to play music, and sing together at special occasions especially, family affairs. It was at times like this that I realised that keeping these skills alive was what my life as a Griot-poet-historian, was all about was just one simple thing. People. Creativity for me was about Community not Celebrity.

The next day was The Africa Oyé music festival in Sefton Park. As we pulled into Sefton Park Drive in Rebecca's car, we hooked up with Levi, carol and the kids in the car park. The sun shone golden in a clear blue sky, decorated here and there with the whispiest of white cumulus, the grass was a verdant green, and I had arranged for as many people as I could to be there for a big picnic in the park. I knew many of the African, and Caribbean artists who were performing, both from my own exploits on the Black music circuit, and just personally as Bredren.

I used to be the compare for the Africa Oyé Festival, when they first started off, and were testing the water in the Black Community. Once upon a time they needed a local face to front the thing, because bad-boys had been shooting each other up, and the nice middle-class White folks, had decided it was better to risk my life before one of theirs. Once the trouble was over, and the area was relatively safe to set up in, I never heard from them again. I had genuinely been promised all the comparing gigs from that point on, and I actually expected to get them, but then I've always been so vulnerably naive. It's to do with being an "Honest Injun" in a cowboy world. Never the less it was a magnificent day. Everyone I could have wished to have been there was there to meet Rebecca. I took about three rolls of film, as I really wanted it to be a moment to remember. A day to remember. And Praise be to Allah ! It was.

I met an old friend, Billy Mitchell. Bill was a member of the Jazz-Bop Elders. A drinking club, and a Jazz, experimental, improvised, and obscure music appreciation society, and a music swap-club that would meet on Fridays in the Flying Picket bar. Bill was a sprightly Sixty something, full of vitality, and energy, he used to promote Jazz artists during the Sixties. When I told him my daughter had traced me after 28 years, he was cynical. He suggested that I may be being fooled. I said ,"Come and meet her, then tell me that." I brought him over to the tribe of about thirty of us, that had by the time I got back been slowly expanding closer to forty-plus, as more and more family, friends, and neighbours turned up. I introduced my mate Billy to Rebecca and took their photo together with some of my other friends, and some semi-in-laws from Brum.

Billy took one look at Rebecca, and turned to me and nodded, in an affirmative manner, as if to say "There's is no mistake, no doubt what so ever." Then later he said to me in a sort of confidential manner, "She is definitely her Father's daughter. People everywhere that day were being so nice to me, saying good things about me, and bigging me up in front of my daughter. When I introduced her to Scotch Kenny who organises the Africa Oyé Fest he said "You kept that quiet". I didn't even bother explaining. It was unnecessary. Tommy Calderbank was talking so cool about me, it was embarassing me. A lot of people in the area did me proud, everyone was really representing with class that day. Even my enemies from down Dingle way. It was so overwhelming, as if the sweet fragrance of harmony had blossomed around us like a bouquet of perfumed hearts, and scented tongues, just to show Rebecca that Liverpool people can be so wonderful when they want to be. People are what this whole Universe is about. We are what the Universe was created for, a soft Summer breeze whispers in my ear. By mid-afternoon Rebecca was exhausted with meeting people, and talking, and smiling, and being a mini-celeb for the day posing for snap-shots with local celebs, and internationally renowned Reggae stars and Calypsonians like Brother Resistance and Muhammad Yusuf, and many many up and coming African musicians. We went for a stroll across the rolling green fields of Sefton Park, exactly where I had strolled with her Mother thirty years earlier. An old neighbour and her friend just stared at us as we walked past amazed, I could see the picture just falling into place on her face. It was surreal, most people who knew me just looked at us both and knew. Some friends of mine had set up a couple of stalls, one guy, a Bajan brother called Bongo who lived in the Gambia, had a stall selling djembés. Another brother, a Sikh brother called Ghopal was selling silver jewellery we browsed his wares. I bought Rebecca a silver necklace that she liked. She cried when we got back and showed the others. So did I.

Back in the day I'd actually been at an Easter Fair in this very Park, Sefton Park... On this very spot with her Mother Lorna all those years ago. My mind kept going back to the Top Rank ballroom days, the Green Jacket Era, stack-heals and flairs, big 'Fro's and loud checks. Street fighting, gangs, and the Shine's against the Skin-Head's. One Sunday nearly thirty years ago, we were all standing in a field in Sefton Park. Just about fifty yards away from us there were some tents from the Easter Fair. Tall off-white canvass marquees, rain, grass and sweat stained. They were set up pretty close together and in between them there was a lattice work of guide ropes. As we stood there just chilling and drinking lemonade from a bottle. I became aware of shapes dodging in and out of the guides ropes, skipping over the tall iron spike tent pegs , and ducking down to emerge a bit closer. Like people trying to sneak up on you undetected. Next thing Hogbass said "Skins!", and pointed in the direction in which I was staring fearfully myself. True enough a gang of about twenty Skin Heads had by now that their cover was blown, decided to rush us. We couldn't run and leave the Dames, so we stood our ground. I remember Hogbass saying "Well we've got a lemonade bottle." Our only weapon. He was nonchalant about is. Cool, unperturbed. A warrior I suppose. His Dad was the Commonwealth Boxing Champion Kid Hogan Bassey. Hogbass was the name they'd gave him in public school. In seconds we were slowly being surrounded by tent-peg-mallet wielding Skins. We took up Bruce Lee poses, as we braced ourselves for an assault. As the mob lurched towards us seething with impending violence one of the Skin's recognised Kif, and said, "It's OK ! I know one of them ! Let them go !" So they let us go. Kif had been at a rumble on Lodge Lane the previous night, and when one the lads was gonna stab Macker this Skin-Head's mate. Kif had stopped him and ... That's the way it went back then. Everything depended on the mood of the moment, but we had a sense of Justice about us, we were chivalrous, like knights from a bye-gone age.

Liverpool can be a tough place. Lorna's eldest son to White-T, Anthony who was 23, had been blessed with a son the same day in September that Rebecca had given birth to my youngest grandson Rudi. The upshot was Lorna had become a Granma twice on the same day, once through our daughter, and once through her son to White-T. Rebecca and young Anthony got on well, they were good siblings. That Christmas Eve, only three months later, young Anthony was picked up by the police, and died in police custody leaving, his young son Fatherless. The police were acquitted no one was charged. This had a profound effect both on Lorna, and Rebecca. Rebecca was so angry. I can't imagine how Lorna felt, but I believe it turned her to slowly drink herself into the next Life. Family is what we all need in times of bitterness and dispair, suddenly we all became Family for real.

The moccasins I still wore, now became embroidered not with the bitter beadwork, of my excluded past, but were a celebration of my fully embraced conscious diversity. There are no coincidences in this life. The practice of perpetually questioning our existence, and calling out the powers that be, is not anything you can label really. It's a perpetually rare strain of something that's always there in every society in every age, if you look hard enough. It all came flooding back to me so vividly. I stood back took a moment amidst the ocean of familiar faces both past and present. The dead and the living, and I drank it all in, the heady nectar of synchronicity. This golden moment of familial bliss and tribal affiliation. This golden moment of belonging. It was the only thing I had to share. But... I realise now that it was a priceless treasure.

Sarah.

It's September 2005. We've been in touch as Father and Daughter now almost five years. As long as I'd known my Pop, until he passed over in 2003, and as long as I've been with Henna. I worry for her now, and it seems so natural. She has gone through a major transformation since she discovered her long denied Father. It's gave her so much self-belief, thats what Sarah her Home-girl was telling me on the phone. Her friend from the age of four, Sarah who was in Greece at the time with her mother, and her own child of four, Olivia. The pixie-like

Sarah was surprised that I had a Scouse accent when I spoke to her on the phone.

"Oh you've got a Scouse accent?"

"What did you expect ? I'm from Liverpool, most people I know speak like this, it's what it's like up here."

"I know but Rebecca told me that you've got an MA, so I expected you to speak more Middle-Class."

"I'm sorry to disappoint you".

"No I love your accent you sound really cute."

"I'm not."

"I don't believe you. Don't come down till I'm back from my holidays, will you. I so want to meet you. Rebecca's told me all about you. She really needs you. It's changed her so much finding her real parents".

"I know. It's changed me."

Sarah tells me that the reason Rebecca is upset is because, her and Rebecca have been arguing over why the police just callously shot the young Brazilian kid in cold blood. I support Rebecca's argument. I tell her that Race was definately a key factor. She still can't see it. I'm used to the denial, Rebecca's still learning about it. They've never fell out before, Sarah tells me, been friends since they were four years old. I tell her it it's a sign of the times.

"Don't you resent Lorna for not telling you you had a daughter for all those years?", Sarah asks me, now that I know she's so close to Beck.

"No. Not at all. I understand that she has had to deal with her own pain, it's not easy having a child torn from you, and an engagement broken off against your will. Even if we were only seventeen and eighteen."

"Have you spoken to Rebecca about it."

"Not really."

"That's surprising. She said exactly the same thing. Your so cool. I'm going to pinch you and squeeze you when you come down here." Sarah giggles mischievously. It disturbs me somewhat. "Sarah have you been drinking?", I ask subtly.

"I am a bit drunk actually. Can you tell?"

"Just a tad, could you put Rebecca on please I phoned up to speak to my daughter you've been grilling me for almost half an hour. Your gonna be embarrassed when you eventually meet me."

"I know ", she says self-reflexively.

"You need to move down here your daughter needs you."

Eventually Rebecca takes the phone, we speak for about three and half hours. I realise that since we've been in touch, it's always Rebecca who comes to visit me. I've never made the journey down to Devon to see her. Although I did visit her once with Henna when she lived in Salford, but that was three years ago. I have'nt seen her or my Grandson for nine months, since last Christmas. Time flies, and I've been skint, but I feel so guilty of neglect. If I could have stolen a car, I would have drove down to Devon that very same night, through the wind and the rain.

Devon.

So I'm in heavenly Devon. Back at the BBQ, people are mellowing out. Later on I'm browsing through the photo's in the kitchen, while I'm making myself another mug of tea. Everyone is in the back yard eating grilled delicacies and listening to Ska. I'm glad I came down. It's been so important for both of us. Rebecca's friend Sarah Literature comes in for a clean glass, joins me, and I'm naming the various people on the photo's for Sarah as we browse the nostalgic collection.

"That's my Mutha, Bec's Gran-Mutha Flo, Florence Annie Lange. That's our Tan, our Tracie, our Malik, our Ashur, our Akim, and our Kyle whose Tan's brother. That's our Maria. That's my Pop, Nugent Eugene Golden, Bec's Gran-Poppa, that's my cousin Gary. She pulls out a Texas snapshot of a family gathering. That's the family tree, that yellow design on those purple t-shirts that everyone's wearing in that picture, it's a family reunion, the Yanks are big into it over that side."

"Really that's amazing", says Sarah eyes widening with keen

interest.

"Yeah... everyone at that event is related to us in one way or another", I tell her as I point to a picture of a big open air picnic that looks like an out-door festival. She pulls out a photo and says... "God who is this. It'se splitting image of Levi". She compares the dusty old, torn school portrait that she's fished out of the archive to my Grandson Levi. I'm as amazed at the resemblance as she is. The smile, the eyes, the nose, the mouth, the teeth, the whole look. Rebecca comes out to the kitchen to see what's keeping us. Sarah shows her the photo...

"Who does he look like" she asks Bec.

"Levi", says Rebecca without hesitation.

"Who is it ?" asks Sarah curious to find out.

Rebecca knows. I stare at it closely and then at my Grand-Son Levi as they call him into the kitchen, to compare his face to the face in the dusty old photo. Everybody's amazed at the resemblance. Except Levi, he can't see it. People start piling into the kitchen to see what the commotion is all about. As I stare at myself in the old school photo I can see my Grandson's face, and I can hear Fred Flintsone in the movie saying to Barney, "Yuh kno' Barn, it doesn't get any better than this." "That's me when I'm seven years old", I tell them. They stare at the photo and then they stare at Levi. "Amazing !" says Sarah.

The next day it's Sunday. Last night I looked out of my window and the candles were still burning in the back yard from the BBQ. This morning I expected them all to have burnt out, all had done except for one. I got up made a cup of tea and sat out in the yard and watched it for a bit before blowing it out. By the time I'd come back in Rebecca was up, and making a picnic hamper from the BBQ left overs. We drove up on to Dartmoor, just Rebecca, Levi and his mate Brian and myself. Rebecca and I get some quality time to talk one on one again, while Levi and Brian play Crick-Ball a fusion of Cricket and Baseball that we'd invented yesterday afternoon on a day out to the beach at Bigbury Bay.

We talked about our visit to the picturesque Burgh Island

with it's tiny little Pirates tavern on the rocks, called the Pilchard Inn. I could see and hear the ghosts of pirates, buccaneers and smugglers that still inhabited the place. The stones, and the wood work spoke to me of lantern lit nights, and tales of exotic far off climes, smugglers booty and the bounty of the sea.

We laughed due to the fact that I'd bought myself a pirates bandanna in Plymouth, and then Toni and Bec had bought me a striped St James, Breton fisherman's shirt. They had seen me eyeing them up in the window of the same... Mariners shop that I'd bought the bandanna in. My belated birthday gift came complete with a key-ring of a pirate wearing the same gear as me.

The tide is drawing in. We ride the big-wheeled ferrybridge back across to the beach. "Look Pops !" Rebecca pointed to one boat moored just off shore that actually had a skull and crossbones insignia painted on it. We buzz on it. The American, and Arab tourists on the ferry buzz on us, each in their own way. I can see both their angles, feel both sets of feelings. It was a good day. On the way back we stopped off to shop for the BBQ, I bought the kids two large bags of mini do-nuts one lot sugar coated, and one lot chocolate. They were made up, they kept them for the BBQ. After the picnic, and hearing about how ill Rebecca had been earlier this year. I am struck with pangs of worry, and desperation. I need to make some money. I need to make up for all those lost years. I buy the lads some ice lollies from a van where adults and kids are queueing up not far from where we parked the car, the guy in the ice-cream van gave me one extra by mistake, but I gave him it back. "You've already gave me them mate. I could have a bonus one there", I say pushing the ice lolly back across the counter. The ice-cream seller is shocked. A Scouser missing an opportunity. I must be on my best behaviour, well I am in Devon. Representing. I try some of the excellent Devon ice-cream. We drive to the coach station. Rebecca is happy, but a bit hung-over from last nights party. She took the knock. She's like me, she can't handle drink. I used to drink then be ill for a week.

Heaven.

I look up from the page. All of a sudden I turn around and it's a different era, I'm fifty not forty three. It's seven years on from that revelatory, sanctifying November evening back on Singleton Avenue, East Austin, Texas, just off Martin Luther King Boulevarde. Time has flown since I wrote all this stuff about my Grandma Eva-May , and now I'm in my daughter Rebecca's kitchen down in Devon, reading this account of her Great-Granma to her, after just printing out a copy of it from the PC in the kitchen. Rebecca is wearing Dreadlocks now, some of them bleached blonde. She's wearing jeans, a pink cotton top, and flipflops. She's sitting adjacent to me sipping a glass of white wine after just finishing the preparations for the BBQ. The BBQ has been organised partly to celebrate my first visit to their new Devon home, and partly to celebrate my daughter Rebecca and some of her friends getting firsts for their BA honours degrees.

She's lost a lot of weight, her final year took it's toll, but she's decided to stay on and do her MA, work hasn't been as easy to come by as she imagined. She's stressed out about that. I know the feeling. I feel for her so much. There's various Rasta memorabilia in red gold and green scattered around the place from Henna and I. Trinkets that I brought up from London from the Nottinghill Carnival. It all adds to the nostalgia, it's like listening to myself, and watching myself when I was at College in Cartrefle in Wrexam at the end of the Seventies, beginning of the eighties. The locks, the Crusading Spirit, the desire to take on the hoards of Babylon single handedly, those first steps of cultural awareness that I took myself during my own journey of self-discovery.

I gave my grandson Levi a darabukka, a small Arab drom that I brought back from Turkey, a scaled down version of the one that I play at home. I taught him an Egyptian belly-dancing rhythm, the Masmudi. He tried it a few times, and soon he'd almost mastered it. So he has my drum-boogy in him. I told him to, " Practise it everyday and it'll get smoother. Next time I come down I'll teach you another one." He promises to do it. I hug my habitual mug of hot, sweet-milky tea, as I read to my daughter about her Great-Gran-ma from the print-out on my knee. The golden pine wood table and work-surfaces around the country kitchen are covered in dishes full of fried chicken, various salads, cheeses, Devon herb-and fruit blended sausages, and chicken pieces seasoned ready for the BBQ gently glowing outside in the back-yard.

"That was your Great-Grandma Eva-May, my Grandma. I thought you might want to hear some of her story", I tell her. Rebecca's eyes fill up. So do mine. "All the different bits and pieces of the puzzle are starting to fall into place", she says her eyes welling up, brimming with tears. Wakantanka mends another break in the Sacred Hoop as the ancestors assemble, and Allah's angels hover above us. The frog-clan brings the gifts of tears. There is much healing in the telling of a family story, to one who has been left out of the Sacred Hoop. Especially when told as remembrance with a Sacred intention. This is what makes me a Griot.

We sit in silence and just study each other, both of us thinking of how alike we are. Both seeing so much of ourselves in each other and in our elders. Both thinking of how much we'd been deprived of access to each other's lives, and to our blood relatives and natural kinship ties. We share a few moments of silence as if in reverence. There are no words for this in the modern language that I know of, but I know many ancient ones. Prayer is one of them. "I've put some more stuff on the PC for you to read at leisure, it's all family stuff, it goes with the photo's I've brought down for you, to scan onto disc. Read that stuff and if you like it I'll e-mail the rest of it down to you. I've got about five volumes of the stuff. The bits that are missing from these poems pop up in other collections. As so do bits of this. Where the context gives them a different reading. An altered, sometimes enriched meaning. Maybe you can be my agent ? You can push it

to a publisher for me down here, and we can split what ever we make between us."
We both laugh again. It's all good.

Rebecca was a Baptist and attended a Church ran by an American Pastor and his wife long before we'd ever met. She was raised by a couple who were Baptist Missionaries. She also attends an Inter-Faith group on a Friday, with her mate Pete. His girl Emma also got a first, in Philosophy. Rebecca studied Community Arts and Social Policy. She defends her Christian beliefs at University where she is dismayed because it's seen as being so hip to attack Jesus. Her thesis was the use of theatre to tackle issues of race and cultural diversity. I met one of the writers she worked with a Sikh brother from Birmingham known for his Burberry turban. Chav Rebecca called him. It was the first time I'd heard the expression, I though it was his name. She's just like her Great-Gran-Ma. She's just like my Ma. She's just like me. It's not long before my Grand-son Levi, Rebecca's other half Toni and his little girl Leah, and some of Rebecca's friends all turn up, and then some more friends and mutual aquaintances, and then finally Pete with a load of serious 70's Roots Rock Reggae Rastafarian Dub-plate selection, but nobody has any herbs, and they are lamenting the fact. I just happen to have some on me for medicinal purposes, enough for everyone as it happens so I'm only too happy to contribute it to the enjoyment of my new found friends, and then the party is in full swing.

Nu Tribes.

Emma is the tribal Earth Momma, she got a first in philosophy but works for the DHSS which she hates. She's a fun person, but she knows what severity is. She studies me curiously. Pete is starting the access to Philosphy degree course in September. Pete is Emma's other-half, he was the lead vocalist in a White Trash Reggae band touring the South West for five years, he practise an ancient form of Hinduism, he's a deeply compassionate poet, angry like Jesus with the money lenders, a sabre toothed Wolfy Smith. Still in student mode Sarah shares with Emma and Pete. Sarah's thing is literature, she's just finished her second year. She's nice they all are. No awkward vibes whatsoever. Simon is a Hippy-philosopher with long black hair. Mellow, chilled out, one of life's veterans. He's also just finished his Philosphy Degree along with Emma, and has landed a job teaching Philosphy on the Access course. Simon's my age, but Pete's still trying to get his head around his Hippy mate being his teacher all of a sudden. Simon received a special award for the highest marks of the whole course. He was found in a box as a baby, hitched to India following the Hashish Trail through France, Spain, across North Africa through Turkey, Afghanistan, and Iran into India. That was my dream journey back in the day. Simon had also won a five year struggle against heroin, much of which was recorded in the his amazingly satirical folk songs tha he performed with the aid of acoustic guitar. Kelly is a young Maori lass from Kiwi, she turns up a bit later. Kelly has frizzy hair and a Samoan look to her. She tells me that she keeps getting mistaken for mixed race, as not many people expect to meet a Moari in Devon. She tells me the other assumption is that she's from London. Kelly's quite fiesty, she knows a lot about Islam as her boy friend's from Zanzibar. Her and Rebecca seem to bond quite well over the cIur thing, but not as much as they do over the fact that they were both adopted. Kelly is a Youth worker-stroke-community artist-stroke-cultural activist. She has been trying to trace her bilgical parents for a while now but with no luck, although she has traced a few cousins. Everyone seems to be supportive of each other. All Rebecca's friends seem to be hip to the post-cInial polemic, and as consciously-radical as Rebecca is over the race issue. I like the general energy of the group it's all good. At this point in time. I'm happy to see that she's in with a good crew, it's not unlike my crew at college in Cartrefle, North

Wales.

Deeper Roots.

As the September evening chill draws in the BBQ resettles in-doors. At one point people are singing along to a Bob Marley compilation. I'm amazed at how everyone knows the words to every song. The whole evening in fact has an air of mysticism about it that seems quite natural. Later that evening my daughter will ask me, "Pops what's our culture?", and I will reply, "I suppose we share the consumer culture of everybody else in the West, but it's not really about culture babe. What's important is that we both have Faith. We're Mixed Race people, babe. Part African-American, part Native-American and part European. We are a New Breed. We are from all cultures and from no culture, all places and no place. We create our own culture as we go along. What ever softens the heart is our culture. Our culture as Contemporary Western Mixed Race people, is what ever we choose to adopt as a vehicle for our Spirituality, and the values of our Faith. Our culture is ours to create from whatever binds us together as One, whatever binds us to our Faith in the Creator. It's more about consciousness, and cultivating Human awareness, and what our reasonings are behind the culture we create. Our Love, our Compassion, our Light, our Inner Truth that's more important than what we dress like, or what music we listen to, how we dance, or what food we eat. The Soul lives beyond all the superficialities of Human diversity, beyond all external differences of race, culture and even religion. We have to transcend, while including what has come before. But I'll you something to hold onto. Native American's have a saying "Mitakuye Oyasin", it means "All my relations", it also we means "We are all related", not just people, but animals and our relatives also, even the trees are known as the 'Standing People'. The whole Earth is living entity. Our

Mother, and our Father is The Sky. We call God - The Great Mystery - Wantanka. But don't get hung up on culture babe, I know where that trip leads. Trust me on this one". I grin a mad grin on purpose. She smiles at me.

"I love you Pop's", she says.

I absorb her words for a moment. Then I just babble as I usually, "For your MA, start to think about how you can use the Inter-Faith group for a comparative study of Raj Yoga, Golden Sufism, Zen Buddhism, the Quakers, and certain Native-American Shamanic centering rituals. Pick the stuff that keeps you in touch with your own Roots as a Spiritual Being. It doesn't have to be a fight. I don't want you to be a copy of me. If you make it fun, and keep it creative, it'll help you study without straining your mind. What we went through, and what we did growing up was of our time, it's gonna be different for you, it is different for you. Faith in your own potential, is the best way to tackle those self-same issues of Race and Identity that make you so angry right now. Trust me. Just do what I say and not what I did, babe I know what I'm talking about. I'm your Dad. I don't want you to suffer any of the shit that I've had to go through, just for being a person of colour with a brain. And always remember you are loved."

"But Pops I'm your daughter. I've got your Spirit ask people what I'm like !"

"I know I can see it in you, and that's what I'm afraid of".

I go into philosopher mode, "Freedom is a state of mind... Listen to me babe. I don't want you to get all twisted up trying to emulate me, or follow in me footsteps. Your already ahead of me. I only got a 2-1 for my Degree." We laugh it off.

Back Up North.

Rebecca and I sit on a small wall by the main road, we're at the National Coach station now waiting for the Liverpool coach to come in. The picnic's over. It's time to catch the coach back up North. There's an air of melancholy. I open my rucksack and take out from the front pocket, a small blue copy of Juz'ama, decorated with an intricate, geometrically formed design of red and yellow flowers, and intertwining green leaves. I'm at an intensely scholarly stage at this point in my Earthwalk. Heavily involved in my Mystical Islamic scholastics. It's a pocket-size version the last thirty or so surahs of the Quraan. The ones generally used in prayers. I explain to her what it is. I take out my carved brown wooden prayer beads with the green silk platting, from Morocco. "These are called Tasbih in Arabic" I tell her. I pass her my headset. She listens to what's on my Walkman.

"What do you think of it ?", I ask.

"It's beautiful. It's very calming, very peaceful."

"It's Quranic recital. That's what I listened to on the twelve hour journey down here." She handed me it back and I listened to see what part she'd heard. "That's Shiekh Minyaoui. You see there's all different recitals on the actual tape... Yeah that's Surah Al Humaaza. The Scandal Mongerer". I recite it in Arabic. Then I translate it for. I tell her about the idea for Abdullah Quilliam Islamic Heritage Centre, and the project launch at the townhall, and what it was all about. Abdullah William Quilliam was the founder of thr first mosque in Britain, a solicitor of white, indigenous Scouse origins, a descendant of whom was an officer on the HMS Victory and sailed with Nelson at Trafalgar.

Sheikh Abdullah Quilliam introduced the concept of the Church organ to Islamic tradition. He used to convert Christian hymns into Islamic theology, and in a Methodist move that would have made John Wesley proud, brother Abdullah converted 150 members of the Liverpool public from all walks of life, starting with members of the Temperance Society. I recite what I recited that evening. I show her how it was composed of some of the Most Beautiful Names of Allah, as found in certain Ayats of the Qur'an, but how I do it in English and in a Southern Baptist-Gospel-style, to make it my own, and of my time, and as serendipity a bit like Abdullah. She can feel the Christian vibe in it when she hears the Qur'an in English. She hears the Bible in the Qur'an. We discuss God's Names and the Universality of our shared World view. I bring up the Quaker's, big favourites of mine. We discuss how brother George Fox the founder of Quakers was in correspondance with Islamic mystics in Morocco, as far back as the sixteen hundreds, and how he'd actually used some Sufi techniques and introduced the use of the Asmaul Husna, the Most Beautiful Names of Allah in the hymns he composed.

Enraptured with trying to catch up with each other's Life narrative's we explore our respective beliefs... and disbeliefs. We listen to some poetry of Rumi that I have being recited by Coleman Barkes... On my headset...

We explored Rumi's eclectic approach... this theme of how throughout the ages, Islamic mystics and Christian mystics have cross pollinated each other's understanding and practise of the Religion of Abraham since the Prophet Muhammad first started following the path of the Nazara, like Esa-Jesus, peace be upon them both. I show her the correct Islamic etiquette to say in Arabic for starting a kutbah or a talk at a gathering , and the correct thing for concluding it. We discuss her relationship to Jesus, Christianity, the Baptist tradition. I tell her how we had to learn Latin at school, and she tells me proudly that Levi is learning Latin at school, and we discuss religious language and how in the Caribbean and the Americas certain fusions of Christianity, and Islam, and African and Indigenous religious forms like Santaria in Cuba, Hundun in New Orleans, Voo-Doo in Haiti, and Candomblé in Brazil all still use the religious language of Yoruba, and some even use Arabic. She has as much to say as I have. It's like talking to myself.

I start to resent all the time missed, all what's been cut out , and denied from both of us due to our skin colour no more no less. I ponder the journey that both of us have been on to transcend our similarly Fatherless fates. I tell her that I've been unhappy because I've been skint since she caught up with me, and that I haven't been able to do some of the things I would have liked. She knew that things have been hard since 9-11. I tell her that as soon the Islamophobia dies down and I can get some work I'll help her pay off her student loan, and try and help her get through her MA. She doesn't care, she says she's glad to have found me. I was owed money from some work I'd done in schools and I was gonna take them all over over to see my Pop, her Grand-Pop, just once before he died, and just so I could see him one more time myself. I never got that money that was nearly four years ago now. I tell her about going on Haj, and my trip to Yemen, and how I went there to learn Patience and Gratitude, and that I should be grateful to God for the time I've had with her, instead of always wanting to see more of her. She says she's the same though. She urges me to move down South. I tell her I'm weighing it up, but it's not that easy right now. The coach arrives. Levi and his chum Brian have been running wild all around the coach station, and they gather to hug me before I get on the coach. I hug my daughter, she is crying.

I say, "Don't cry. I'll be back down. I would have been down sooner but I've been skint babes."

She looks at me her eyes flooding with tears. "Thanks Pops !", she bravely says.

"I thank you for having me down here, and for a wonderful weekend. Extend my gratitude to Sarah, and to all your friends... And don't cry babe... I'm gonna be back down here.. don't worry. Insha'Allah. I can phone you, in fact I'll text you when I'm on the coach and let you know when I'm at Bristol, Birmingham, and Stoke. It's 4-30pm, I should reach Liverpool about 2-20 am tomorrow morning. So I'll keep you informed every step of the journey."

She smiled. Her eyes still full of tears. As the coach pulled out I watched them walk, waving to me. I wave back not knowing when I'll get another chance to see them again. As I try to think, try to plan my future there and then my heart explodes, and I pray to Allah for their protection, and for victory over my enemies, and for patience and gratitude, and for the first time in a long-long time, I pray for myself. Then I put on my Quran tape and practise my Quran recital with the Walkman-sized Sheikhs in my head-set, as I attempt to patch up my heart for the long haul up North.

The Mixed Museum.

Dr Chamion Caballero is a senior research fellow in the Weeks Centre for Social and Policy Research at London South Bank University. Her research interests include race and ethnicity, particularly mixed race, families, social history and qualitative research methods she is also co-author of the book 'Mixed Race UK', and the BBC TV series 'Mixed Britania'. She also co-hosts
The Mix-d: Museum which was founded in 2012 as a means to share more widely, and permanently, the findings of a small British Academy-funded research project undertaken in 2007 by Drs Chamion Caballero and Peter Aspinall into official accounts and first hand experiences of racial mixing in 20th century Britain.

She held a 'Seminar on Mixed Race in The UK', at The Black British History Archive in Brixton, London, November 2019, following the launch of professor Lucy Bland's book "Brown Babies: Stories of the Children of White British Women, and Black American Servicemen Post WW". As I appeared in Lucy's Brown Babies book, I was asked to be a speaker at the event. This anedited version of what I presented to the audience;

"My story begins when Master Seargent Nugent Eugene Golden, USAF, was stationed @ Sealand Air Base on the Wirral from 1952-58, from there he would meet my mother, Florence Annie Lange, from Everton, in Liverpool.

I was born in 1955. The last thing I remember about my Pop was a birthday card I received for my 3rd birthday, from Japan, which I still have. It had a kid in a cowboy suite on the front, and the words "Howdy Pardner!" I had one photo of him taken in Anchorage, Alaska, but his face was hidden by shadow, all you could see was black. I knew he was half African-

American, half Native-American, and that he was from Texas. I knew I had his face, and even aspects of his personality, because my Mom, and other people who knew him told me so. I knew about the race situation Southern States, and the Ku Klux Klan, vaguely.   Wrestling on TV was big viewing amongst the Mother's of the time. I identified with Masambula, Johnny Quango, and Billy Two Rivers. When we played Johnny Quest, I was Haji. When we played Robinson Crusoe I was Man Friday. By the age of five my Cuban-American Step-Dad, and Father of my sister Tracie-Bellinda Arturo Villado, came on the scene. Arturo was a Cuban who had left Cuba for New York, and worked as a merchant seaman for the United States Lines. He sailed on the American Courier, and the American Scientist. Arturo was the one who I would call Dad from then on. He brought me all the coolest kids stuff from the States, a chemistry set, art materials, a Stetson, real cowboy shirts, jeans, and hand carved cowboy boots from Texas.

Needless to say my favourite things were an Eagle feather head dress, a buckskin suite with fringes, beaded mocassins, a tomahawk, a sheath-knife, my bow and arrows, medicine beads, and a tom-tom. He also brought me a book on the various tribes, and customs, which I studied religiously like it was a Bible. Arturo played Spanish guitar, and he would jam with the Caribbean Calypsonian guys on Granby Street, out side PeeWee the barbers, people like Zanks, and Lord Woodbine, who was the Beatle's first manager, and who sold me my first drumkit which he said used to belong to Ringo. I also picked up a love for the bongo, and Afro-Cuban music from Arturo. Two years after Arturo showed up my sister Tracie was born. She was a bit lighter than me, fair haired, green eyes, but she had easily recognisable Afro-Cuban features, what they'd call a High Yellah in the States.

Mixed Relations.

My Mother was part German, Dutch, Scottish, and

English. She had 3 brothers and three sisters. My Aunty Ethel May married a Malayan seaman, my Uncle Osman, who was half Malayan, and half Afghani , born in Singapore. Beatrice Alice married a Somali seaman, my Uncle Hussien. And my Aunty Maggie, the oldest of the sisters married my Uncle Omray Roberts, who was a devout Welshman, and a big an of Dai Francis from the Black and White Ministrel Show, which we'd all watch every Sunday, religiously. Also my Mother's youngest brother my Uncle Billy, was a merchant seaman. He jumped ship in Kuwait for 2 years and came back a Muslim, fluent in Arabic, and called Muhammad Khalil, a name he'd taken from a Sudanese student friend of the family back in Liverpool. Billy also spoke German, Dutch, Swedish, Norwegian, and Danish, and was very much into researching his Northern European, Viking roots. He was also a Beatnik, he'd take me with him when he went to the river front to look for a ship. I remember going into a Beatnik cafe with him once, down on the dock road when the over-head railway was there. The smell of coffee, and herbs, and the Strange World of Gurney Slade vibe to the place, with the coloured glass balls hanging from the walls covered in fishing nets. The music and secretly hip atmosphere.

Now although the Black Community was only a fifteen minute walk from where I was born in Everton, and I knew it quite well, and had Family there, it was a world way from the White working-class area of Everton. In Everton we grew up divided between Catholics and Protestants. Never the less on the Street I was given the name "Gene The Niggah", by certain Catholic gangs. There was one other mixed race kid, my mate Benny. He lived a little bit closer to the Black Community, but to get to his house I had to run the gauntlet of these Catholic gangs, and as I'd sneak through their turf with my head down, I'd be waiting to hear the cry, "There's the Nigger! Let's get him", and I'd be ready to run. Benny and his sister Marie were half Nigerian, they had an older sister Sadie, whose Dad was Arab, and a younger brother Abel, who was alabaster white, red hair, blues eyes. This was normal in Liverpool 8, and still is today.

Families can have siblings with seperate Mothers, and or seperate Fathers. Also there are a lot of Foster Families, like the one my Mother eventually ran as she got older. We grew up from our teens onwards many Foster brothers, and sisters. Some people's adopted siblings were often closer to them than bilgical siblings. No one distinguished between, half, step, foster, or adopted siblings, brothers and sisters were brothers and sisters. I know many Families were this is the case, once you were Family you were Family. I put this down to the old Matriarchy system of inclusion, which is similar to the Native Anerican system of making blood brothers, but also due to the fact women had to be decision makers, as many of the men had been off to the war, or were often seamen, away at sea for long trips. Your Mother's friends were your Aunties, her kids were your cousins.

Grammar School.

I'm eleven years old. I pass the "11 Plus". I win a scholarship to the Liverpool Collegiate Grammar School For Boys. This is one of the best schools in Liverpool, very prestigious. We do Latin. I loved Latin. We sang the school song in Latin: "Vivat haec soldolitas, decus Esmedunae, vivat haec soldolitas, decus Esmedunae. Nulli usquam phosabenda, semper in celum tollenda. Magnum virum cunae." I never knew the meaning of it until I came across a Collegiate Ulumni page on line, and it was there.

Then one day in Latin class we are memorising by rote the words for cIurs. The word for black in Latin is 'Niger' (pronounced nigger), so the whole class is chanting "Niger-Niger-Nigerum-Nigeramus-Nigeratis- Nigerant." We do this for a while just drilling the word, and it's case endings, over and over, until it's engrained on our cerebral cortex. Next the Latin master goes through the class picking out individuals to recite on their own, just to test who has memorised it. If they stumble, we drill it as a class again, then we go back to testing individuals. Of course everyone is sniggering all the way through the lesson, as I'm the only "Black" kid in class, one of about 5 non-White kids, in amongst roughly a 1'000 pupils in the whole school. When it came to my turn to me to recite I had no problem memorising the order, amidst the muffled chuckling, and secret sniggering of my peers. I can't remember how I felt actually, but I remember the smug, sardonic, sinister, sadistic grin, on the Latin Master's face. He thought he was so cool. I just thought he was a square. I recited Amo Amas Amat, Amamis Amatis, Amant, but to myself.

At The Collegiate the snobs refered to me as "The Native". They never addressed me directly, but through who ever I was with at the time, they'd say, "Tell your Native friend this, or tell him that." I'd be standing there right in front of them, next to the person they'd be speaking to, but they'd just ignore me. Never the less I was not totally isolated at The Collegiate. In the second year I made friends with David Norman. David lived in Cadogan Street, in the heart of the Black community, and he was White. His Mother had then married a guy from Antigua, so David and his brother Peter were White, and his younger brother, and sister where mixed Race. His best mate out of school was a mixed race guy called Andy, the both boxed, and were in the army cadets. Andy went to Paddington Comp, the local Black school, in Liverpool 7, halfway between Liverpol 6, and Liverpool 8. All the kids wore big Afros. Motown, and the Afrocentricity of the late 60's, and early 70's was just starting to emerge as a counter-culture. People in the school were buzzing about it.

So one day David and I are standing up against the wall in the play ground, reading comics. We're second years, and the Cock of the Third Year approaches us with his side-kick, and his henchmen, and he says to David, "Tell the Native we don't like him." David ignored him. Then he snatched the comic from David's hand and scrunched it up. Now it was cold, and David was wearing these big furry mittens. He just shook them off his hands, and delivered a furious flurry of jabs to the face of the bullying jackanapes, and boxed his ears good style. His henchmen came at me, but I'd been practising Ju Ji Jitsu since I was 7, so I was able to toss them all over the place with little effort. This is the 1960's no one had seen Bruce Lee, or Kung Fu, but they had seen lots of cowboy movies, so the nearest they could make out was that I'd used Indian fighting. After that they called us the Lone Ranger, and Tonto. I was always the 'Other'.

I also had some cool friends who were Soul Boys, into Tamla Motown, scooters, and Mod fashion. David Soorngard, whose Father was a Norwegian seaman, and whose brother, and sister also went away to sea, had a collection of Motown LP's all imports, on the original Detroit label. His crew were actually honoured to have a GI kid hang with them.

By my teens I was beginning to turn Black, and identified myself as Black. Richard Pryor had made the "N" word a harmless joke. Malcolm X, The Black Panther's, and Angela Davis had made being Black, a badge of honour. The Last Poets, and Hip-Hop made it both a weapon, and a term of endearment. One drop of Black blood, and your a Nigger, that's how it worked during slavery, that's how it worked when I was growing up, and that's how it works even today. I embraced my African-American heritage, and my Mohawk heritage to the max. During the next thirty years I would become a community arts/cultural activist. During which time I would visit many Black Arts, and Community arts centres, up and down the UK, as part of my college training, and after college through the work of the Manchester based, Black Arts Alliance, and Cultureword. I would imbibe all things counter-cultural, post-colonial, and post-modern".

Irene.

Now I'm 65 as I type this, and again the story of the Brown Babies continues, as does the struggle against all forms of discrimination. When I bought a copy of the book "Britain's

Brown Babies", for my daughter Rebecca, she recognised her story.

She said, "That's my story Pop's!"

I said, "It's all our stories babe."

She looked at me and it hit me. Yes! her story was the same as the stories of all the other people in the book, "Britain's Brown Babies". All the babies who were also adopted for being off-Black, as opposed to off-White. She was not just a random chocolate drop brought up in Tewkesbury, there were many random chocolate drops, dotted around the country, and together we were all unique.

We all had our own stories, but it was the same story really, at the core. The story of how Racism had robbed us of family ties, people, memories, and experiences. What Lucy Bland's book did for me, was give me something to hand down to my daughter, something that was as uniquely relevent to her life history, as it was to mine. It gave her some pertinant stories to tell my grandsons, and insha'Allah, they can pass it on to their kids also, and never have to feel excluded, because their historic origins as 'British Brown Babies' has been documented, and put into a book. It gaves us an existence within a very specific socio-historical, cultural context, like the Windrush Generation. Ethnically, even my grandsons identify as Mixed-Race, because they are proud to be mixed race.

Just last Month Irene my Spanish sister, the one my sisters in Texas and me speculated about, the one in Pop's Country song, traced me, and her Texas siblings via Facebook. She looks like me, everybody thought it was my daughter Rebecca, as they are of similar ages. Exchanging stories I cried. I sent her the song, that song, Pop's cassette song, her Mother's name is Maria. She was that baby. She cried.

Ironically Irene was in the band that had the hit single with the song 'Macarena'. She toured the States, and also Globally with the band. She writes, and has also been involved in several publications in Spain. She makes bespoke life like ethnic dolls, her work is breath takingly realistic. She is so happy to

213

have contacted Bec, Wanda, the whole Austin crew, and myself. We met up in December 2019. I had to brush up on my Spanish. Her English is very good. She brought me a set of castanets, which she plays. Seville is the birthplace of Flamenco, her boy friend Victor brought me a vast collection of Flamenco music.

I took them to the Beatles museum, the Walker's Art Gallery, and the Trans-Atlantic Slavery Gallery. She cried when she saw it. We got a photo taken by an exhibit of a Ku Klux Klan gown that they had in a glass case Irene is holding up one finger. Her and Victor also taught me to swear in Spanish. Irene taught me how to make Seville style tortilla. I cooked a pan of Scouse for them, and their friends Miguel, and Pilar. I brought out the only book I had in Spanish, it was a book of Spanish poetry, given to me by my Jungian-Sufi friend, Peter O'Halligan. Pilar was amazed, by sheer coincidence the only thing she had ever been given by her Father, was a copy of that very same book. Synchronicity is a strange thing.

Irene showed me documents about my Father, and Grand Father that she had traced, and about medals they had received from their time in military service. I cried, I don't know why. I showed them the old photo I had of Pop in Anchorage where you couldn't see his face. Victor studied it closely, and noticed a message written on the back. It was message to me. I had possessed the photo for over 60 years, and I had never noticed that Pop had written a message on the back of it. I must have been so focused on just trying to make out his features. Victor couldn't believe I'd had it all that time, and not noticed it had writing on the reverse side. I couldn't believe it, but there it was. The message was, "You can't see my face but it is me."

In the beginning there was absolutely nothing, apparently, or so I'm told, then there was The Big Bang, which scientists call, 'The Singularity', and it just got more, and more complicated, as time went bye.

Printed in Great Britain
by Amazon

10763921R00122